The Gobbler

The Gobbler

ADRIAN EDMONDSON

HEINEMANN : LONDON

First published in Great Britain 1995
by William Heinemann Ltd
an imprint of Reed Consumer Books Ltd
Michelin House, 81 Fulham Road, London SW3 6RB
and Auckland, Melbourne, Singapore and Toronto

A CIP catalogue record for this title
is available from the British Library

Hardback ISBN 0 434 00149 X
Paperback ISBN 0 434 00362 X

Phototypeset by Intype, London
Printed and bound
by Clays Ltd, St Ives plc

1

Julian couldn't believe that Doctor Sachs had swallowed the lie about his drinking.

'Oh, not a lot, half a bottle of wine a day, the odd bourbon,' he'd said, as beads of whisky perspiration broke out on his forehead. He'd lightly clenched his fists to hide the slight tremor in his hands as Doctor Sachs asked him how much he smoked. 'I'm cutting down at the moment, maybe ten or fifteen a day. A couple more on an opening night,' he'd added with an ingratiating smile.

Julian Mann knew how to handle Sachs – a bronzed tailor's dummy in a Savile Row suit with more bedside charm than medical curiosity – Julian knew how to handle all the showbiz doctors whose surgery walls were chock-a-block with signed photos of the stars: you simply had to turn up on time, indulge in a bit of chit-chat about this or that gala première, answer a few simple questions to prove you weren't clinically dead, then give the doctor a quick flash of the teeth and a flattering laugh to prove he was as much a part of the great show-business aristocracy as yourself, and Bob was your uncle.

But this time it hadn't worked.

Maybe collapsing on the way out of the surgery had scuppered him, Julian thought to himself. Though he hadn't really collapsed, he'd just stumbled to the floor clutching his chest, crying out 'Oh my God, a heart attack, I knew it!'

Later, as he recovered on the couch with a cup of sweet tea and a chocolate Bath Oliver, Doctor Sachs had told him it was stress: anxiety was apparently making him breathe too shallowly, reducing the amount of oxygen in his blood, and causing the muscles across his chest to stiffen and contract – but he'd been 'really pretty sure' that it was nothing to do with Julian's heart. However, 'on balance' Sachs had felt unable to give Julian a clean bill of health until he'd learned some breathing exercises and made some kind of effort at taking regular cardiovascular exercise.

Julian needed a clean bill of health so that Picador Pictures could effect completion insurance for their new film *Blood Train*. Film insurance underwriters required all leading players to undergo a medical as a matter of course, though Julian couldn't help taking it as some ghoulish personal slight that a doctor should have to testify whether he was going to live through the next three months or not. *And now he'd been failed!* He'd toyed with the idea of demanding a second opinion but quickly rejected it in fear of what a real doctor might find.

And that was why he was now standing in his trunks on the side of the old Chelsea Baths. He hated public baths – all cracked Victorian tiles with dirty grouting, and algae in the spittoons. The smell of the showers drifted through from the changing rooms – the smell of old wet soap and athlete's foot. The management had attempted to liven up the pool by changing the name from 'public baths' to 'sports centre' and hanging a few strings of bunting across the rafters, but it didn't work for Julian. He'd gone to his private health club first, only to find that his membership had lapsed five years before. He'd complained that he'd only ever used the club once, but they wouldn't let him in for a swim until he'd bought another membership for two and a half thousand pounds and paid subscription fees of nine hundred pounds for a year. Three and a half thousand quid seemed a bit much for a swim. Not that Julian was mean – he could be quite purposefully and senselessly extravagant at times – he just resented being made to fork out that kind of money for the sake of some upper-class twit doctor in Cadogan Square.

If it hadn't been a bastard medical he could have had a little drinky on the way, he thought. He'd have been more relaxed, able to breathe more easily. His blood would have been bursting with oxygen, and he wouldn't have felt the huge tightening of luggage straps around his chest, wouldn't have felt the terror and the panic, and the enormous and instantaneous sense of grief at the loss of his own life. He wouldn't have cried, wouldn't have begged for help. He'd have had his ticket to Hollywood, and he wouldn't be standing on the edge of the pool where the word 'municipal' was beginning to stand for all that was rotten and fetid and dull and unsuccessful.

The door leading from the women's changing room opened. Two lithe young figures strolled casually out and turned in Julian's direction. He pulled his stomach in. He imagined they must be nineteen or twenty – definitely above the age of consent, anyway. Julian enjoyed the look of surprise on people's faces when they saw him in places they wouldn't normally expect to find him. He pulled his easy roguish smile and waited for them to recognise him – and it was hard not to recognise Julian with his trademark eyes.

Crueller members of the press claimed that the strangely prepossessing asymmetry of his eyes was the result of a contact lens and an affectation, but although it moved synchronously with his left and looked just as functional, Julian was actually blind in his right eye – thanks to a childhood fight with his older sister in which, having run out of sucker-tipped arrows, she'd jabbed at him with the bow. In consequence his right iris was a fiercely brilliant, arresting light blue in contrast to the rather ordinary brownness of his seeing eye. The effect was at once startling and attractive – two attributes which in Julian's mind easily outweighed the sole disadvantage of only being able to see in two dimensions, and the occasional stumble that induced. He sometimes wondered, though, whether his seemingly increased desire to touch and feel might be the result of his senses trying to balance themselves out.

The girl in the shiny, clinging, black one-piece with the long, reddish hair looked his way first. He met her gaze with an almost imperceptible widening of his seeing eye. Enough

3

to signify his interest, yet small enough to be denied in the face of a rebuttal. She looked away. Her look had been too brief, he thought, she couldn't have seen him. She hadn't had time to let her brain assimilate the information, or perhaps her brain had dismissed it as being too fantastical to be true.

The dyed blonde bob with the heavily lipsticked mouth and prominent nipples would be next. Julian waited until she looked and then widened his eye again. She didn't react but kept on looking. Julian lifted both eyebrows in a gesture of engaging humility – *for one as famous as himself* – but she still didn't react. He was confused – was she looking at him? Or was she gazing at something behind him? Was she cross-eyed?

The two girls were approaching his corner of the pool. They were gorgeous. Their breasts somehow more discernible through the thin, stretchy lycra of their swimsuits than if they had been naked. Julian pushed his charisma button. Nothing tangible of course, just that special way he had of suddenly exuding immense physical presence – the sort of magic that had won him 'Best Light Entertainment Performance' in 1980 and '84.

The two girls passed behind.

Julian knew the sort, he thought to himself. There were some who were more polite than others – they didn't want to let him know they'd recognised him because they didn't want to embarrass him, they respected his right to freedom from public harassment. He quite liked this game – the polite ones were always the easiest to hook because they could never resist a look back. They'd wander a few yards past him, then, when they were sure they weren't going to compromise his privacy, they'd sneak a quick glance back, and they'd be trapped, caught in the act – his smile would broaden and they'd understand that he'd known all along, that they'd been involved in playing a game with him – and in Julian's book that was practically a relationship.

He watched the two young sex angels saunter round the

deep end and through the heavy swing doors to the sun-bed and sauna rooms beyond. They never looked back.

He looked down at his body. It wasn't that bad – wasn't bad at all really. There was his stomach, but he always pulled that in. His chest had a slightly doughy look to it, but it was nothing a week in the sun wouldn't put right. He knew he was pretty good-looking for a man of thirty-eight – his legs were very good, always had been, and he'd never had to do anything to keep in shape, which was surprising considering the amount he could drink. He put it down to a fast metabolism and the ability to shit the longest turds in the world.

He was no matinée idol, but only a very few female journalists could ever resist writing gushing accounts of his 'physicality', and the word 'electricity' was much overused in their pieces. Indeed, he was more than a matinée idol, for along with his acceptably roguish middle-England good looks, he had real talent. There were a lot of well-regarded, jobbing humourists in the TV comedy world, but Julian's status was down to more than just hard work. He was what they liked to call a natural, and it was this spark of genius that held the key to his attractiveness. It was the spirit of the man, the adrenalin rush of watching something dangerous, the heart-stopping way his work seemed to tread such a perilous path between uncompromising brilliance and abject failure – along with all the flattery and come-to-bed charm he poured upon his female interviewers.

Looking down at his reflection in the water he was pleased to see the dark sweep of his full head of hair staring back up at him intermittently through the ripples. 'God of Comedy' by David Hockney, he thought to himself, then laughed quietly at his own presumption.

The pool was empty save for a pair of geriatrics inching their way noiselessly up and down. Julian dived to the bottom of the deep end and exhaled. Not all his air, but enough to keep him comfortably balanced at the bottom. He closed his eyes, and enjoyed the silence. He'd stumbled upon the joy of lying at the bottom of a pool whilst in a drunken sulk on holiday in the Seychelles. It was like lying in space; it gave him a sense of peace and equilibrium, half-satisfying the impulse he often felt to kill himself, without going through any of the pain. If he didn't panic he could stay there for a surprisingly long time, floating like an astronaut on the end of his line – a long way away from the struggle. He could shut down his physical senses and just think.

Julian thought about the mesmerising rise and fall of the two girls' tantalisingly athletic buttocks. He remembered their cruel lack of recognition and tried to blot out his unfulfilled sexual fantasies – he must have got their ages wrong. He preferred his slightly older fans anyway, he thought to himself, the ones who'd discovered him when they were teenagers and who were now in their twenties; they were young, independent and firm-breasted, and they still thought of him as their very own, the one they'd laughed at first, the one who'd taken away their comic virginity; they were much more amenable to his casual groping and not as easily diverted by the new pretenders to the comedy crown.

The comedy crown! Memories of the BAFTA awards shindig of the night before came flooding back into his mind and all thought of the girls vanished in a mist of anger.

Why had he even gone? Why had they lied to him? If they'd told him they were going to give Best Comedy to some load of old bollocks about two pensioners in a houseboat he wouldn't have been there and he could have saved them all the embarrassment!

He should have guessed, he thought to himself – his sitcom *Richard the Nerd* was into its fifth series and they'd never give a BAFTA to such an established programme, even if they managed to see through the regular battering the show suffered at the hands of broadsheet reviewers, the cries of horror and alarm that seven million people could so regularly tune into his 'crass' and 'banally obvious' characterisation of a monumentally evil but staggeringly stupid King Richard III; even though it was BBC 2's most popular series; even though it

6

had been voted the No.1 comedy by *Daily Mirror* readers for three years in a row.

Mind you, they'd chosen the wrong clip so it hadn't stood a chance in the first place! *Why show the episode with the crap child actors coming back to haunt him as the Princes from the Tower, when they had Julian falling into the giant malmsey tub whilst trying to murder the Duke of Clarence in the bank?* There was a half-hour virtuoso solo performance, a blinding giddy roller-coaster ride through farcical paranoia and overweening ambition, and an obvious comedy classic!

Julian hated the BAFTAs – the great dining hall of the Dorchester crammed with his professional enemies and the sea of media executives and their lackeys either trying to cash in on his success or gloat at his failure. He hadn't been since his defeat in '85, and though he'd been nominated four times since, he'd always made it quite clear that he wouldn't turn up unless they could promise him that he'd won. *The cheating, lying bastards!* Still, at least neither Harry Enfield nor Steve Coogan had won it.

'And what did you get for your last Christmas Special?' the sneering LWT Light Entertainment lackey sitting next to him had asked towards the end of the increasingly drunken evening.

'Almost ten.'

'*Almost* ten, but not quite?'

'What's wrong with that?'

'Cilla gets seventeen, Barrymore gets eighteen.'

'Yeah – but I'm *funny*!'

The pinch-faced lackey hadn't even flinched, but casually retrieved another cheap cigar from the depths of his rented dinner jacket. 'That's the trouble with you alternatives – you strut about as if you own the place but you never get the viewing figures do you?'

'I'm not an alternative! There're the fucking alternatives!' Julian had shouted, stabbing his finger at a tableful of shabby-suited revellers basking in the warm sun of the Establishment.

'That's part of the Oxbridge lot, that is,' sneered the lackey.

7

'Yeah? Well, I'm not one of them either! I'm a comic actor – I'm *funny*!'

'Yes, but it's not popular comedy is it?'

Provocative bastard! 'It is.'

'You're not universal.'

'I am!'

'No, you haven't got the common touch, you're too educated.'

'I've got an 'A' level – what the fuck's that got to do with it? I'm the same tradition as Hancock, and Williams,' Julian had slurred, his elbow crashing into the collection of glasses on the table in front of him and attracting the attention of the rest of his table and a couple of tables beyond. 'What the fuck's class got to do with it? My comedy goes beyond class – I'm just *funny*.'

'You went to university.'

'I did not! I went to fucking drama school!'

'Yes, well it's all the same, isn't it?'

He remembered grabbing the man's throat and pushing him back in his chair. 'Look you cunt,' he'd said, feeling the alcohol surge into his eyebrows and hood his eyes, 'I've really got no fucking interest in the views of some lowest common denominator producer like you who pitches every boring fucking show he makes at incontinent grannies and shop assistants – because d'you know what I am? I'm the new Peter Sellers, that's what I am – I'm making a film, not some stupid, fucking, English, bastard, half-cocked, pretend film, but a real film, an American film, an American *funny* film and you bastards in television can just sit there and eat your own parochial shit and choke to fucking death!'

'You'll never work at LWT again,' the man had croaked, clawing at Julian's hand, as three of his friends rose half-heartedly to break up the impromptu entertainment.

'I wouldn't work there if you got Cilla Black to suck my cock!' Julian had shouted, eliciting a small round of applause from the Oxbridge table.

The lifeguard's smoothly muscular arm took Julian by surprise at the bottom of the pool as it snaked round his chest and squeezed the reserve oxygen supply from his lungs. Julian gasped and his lungs filled with water. He could feel the chlorine burning his throat. He panicked, choking underwater as he struggled to fight off his supposed attacker, and finally passed out as the lifeguard's elbow accidentally jabbed into his temple.

Coming round on the side of the pool Julian was aware of the vicious rasping of the man's unshaven chin on his cheek, and the overpowering smell of pilchard and tomato paste on the breath he was blowing into his lungs. Later, Julian was to swear that it had been the fish paste, not the lungful of water, that made him vomit.

As he lay retching onto the cracked tiles of the poolside Julian noticed two pairs of pretty young feet skipping back to avoid the splash of his spew, and glanced up into two lycra-wrapped pudenda.

'The girl on the desk said it was Julian Mann,' said the shiny, clinging, black one-piece.

'Yes, look at his eye,' said the high-cut scarlet peach.

'He's a lot fatter than he looks on the telly, isn't he?'

'And older – he must be nearly fifty.'

Julian slumped to the floor and pretended to have passed out to avoid having to make a response – not just to the comments of the two girls but to the barrage of concerned questions coming from the over-eager lifeguard. In retrospect this was a mistake, for by the time they were wheeling him out to the ambulance on a stretcher the press had arrived, and the next day he was front-page news in most of the tabloids for his supposed 'suicide attempt'.

2

Julian was one of the last to learn of his 'suicide attempt' as he rarely rose from his bed until lunchtime unless he was working, and he was generally a few hours, sometimes days, behind everyone else, because he had a policy of never answering the phone unless he was drunk. This habit had formed simply from having few real friends and realising that most of the phone calls he received spelled trouble – most were *business* calls from his agent or his accountant and he hated *business*, and the few calls from his parents and his sister made him feel so unutterably guilty at not having called them first that he preferred the less damning, insistent ringing of the unanswered phone.

On the morning the papers splashed photographs of an ashen-faced and seemingly unconscious Julian being loaded into the back of an ambulance the phone started ringing at half past eight, and didn't stop until Julian pulled it out of the wall socket about two hours later. He then swallowed an antacid tablet and a hundred milligram Vitamin C lozenge – to counter the effects of the drinking binge he'd embarked upon on his almost immediate release from casualty the day before – turned over, and went back to sleep.

He was awoken ten minutes later by his wife, Wendy, who'd just returned from taking their twin six-year-old sons to school and from doing the weekly supermarket shop.

Wendy was a full ten years younger than Julian though he thought she somehow looked older. It wasn't that she had more wrinkles or grey hairs than he had, it was the way she carried herself. She'd been a young, girlishly vibrant, excitable twenty-year-old when they'd married eight years before, yet now her every movement seemed burdened by the weight of premature middle age. Julian might not have been the most sprightly thirty-eight-year-old in the world, but his soul was still ready to whoop and holler at the faintest whisper of a party or 'good times' – whereas Wendy now seemed consumed by leaden-footed pragmatism.

He liked to remember the halcyon days of their courtship; dancing together on the pool table of the Strathallan Hotel in Aberdeen; deliberately capsizing a pedalo on the boating lake in Scarborough (a difficult feat which had taken all their combined strength and initiative, and a bottle of cherry brandy); making love in the woods behind her parents' house on the very first time she'd taken him home to meet them.

Nowadays Julian often reflected ruefully on how the pert young sex goddess he'd married had turned into such a frumpy housewife. He hated her cardigans. He'd once collected them all, taken them into the back garden, and tried to set fire to them – but he'd been too drunk and it had been raining too hard. Confronted with the soggy pile of wool in the sober light of the next morning he'd tried to work up the courage simply and honestly to discuss how much he disliked them, but hadn't been able to.

Wendy could be a difficult woman to reason with, even for people other than Julian. Her father had been a Reader in Psychology at Reading University where her mother still worked as a librarian, and being the only child in that fiercely academic and logical household Wendy had learned to argue with a pedantic zeal that had left even her tutors begging for release. In the face of her parents' overbearing scholasticism she had also learned an unfortunate inability to let go, and a scepticism about her own natural beauty, and though leaving home and going to university had helped her overcome these to some extent, and her subsequent elopement with Julian had excited her more impetuous side, she now seemed to be slipping once more towards the humdrum. It seemed to Julian

11

that Wendy's rebellion had never gone far enough – after the initial excitement of the coup things had evened out and gradually returned to the status quo, and now he felt that the young firebrand he'd married might as well have joined the civil service.

He knew that bringing up two wilful young boys had taken its toll on Wendy. She had wanted a girl, had imagined herself with a daughter, playing with her and dressing her as if she were an outsize doll, and so she had been slightly perturbed when the ultrascan had detected *two* foetuses, and most confused when two little *boys* had very painfully emerged.

She'd decorated their nursery with lace and frills all the same and had enjoyed the first eighteen months or so when she could legitimately dress them in smocks and dresses without public disapproval. Even now, at the age of six, the boys still had their blond hair cut in feminine bobs, each looking like a miniature version of Sarah Bernhardt playing Hamlet. But that didn't prevent them from being boys – boys who seemed intent on testing the breaking strength of anything and everything, including their mother.

Now, in the linen-swagged marriage bed on the fourth floor of their house, Julian was lying sprawled amongst a cornucopia of broderie anglaise pillows. He felt his shoulder being shaken and as his mind wrestled itself into consciousness he instinctively put out an arm and pulled Wendy towards him. She didn't resist. He could smell the cigarette smoke in her hair and found it unpleasant. He was a heavy smoker himself but was constantly amazed at how Wendy could smell so much like an over-full ashtray. Other people smelled of smoke, he thought, Wendy smelled of dog-ends. It was a far cry from the days when she'd resolutely made them both munch their way through a whole packet of polos whenever they'd visited her parents. He stroked her tangled shoulder-length hair, brittle and wiry from being dyed strawberry blonde continuously since her first term away from home, then took to patting her softly on the back of her head, slowly and rhythmically, tenderly, lovingly; the consummate actor at work and at home, he thought to himself.

'I didn't know you'd taken up swimming,' Wendy murmured.

Julian wondered whether she could feel his heartbeat quicken through the quilt. Had she found his wet trunks? He couldn't recollect having them with him when he'd escaped through the busy service bay of the hospital. In any case, he was sure they'd never have survived the subsequent evening's entertainment in Soho.

'Well, I've been thinking about it for a long time, you know, need to get into shape really,' he said noncommittally – when Wendy murmured she was usually scrabbling around on the edge of something big.

'How many lengths did you manage?'

'Not many,' he said. At least he hadn't lied yet.

Wendy lifted her head and looked into his eyes. She leaned forward and kissed him – a fulsome, loving kiss, their lips squashing together for a good five seconds before she peeled off and buried her face in his neck with a huge sigh. Julian's head filled with the image of a hand grenade rolling pinless across the bed and lodging itself under his ear.

'Bit of an incident at the pool, actually,' he said.

'Oh yes.'

He was encouraged by her seemingly casual interest. 'I was just doing a couple of widths underwater when the bloody lifeguard jumped in and tried to save me! Thought I was drowning apparently. Stupid twat. And you'll never guess what happened next . . .'

'They called an ambulance, and the press, and as you were wheeled out the photographers took lots of lurid snaps of you which they splashed across the front pages of this morning's newspapers under banner headlines announcing that you'd tried to commit suicide.'

Julian was so busy listening to the tone of Wendy's voice –

13

searching vainly for any sign of vindictiveness – that he had to replay her words in his head to take in what she'd said.

'Suicide?' he asked.

'Yes.'

'Front page?'

He could feel her head nodding against his cheek.

'*All* the papers?'

'Lead story in the *Mirror*, the *Star* and the *Mail*,' Wendy breathed into his ear. 'You even get a mention on the front of the *Telegraph*,' she said, sitting up, 'with a small photo. And Matt's cartoon has you and John Major sitting together at the bottom of a swimming pool – but I didn't get the joke.'

'*The bastards!*' Julian shouted, making the necessary public show of outrage at this monumental intrusion into his private life, but secretly proud at making it onto the front pages at all and getting to be the subject of a pocket cartoon. *That was one in the eye for the anonymous Best Comedy-winning pensioners on their houseboat.* He was overcome with curiosity to know how they'd labelled him – was he still 'Britain's Funniest *Mann*'? He was never annoyed by the press as long as they prefaced any article they wrote about him with the words 'comic genius'.

'Why didn't you tell me last night when you came in?' asked Wendy, taking one of his hands in hers and stroking it gently.

'Well, you were asleep.'

'What time did you get in?'

'About three o'clock,' Julian lied.

'Oh,' said Wendy, keeping her eyes fixed on his hand.

He could see immediately that he'd given the wrong answer. *So why didn't she pick him up on it?* He could do without a full-scale inquiry into his movements of the night before, he thought to himself, but at that moment the embarrassment at leaving his obvious deceit just hanging in the air between them seemed even more excruciating.

'Didn't you see all the paparazzi when they wheeled you out of the pool?' asked Wendy, breaking the awful silence.

14

Julian thought hard for a moment. 'I must have had my eyes closed,' he said.

The corners of her mouth relaxed in a fleeting smile. He could still make her laugh.

'You see, I'm so bloody famous I can grab the headlines with my eyes closed – because I'm the King of Comedy,' sang Julian, picking up on Wendy's short-lived smile as the first recognisable chink in her armour, and flashing one of his irresistible childish grins, 'and, "When you're the King you can do anything you bloody well like!",' he added, reciting Richard the Nerd's catch-phrase.

Wendy's grim expression relaxed into a philosophical grin. 'That might not be strictly true. Paul's holding on the phone for you, says it's very important.'

'Holding on the phone?' asked Julian, 'but I pulled the socket out.'

Wendy fixed him with a long-suffering stare.

'Yes, but it still rings downstairs, Julian. It was ringing when I came in. He's been trying to get you since half past eight this morning.' She plugged the bedroom extension back into its socket and picked up the receiver. 'Hello, Paul? Sorry it took so long, I've got him here.' She carried the phone around to Julian's side of the bed, but as she reached him she hesitated and pushed the mute button on the console. 'Look, I'm not cross, I'm really not cross. I'd just really rather you told me things before some arsehole of a *Sun* reporter does, that's all. They were all waiting by the door when I brought Sean and Jamie home from school yesterday . . .'

His family – door-stepped! A flash-flood of guilt swept over Julian and he shot out a comforting hand for Wendy to hold. She ignored it, and looking up into her face he detected a tiny quiver in her bottom lip as she struggled to keep a lid on her emotions.

'. . . there were about ten of them and it was really quite frightening for the boys. They kept shouting through the letter box after we'd got in and the boys got very confused –

I was in their room till midnight explaining that you weren't dead. Of course, I didn't really know how hurt you were, or whether you'd hurt yourself at all, or whether you'd meant to hurt yourself . . .'

She seemed about to carry on, then obviously thought better of it. Julian could see she was trying hard not to press home her advantage and bawl him out. *Why was she always so fucking reasonable?* If she'd only get angry he'd have something to fight against, he thought to himself. Her reasonableness just left him feeling castrated.

'Are they still outside?' he asked, ready to bound down the stairs and take out his frustration on *them*.

'No, I told them you'd gone to France, and when you hadn't shown up by four this morning I think they believed me and left.'

'France?'

'Well, I don't know, Julian!' She was on the edge of losing her cool but fought valiantly to regain control. 'I didn't know where you were,' she said in heavily measured tones, 'and it was the first place that came into my head.'

'You could have said Hollywood,' he muttered under his breath, then immediately regretted it.

She let her head fall forward with a sigh, pressed the mute button again and handed the phone to Julian, then walked to his chair and began to sort through his washing.

Julian felt ashamed. He'd been thoughtless, irresponsible and selfish, perhaps even cruel. It struck him, not for the first time, that if he didn't live with her he wouldn't feel this way – as a carefree bachelor he could attempt to drown himself as often as he liked.

He could hear an ant-like voice shouting 'Hello' from the phone and put the receiver to his ear. 'Paul?'

'Julian?'

'Yes.'

'Look, it's all getting a bit hot and we need to talk.'

'What time is it?' asked Julian.

16

'It's nearly eleven.'

'Is it? It's a bit early.'

'We have to meet,' said Paul, surprising Julian with his assertiveness. Usually Paul was unseemingly deferential. 'Do you want to come to the office or do you want me to come over to you?'

Julian looked over at Wendy – she was standing with her back to him dropping his socks into the laundry bin. From the drooping raglan shoulders to half-way down her thighs she was one big grey amorphous mass of martyrdom.

'I'll come to you. I'll be there in about forty-five minutes,' he said, then put the phone down, nudged his head under his pillows and waited for Wendy to go away.

Wendy busied herself tidying up the room and changing the towels in the *en-suite* bathroom before heading for the door where she turned and looked at the unruly shape of Julian hiding beneath the bedclothes.

When she'd first interviewed him for the Student Union newspaper at Bristol University, she'd been a high-flying third-year English undergraduate with a glittering academic future, and Julian had been the bright young brash Prince of Comedy, the man who arrogantly proclaimed himself the leading comic force in Britain on the strength of the ten overblown characters he trotted out on his TV sketch show every week. He'd been in Bristol on a UK tour, taking easy money off the students with five comic monologues and a support act.

As a champion of political correctness and scourge of low-brow entertainment, Wendy had armed herself with three type-written sheets of hard-hitting questions, but he'd amused her into bed right there in his dressing room, and from there onto his tour bus. She'd forgone her final term and her degree, and joined him on his twelve-week tour of one-night stands, enjoying the first (and last) reckless decision of her life, and desperately believing their joint assertion that she didn't need her degree because she was going to become a prize-winning novelist.

17

Though their life together had been brilliant at first it could never have barrelled along at that breakneck pace for ever, and she knew the responsibility of the twins had helped to curb their spontaneity. But she was intelligent enough to realise that relationships could see-saw up and down, and that they needed work, and although theirs had only ever 'see-d' and the 'sawing' still seemed some distance away she liked to tell herself that at heart Julian was the warmest, most loving and most exciting man she had ever met and that she still wanted him to be her companion for life.

She crept up to the bed and stood there for five minutes quietly watching Julian's sleeping form until his face rose up slowly out of the sea of pillows to see if she had gone.

'Don't forget it's Tom's first night tonight,' she said, 'so we'll have to leave here at about six thirty, OK?' Then she walked back to the door and closed it quietly behind her as she left the room.

3

An hour later, dressed in his favourite, beaten-up, light-brown leather bomber jacket with a chunky logging shirt, jeans and brogues, Julian closed the door of the house behind him and headed for Gloucester Road tube station.

Julian liked travelling by tube – to him it re-emphasised the fashionably working-class credentials he'd adopted as a young interviewee. Admittedly these had been whittled down over the years until only two remained – drinking in pubs and occasionally travelling by tube – but if interviewers casually asked how he'd travelled to wherever it was they were, he enjoyed answering, 'Well, public transport of course. Why? Didn't you?' Though of course he only ever used the tube between eleven in the morning and two in the afternoon, when the network was deserted save for foreign students and a peculiar breed of anachronously dressed, middle-aged Londoners who never seemed to recognise him.

His stride was brisk and purposeful as he stepped out against the light autumnal breeze and it hardly faltered as he nipped into the Hereford Arms for a quick pint of Kronenbourg and a large Wild Turkey – his preferred bourbon that they stocked especially for him – and from there to the Seven-Eleven four doors along where he had to settle for a quarter bottle of Bell's and a packet of Rothmans. But marching out of the shop his determined gait was brought to a sudden halt as he came face to face once again with his screwed-up disciple – the psycho fan.

'Hi Julian,' she said, her voice weedily thin and annoyingly familiar, her accent strangely cosmopolitan.

19

'Hi,' Julian mumbled. He'd tried pushing past her once but she'd doggedly kept up with him along the whole length of Piccadilly, back and forth across four lanes of traffic, shouting out 'Please wait, please wait' at the top of her shaky little voice, and finally trapping him in a perfumerie in the Burlington Arcade.

How did she always know where he was? Where he was going to be? She had always been able to find him in the most unlikely places and over the last few months especially she'd seemed to be onto his every move.

'Just seven things to sign today,' she said with a nervous laugh, delving into her large woven shoulder bag.

She wasn't a psycho really – 'psycho fan' was just a term Julian had invented as a shorthand way of referring to this incredibly avid admirer who frittered her entire life away waiting for him at every TV studio, every stage door, and more recently it seemed like every street corner; 'psycho fan' was a way of expressing his resentment at her clogging up five or ten minutes of his day every time they met with her mind-numbingly inane chatter and her bagful of new mementoes to sign.

'This is the cover to the Australian video release of *The End of the Pier*,' she said, handing him a clipboard with a pen attached and placing the video jacket upon it. *The End of the Pier* was a series of half-hour dramas he'd made in between the last series of *Mann of the Moment* and the first of *Richard the Nerd* – it had been his pioneering attempt to make the transition from comic to dramatic actor – and it had been a complete flop. Being reminded of it again made him even grumpier. He scrawled 'Best wishes, Julian Mann' across it with such venom that he almost tore the glossy paper.

'Thanking you,' said the psycho fan, oblivious to his anger, neatly folding the jacket along the spine and slotting it into her bag. 'And then there's this from last time,' she said, handing him a ten-by-eight photograph she'd asked a passerby to take of Julian and herself outside the offices of Carlton Television the week before. *How had she known he'd be there?*

20

'I had it enlarged because it came out so well,' she grinned.

Julian scribbled 'Best wishes' across his resigned and resentful face in the photograph – *what did she see in this picture?* – he'd stopped signing 'Love and kisses' six years before in a pathetic attempt to get her off his back, as if that would negate the intimacy she obviously felt existed between them. 'Julian Mann', he scratched across her face and his neck, going back to dot the 'i' and landing it plumb in the middle of her forehead, making her look like a Hindu.

'Just got to get these out without tearing them, sorry to be taking so long,' she said, struggling to ease some sheets of newspaper from her crowded bag – a task made more difficult by her shaking hands.

Why was she still shaking in his presence after eight years of this?

Julian looked back at her image peering out through the curlicues of his signature – she wasn't an unattractive girl, not an obvious trainspotter like some of the keener fans. She must have been in her late twenties and was dressed in a high street version of the New Age look. She had long, hennaed hair with two braids hanging forward of her ears, framing a very paleskinned face intersected by a long, thin, heavily lipsticked and rather crooked mouth, and a pair of straight black eyebrows which almost met in the middle above blue eyes outlined in kohl. She didn't meet Julian's most fanciful conception of attractiveness but early on in their acquaintance, at least, she had held an appeal of her own.

The first time he had had his photograph taken with her he'd put his arm around her shoulder and felt her tremble under his grasp. He'd known she'd been ripe for a kiss and had obliged her on the spur of the moment – it was something he liked to do and it always raised a pleasing caw of jealousy from the other girls hanging around the stage door. The psycho fan had responded with enormous physicality, pressing her body so hard into his that he'd thought she had been trying to meld them into one. The kiss became a regular occurrence thereafter, and it was only after a year or so that Julian had

21

begun not to enjoy it. It began to feel dangerous. He had few maxims in life but one that seemed to click was 'Never fuck a fan' – it was a saying he'd heard attributed to John Lennon, and he'd thought it a remarkably wise one. The desperation in ardent fans was unattractive and frankly quite scary. They couldn't be labelled mentally ill for simply turning up at stage doors repeatedly but there was definitely something touched about that kind of behaviour.

And it wasn't as if Julian was short of other people to fuck with. Naturally he'd like them to be fans of his – he wanted *everyone* to think him a genius and be in awe of his talent and magnetic personality – but they had to have something else in their lives as well. He couldn't entertain the notion of them being solely dependent on him for their existence – it gave him too much responsibility. He knew that from being married with children.

'Here we are,' she said at last, carefully unfolding the front page of that morning's *Daily Mail* and smoothing it across the clipboard. 'That's your first front page since the twenty-fourth of March 1988 when the twins were born and you gave a free glass of champagne to everyone in the audience at the Globe.'

Julian looked at himself being loaded into the ambulance on the stretcher. He looked awful – although the mean quality of the newsprint hadn't done him any favours either.

'You were doing *Accidental Death of an Anarchist* and it was the seventy-ninth performance of the run,' the psycho fan babbled on.

Julian grabbed the cover of the *Daily Star* from her trembling hands. It carried a close-up shot of his face, blotched and pale, with what looked like a rivulet of sick running across his cheek down towards his ear. His hair was mussed up and a lank swathe of it lay plastered across his forehead so that he resembled Adolf Hitler. He tugged at the other sheets of newspaper sticking out of the psycho fan's bag.

'Careful, you'll tear them!'

The front page of the *Mirror*, page four of the *Sun*, page seven of the *Express* – each carrying a similar photograph. His eyes raced over the text to find 'comic genius' or 'funniest Mann' but lighted first on a paragraph headed 'downward spiral' and another in the *Mail* pronouncing him an 'also-ran' and he had to look away, his teeth grating as his jaws clenched at the outrageous humiliation of it all.

'Would you sign them please,' asked the psycho fan, thrusting the pen into his hand.

'No, I fucking won't,' shouted Julian, throwing the sheets of paper into the air, along with the video jacket and the ten-by-eight photograph, where they were caught by the breeze and carried off. The psycho fan toppled backwards trying to catch them. 'It's all fucking lies and you shouldn't read that kind of stuff,' he yelled after her, his face hot and red, then, seeing her careering around the busy pavement trying to catch the errant sheets of paper, and sensing an opportunity to make an escape, he turned and stepped briskly in the opposite direction. As he reached the crossroads he glanced back to see if she was following. She looked panic-stricken – torn between rescuing her precious mementoes and chasing after him.

'I'll try and catch you at the theatre tonight!' she cried, running madly after the video jacket as it was sucked along in the slipstream of a passing van.

She looked pathetic struggling against the traffic and the surge of indifferent pedestrians, and an absurdly chivalrous streak within Julian wondered whether he should lend her a hand. Was he helping himself by running away, or was he merely storing up more trouble for the future? The sudden beeping of the pedestrian crossing forced his hand and he darted across two sides of the crossroads and legged it towards the tube station.

How did she know he was going to the theatre tonight? He'd only found out himself an hour ago! This all-encompassing knowledge of his every move was beginning to feel sinister and threatening.

As he waited impatiently on the station platform, casting

23

nervous glances towards the steps down from the ticket booth, Julian helped himself to a long draught of the scotch and tried to put thoughts of the psycho fan behind him by thinking about Paul and his 'need to talk'. And as the eastbound train arrived and Julian finally gained the safety of a carriage some strange similarities between Paul and the psycho fan suddenly struck him – their unfailing confidence in his 'star quality', their desire to dwell on the minutiae of his life, and their uncanny ability to catch him at moments when he was least expecting them.

How he wished he had a different agent – an agent who would simply phone him three or four times a year to say 'I've got you the best part in the best film for the best money' and then ring off. Though he knew it couldn't be as simple as that. He knew he'd probably never find another agent quite as fawning as Paul, or as adept at getting him out of things he'd agreed to in the afterglow of long and splendid lunches with flattering producers. And what other agent would book his holidays for him, fill in his poll tax forms and arrange late entry for the twins to the best private school in Chelsea?

Yet, unfortunately, by virtue of having so much control over his life, Paul had become just another figure of authority in Julian's eyes – like a teacher or a parent – and had brought out in him his hated but dutiful desire to play the perfect son. The same kind of cheating, lying and deceitful ways he'd used to prove himself a worthy son to his father, the kind of oily charm he had used to impress the parents of his school friends, had now been transferred to the likes of his agent and his bank manager. Meanwhile the rebellious schoolboy within gradually learned to despise them all more and more and to feed on his self-loathing until the smarm could barely hide the malice and resentment festering just below the surface.

Julian took another slug of whisky and wondered how easy it would be to hide his malignant hatred today. No matter what Paul's news was he'd already had the contract for *Blood Train* – so he knew the film was all right. The film would show the bastards who thought he was an 'also-ran' on a 'downward spiral'. This was a real film, an *American* film – a comedy about a psychotic mass-murderer's soul being accidentally transferred into the body of a mild-mannered train conductor – a genuinely funny film written by people who'd written for Steve Martin. *And to be directed by Bill Tyndall!* The award-winning English advertising director who'd just made a low-budget movie with his own money that had already grossed over eighty-five million in the States. *This man was hot!* – and great fun to work with, as Julian already knew from the series of cider commercials they'd made together in Spain the year before.

That had been a wild fortnight, he thought to himself. They had made each other laugh hysterically all day and had drunk each other under the table every night. As the tube clattered out of Hyde Park Corner station it occurred to Julian that in Bill he might have found a soul mate, and sitting there, smiling into the middle distance, he drank a toast to Bill and berated himself for not seeing more of him. After all it was Bill who had sent him the script for *Blood Train* in the first place; Bill who seemed to be the only man in Britain to understand Julian's potential for films; Bill who had communicated his vision of what Julian was capable of back to the faceless executives in America; Bill who had handed him his ticket out of the grubby little world of Britain's comedy circle – his ticket to the future.

It had been a long time since Julian's 'year', 1979/80, when his face had been on the front of every magazine and his name on everyone's lips, bang in between Rowan Atkinson's year and Rik Mayall's.

He'd stepped straight out of drama school into a touring revival of *Charley's Aunt*, 'acting the bollocks' off Lord Fancourt Babberley. The production had done so well in the provinces that the producer had chanced his arm on a West End transfer which became an immediate hit, running for eighteen months, and sweeping all before it at the 1979 *Evening Standard* Awards.

Television had picked him up so quickly that a year later he was collecting the BAFTA for Best Light Entertainment Performance for his work on *Mann of the Moment*, his own sketch show that had had critics rushing to label him the new John Cleese or Eric Morecambe.

He was still famous now of course, but he was no longer a 'find' and practically everything that could be written about him had been written. But now he was going to get a second chance, a second career, and maybe a second 'year'.

Julian toasted Bill again to the consternation of his few fellow travellers and by the time he got to Piccadilly Circus the Bell's was finished. He slipped out of the tube station and into the White Horse and downed another pint of Kronenbourg and a large Jack Daniel's. He ignored the mannerless gawping of a fat old man looking up from behind a *Daily Mail* with his face on the cover, ate a sausage in a bun with lots of mustard, and ordered another round of drinks.

He didn't usually drink this much at lunchtime without at least some pretence at celebrating something, but he knew that Paul had something important to say; which meant there was trouble; which meant he would rather be insensible.

4

On the upper floor of the cramped suite of offices he rented in D'Arblay Street in Soho, Paul sat behind his reproduction Edwardian desk in his sharply cut, velvet-collared tweed jacket with yellow waistcoat and matching handkerchief, and nervously rehearsed the speech he was going to make to Julian. It was sober, dispassionate and fair, a speech by which he could rebuild some measure of honour and pride, a speech that would inform Julian calmly and reasonably that it was Julian's persistent lack of just consideration and respect that had forced his decision – the decision he'd made whilst waiting for Julian to pick up the bedroom extension that morning – that he couldn't bear to represent him any longer.

It seemed an extraordinary decision to have come to, having come so far; as an agent's assistant he'd taken Julian on – much against the advice of the agent he was working for at the time – after seeing him steal the show as Bottom in a Central School of Speech and Drama production of *A Midsummer Night's Dream*. He'd got Julian the job in *Charley's Aunt* and had forged a very good deal out of the subsequent flurry of enquiries from eager television producers. He'd nervously set up his own agency and Julian had happily followed along with him, so that it seemed to Paul that the successes of that first astonishing year were somehow shared.

Yet, this morning, after auto-redialling for two hours, then holding for a further fifteen minutes for his perfunctory phone conversation with Julian, Paul had asked his secretary to gather together every single file and artefact tainted with Julian's

27

name. The assembled pile had filled four large boxes, with various framed awards and magazine covers perched on top.

Paul knew that Julian had more or less despised him since they'd first met – the way he seemed to despise everybody – and that Julian had never looked for another agent only because he was feckless and lazy, but he suddenly wanted to be shot of the endless saga of broken promises and disrespect. He knew that Julian was his star client but he couldn't swallow the casual humiliation any more. His greed had finally been outstripped by his desire to lift his head a little higher.

This sudden gaping fissure in the façade he had kept up so fastidiously for so long frightened Paul, and he felt shaky and anxious, and deeply embarrassed by memories of his kowtowing subservience. He wondered whether he oughtn't postpone the meeting and give himself time for a little more reflection, but just at that moment he heard the entry phone buzzing erratically in reception on the floor below.

Outside in the street Julian was tapping out 'Land of Hope and Glory' on the door buzzer.

'Hello,' crackled a young woman's voice over the intercom, 'who is it?'

'It's Julian,' Julian slurred.

He heard a slight but nevertheless audible titter from the speaker before it was cut off and the door lock began to buzz. He pushed at the door – it wouldn't open. He pushed harder, then shoved at it with his shoulder – it still didn't open. The lock release stopped buzzing.

Julian looked round with arms outstretched as if to beg pity from the whole street for this obvious confirmation that the entire world was against him.

'Are you in?' crackled the voice.

'It's me, Julian, I can't . . .'

The door lock buzzed again and he was startled into action, lurching against the door through a fog of alcohol and anxiously kicking at the bottom corner. The lock release stopped buzzing again.

'OK? Are you in now?' came the voice.

'It's this fucking door! Why don't you get a new door?!' Julian yelled, looking round for something to break.

'Hang on, I'll come down.'

Moments later the door was opened by Elaine, Paul's receptionist, whose chief qualifications for the job were a CSE in typing and an addiction to blue eye-shadow. She was wearing a white blouse with diaphanous panels down either side through which Julian caught glimpses of a lacy white bodice. A good deal of her breasts were fleetingly on show. Julian looked up at Elaine's face, and she smiled. His mood immediately lifted at the prospect of being able to stare at her underwear for the next few minutes.

'I was pushing the wrong side of the door,' he grinned sheepishly, hoping his practical ineptitude would make him seem even more charming than ever.

Elaine opened the door wide so that Julian could pass through into the hall. There was plenty of space but as he moved through he leaned to his right and allowed his upper arm to brush across Elaine's breasts. He stopped and turned round to watch her close the door behind him. 'And how are we, my fair Elaine?' he asked, pulling what he thought was his roguish smile.

'I'm very well Julian, and how are you?' she replied, tittering at the superfluousness of her enquiry.

'I'm extraordinarily well this fine May morning,' he said, throwing out his arm with a theatrical flourish towards the stairs. 'After you.'

'It's September,' said Elaine.

'Who cares? I still insist you go first,' he said, then added, 'belovéd.'

Elaine smiled and tottered through on her high heels, and as she passed his outstretched arm he let his hand drop and clasp onto her bosom. With surprising strength and deftness, but without verbal complaint, Elaine wrested Julian's hand away and mounted the narrow steps towards reception

29

on the first floor. Julian ogled her buttocks which pushed against the material of her short black skirt as she climbed, and remembered the last Christmas party when he'd managed to wrestle Elaine under the mistletoe. He ran after her and lunged at her behind, impersonating Sid James's leering chuckle as he did so to hide any suspicion of outright harassment. But as his outstretched fingertips embedded themselves in the soft flesh of her upper thighs he lost his footing and crashed gracelessly onto the stairs, the tip of his nose scraping painfully against the coconut-fibre stair carpeting as he fell.

'Is that you, Julian?' came Paul's voice from round the bend of the stairs.

'Yes it is,' Julian heard Elaine say. He twisted himself round and managed to sit on a step, put a finger to his nose and was shocked by the excruciating pain. *This was really going to hurt when he sobered up!* It felt as if someone had slashed at his nose with a cheese grater and squeezed lemon juice into the wound.

Paul's flat face appeared round the corner of the stairs behind him, his thin nose barely capable of supporting his horn-rimmed spectacles. 'Trouble?' he asked, in the degenerate tones of the fading aristocracy which Julian knew belied the struggling grammar school boy he was underneath.

'Just had a little argument with your carpet. You haven't got a hanky have you?'

Paul handed him the billowing yellow handkerchief from his top pocket. 'Had a few too many?'

'No, I've only had the one.'

Paul winced. It was this kind of outright bald-faced lie, the sort of obviously feigned respect that a wayward schoolboy might reserve for a particularly hated housemaster, that really irked him. 'Why don't you come and sit in my office? And I'll get you a drink.'

'Black coffee for me please, Paul,' answered Julian, pressing the handkerchief softly to his nose, and blanching in agony. The pleasant drunken euphoria of a minute before seemed to be escaping from him at alarming speed.

'You sure you wouldn't prefer a lager?' asked Paul. 'I can send Elaine out to get some if you'd like.'

'No, it's all right,' said Julian. 'Got any whisky?' He wondered briefly if the drink was eroding the brain cells that controlled his tongue.

'I've got some gin.'

'That'll do.'

Julian stood, lit a cigarette, and clambered up the stairs into Paul's office on the second floor. He saw his reflection in the mirror behind Paul's desk. *Coco the Clown!* Going closer to examine the bright red raw patch on the tip of his nose, he leaned into the mirror to get an even better look and accidentally pressed the inflamed tissues onto the glass. He cried out at the pain, then panicked – it seemed as if his nose was stuck to the mirror, as if the moisture weeping through the broken skin was actually a glue of some sort. He pulled himself slowly backwards until his nose sucked free of the mirror, leaving a nasty, red, gooey patch of indeterminate skin cells and blood.

'Do you think we ought to get a doctor round to look at that?' asked Paul, as he opened the doors to a small wooden cabinet in the corner of the room.

'It's only a flesh wound.'

Paul pulled out a bottle of gin, a bottle of tonic and two Edinburgh crystal glasses and put them on his desk. 'The tonic's a bit warm I'm afraid.'

'That's all right, I won't have any then,' said Julian, and grabbing the gin he poured himself half a tumbler and took a swig. It was horrible – like drinking aftershave – but he could feel an immediate effect, and a very pleasant one. He took another deep draught then sank down in the deep, well-worn leather armchair opposite Paul's desk and waited. A beatific smile spread across his face.

'Bob Carter from Picador rang me this morning . . .'

'Ooooh,' mocked Julian, his attempts at suppressing his laughter sending cigarette smoke streaming from his nostrils like steam from a cartoon bull. 'I'm sorry,' he said. 'Sorry, carry on. You say Bob rang?'

'Yes, Bob rang . . .'

'Ooooooooh.' He laughed – it was a great follow-on gag: he'd said something embarrassing, he'd apologised, and then he'd immediately repeated his faux pas – the comedy of confounded expectation expertly performed by a true professional, he thought to himself. But Paul wasn't laughing, he just sat there disconsolately picking at his nails. This was new behaviour from Paul, Julian thought to himself, it looked like a sulk – something he'd never seen before.

Julian sighed, looked towards the window and tried to think of a single reason why he shouldn't just up and leave. He drained the glass of gin, felt the spirit bite into his mouth, and sucked in air through his teeth in an effort to cool the burning sensation. *This gin was certainly doing the trick.* He made a mental note to drink a lot more of it in the future. 'Come on then, what did big Bob Carter from Picador want?' he said, dragging his mind up through the crashing waves of boredom that seemed about to close in on him for ever, willing Paul to get it all over with so he could just go.

'This is very difficult, you know,' said Paul.

'Is there any way I could make it easier for you?' Julian replied, responding to Paul's growing petulance with sneering disdain.

'They don't want you in the film any more . . .'

'I'm glad, I never wanted to be in it anyway,' said Julian without a moment's hesitation. His reaction was so fast that he almost believed himself for a second.

'. . . after the incident in the pool they think you're too much of an insurance risk,' added Paul. But Julian wasn't listening. His head was reeling with an image of his dream second-coming spinning out of the sky like a stricken Spitfire and smashing into the ground in a ball of flame.

'It was a piece of shit anyway,' Julian managed to say. 'I was only coming in to tell you to get me out of it.'

The room went quiet. Both men were very still.

Anger seemed to be creeping up on Julian like the licking flames of a rapidly spreading fire. He broke the silence by grabbing the gin bottle, spun the top off with one flick of the wrist, and drank heavily from the bottle. Then, feeling the gin washing away at any residual decency and yawning with the nervous excitement of a schoolboy about to spit in his teacher's eye, he lifted both feet high into the air and slammed them down onto Paul's desk with a heavy bang, scuffing the green leather of the desktop with his heels.

Paul flinched and looked up.

Julian met his eyes and stared him out, lifting his eyebrows as if to say 'So what? I'm the biggest fucking artist you've got on your books so you'll just have to sit there and take it, won't you?' and took another long pull at the gin bottle.

Paul sat rigid in his chair, barely breathing, trying to keep a lid on his nervousness. In his head he went through the first few points of the speech he'd been rehearsing but then realised that Julian's drunken, almost horizontal state had cheated him out of all that. It was difficult to argue with Julian when he was sober – it would be impossible when he was drunk. Julian would maul him like a lion, would torture him like a cat might torture a moth, scraping gently at his wings until all he'd be able to do would be spin around on the floor like a demented beetle. So the speech would have to go unsaid, his pride would have to be restored some other way, some other time.

'So we sue them for breach of contract, right?' Julian burped. 'I mean we still get the money, don't we?'

Paul took a deep breath. 'We might have had a chance of claiming some of it, Julian – but you never signed your contract.'

'I don't like signing contracts.'

'That's why you have so few rights in this particular instance,' said Paul, dejectedly remembering the three months of extraordinarily arduous negotiations with Picador.

Julian was silently furious. *He'd* intended *to sign it for God's*

33

sake! The money was already earmarked for the two whacking tax demands that were stuffed down the back of the 'To do' drawer at home.

Julian got up, moved unsteadily to the window and looked out. D'Arblay Street was full of nameless people in sharp clothes walking to and from smart little advertising agencies and film companies. It annoyed Julian that none of them looked up and noticed him; annoyed him that they were all so smugly successful in their pathetic little jobs; annoyed him that none of them came in through the door below, rushed up the stairs to Paul's office, and sorted the whole bloody mess out for him. He hated them all.

'Maybe I wouldn't be in this mess if I had a decent fucking agent,' he growled, and turned to give Paul his evil eye, but Paul wasn't there.

There was a sharp squeal of taxi brakes from the street below and Julian turned to the window. The taxi had stopped outside Paul's door and Julian saw Elaine scurry into view. The speed of her appearance puzzled Julian – she must have been waiting at the door.

Julian turned back to the room hoping Paul would have returned so that he could ask him what was going on, but he still wasn't there. He looked back out of the window and saw Elaine struggling to load a box of files and papers into the back of the cab. She seemed nervous – eager to get whatever she was doing over and done with before anyone spotted her. Julian wondered whether Paul was doing a moonlight flit in broad daylight, and his regard for him increased considerably. He stumbled across to the desk, demolished the last of the gin, and set out for the stairs to investigate. If naughty goings-on were in the air he wanted to be in on them. The very idea of an 'adventure' filled him with a sudden rush of pleasure, expunging all feelings of anger and frustration from his mind in an instant.

'Paul! Paul!' he shouted, and stuck out his foot to negotiate the first step – but missed. His momentum carried his foot

34

down to the second step where it buckled beneath him and he soon found himself sledging down the stairs on the folded leg. He hoped the bend in the stairs might stop him but the sudden jolt as his knee hit the wall caused him to topple sideways and he slid down the rest of the stairs headfirst on his back. He came to rest on the landing and found himself looking up into the faces of Paul and Leon. Leon was a tall, muscular youth who took care of the photocopying, ran errands, and occasionally made love to Paul during the lunch break.

'What's going on, Paul?' asked Julian.

'I think you've just fallen down the stairs,' said Paul.

'Are you running away?' Julian was content to remain lying on the landing floor. 'Can I come with you? Come on, let's run away together. But I vote we hit the Groucho first and get drunk.'

'Julian . . .'

'Yes?' Julian looked into Paul's face and could see that it was suddenly shiny with perspiration.

'Julian, I . . .' Paul's right hand started shaking uncontrollably at the end of his sleeve, as if someone else had control of it.

'Want to have a wank? What?' asked Julian.

'I don't . . . don't . . . want . . . to be your agent any more,' stuttered Paul. Then he burst into tears. He turned to make his escape up the stairs, to get away from the embarrassment, but to his great consternation he found he couldn't get his feet to climb the first step. It felt like his whole body had suddenly been disconnected from his brain to compensate for the great waves of fear and relief that were surging through his head. His right hand was banging violently and involuntarily against the wall and his legs began to shake.

'Are you all right, Mr Morrison?' asked Leon, his mouth hanging open in shock.

Paul made a superhuman effort to make the first step but couldn't even see it now through the haze of tears and snot.

35

He let out an anguished animal cry, like a fox caught in a trap, which stilled the whole building. A dark stain spread down the inner thigh of his trousers, his knees buckled beneath him and he fell onto the stairs where he lay whining and shivering like a whipped puppy.

'I think you'd better go now, Mr Mann, sir,' said Leon as authoritatively as he could.

Julian raised himself onto one elbow. 'What the fuck was that? It was like the fucking *Exorcist*!'

Leon helped Julian to his feet and firmly manœuvred him to the stairs.

'Hey, steady on, what d'you think you're doing?'

'Mr Morrison said he'd like you to leave once he'd told you.'

'Told me what?'

'About not wanting to be your agent any more,' said Leon, almost carrying Julian to the bend in the stairs.

'You what?'

'I think you heard, Mr Mann.'

'Doesn't want to be my agent any more?'

'That's right, sir,' said Leon, supporting most of Julian's weight as he jostled him down the last few stairs, through the open front door into the street, past Elaine and into the waiting cab.

'But . . .'

'These are all your papers, Julian.' Elaine pointed to four large boxes in the back of the cab. 'Now they're important – so try not to lose them, OK? Oh, and here's today's *Telegraph* – there's a great profile by Jeff Healy I think you'll like, he calls you Britain's most singular comic talent since Tony Hancock.'

Leon strapped Julian into the back seat, pulled back out of the cab and closed the door. Elaine stuck her head through the open window and Julian leaned forward to get a better view of her breasts.

'Sorry it had to end this way. I think you're very funny as well you know,' she said.

'Come on, Elaine,' said Leon, pulling Elaine back from the window.

'But . . .' said Julian.

'All right, cabbie,' shouted Elaine to the cab driver, who raised a hand in acknowledgement and pulled away.

Julian turned in his seat and watched in confusion as Elaine waved goodbye. The cab turned the corner into Wardour Street, and she was gone. He looked round distractedly, unable to focus on the world spinning by.

'Glad to see you're still with us then,' said the cabbie, turning in his seat to get a better look at Julian. 'Bit depressed, were you?'

'What?' Julian didn't want to understand what the cabbie was talking about.

'When you gonna do another series of that *Richard the Nerd*?' asked the cabbie, smiling at Julian in his mirror. 'Me and my wife love that.'

'Why don't you just fuck off?' snarled Julian, and he opened the *Telegraph* and fell into unconsciousness on the back seat.

5

'Hoy, we're there! Hoy, mate, come on!'

Julian half-opened one bleary eye and lifted his head. A long trail of slaver fell from the corner of his mouth and recoiled tantalisingly like a yo-yo before the thread snapped and it sank messily into the leather of his light brown bomber jacket. He wiped his chin clumsily with his hand and caught the end of his nose with his thumb. The thin scab that had formed was immediately broken and Julian was startled into full consciousness by the excruciating pain. Looking around and unable to comprehend what was happening or where he was, it occurred to him that he might have been in a fight.

'Come on, out you come,' said the cabbie, offering a hand to Julian who shrank back in terror.

'Don't hit my face!' he yelled out. Then, after no blows rained down upon him, he cautiously opened the protective shield of his forearms and looked through the gap. He could see a plump, balding, grey-faced little man whose outstretched hand wasn't in the shape of a fist as he'd previously imagined, but open and helpful.

'Where am I?' he asked, stumbling out of the cab.

'Rosary Gardens, that's right, isn't it?' asked the cabbie, shutting the door to the passenger compartment and climbing in behind the steering wheel.

Julian looked around in panic. He could see a mass of large, red-brick, four-storey Edwardian terraces on either side of the street – which seemed right to him – but he couldn't see his bust of William Shakespeare anywhere. It was a cheap plaster bust that he'd adorned with a comedy arrow-through-the-head that had once belonged to Tommy Cooper, and he'd put it in the bay window of the front drawing room specifically for this kind of emergency. It often came in handy when he arrived home the worse for wear and couldn't distinguish his house from the hundred or so identical ones in the street.

'This isn't my street! Where am I?'

'I think you'll find your house just behind the van there,' growled the cabbie, pointing to a Luton van on the opposite side of the street as he pulled away.

'But what time is it? Stop, help me!' Julian screamed desperately at the departing cab, getting only a casual V-sign out of the driver's window in reply.

He struggled to find some point of reference. He didn't know where he was, or what time it was, or where he'd been. He wasn't sure whether he was sober or drunk. All he knew was that he was severely confused, and that his nose hurt. He looked at the van – it completely blocked any view of the drawing-room windows of the house behind it. He moved towards it to check them out and tripped over a framed photograph that was perched on top of one of several boxes set on the pavement. The thin glass in the frame shattered. Julian swore and kicked it out of his way, then noticed it was a photograph of himself on the cover of the *Radio Times*.

He tried to squat and had to settle for sitting on the kerb. He looked more closely into the nearest box and saw the pilot script for *Save Our Souls*, his proposed new sitcom by his regular writing team, Halford and Dixon – the show he'd recently pulled out of, much to their chagrin. He dug his hands into the mass of papers and pulled out a contract for a yoghurt voice-over he'd done, a copy of a letter from Elaine confirming the details of their last family holiday to Kenya, and a small award statuette he'd received from Romania, inscribed with an odd jumble of Cyrillic letters and then the words 'Richard the Nerd' in English. It was as if someone had put his life in a box, he thought.

Why had he come home with these boxes? It was like some paranoid's nightmare. Was *he at home?*

This thought renewed his earlier panic attack, and scrambling to his feet he struggled unsteadily across the road. As he lurched round the front of the van his eyes fell immediately on the skewered Shakespeare staring imperiously down at him from pride of place in the front window, framed by fold upon fold of the salmon-pink ruching that he hated so much.

He often thought he wouldn't mind living in a house that looked like a brothel if the filthy sex and degradation came with it, but Wendy had made their house into a Disney version of a whorehouse, a safe, kitsch model of the real thing.

As he surveyed the curtains he thought, not for the first time also, that the whole house had been a mistake. It was far too big for the four of them. A family of fifteen could have lived in it quite happily – a point his card-carrying sister had made quite disdainfully every time she'd visited, until Julian had stopped inviting her round altogether. Helena was a hard-working computer programmer who lived in Milton Keynes with her equally hard-working husband and she had come to sneer at Julian's easy success which she thought so undeserved because he'd never 'put the hours in'.

Indeed his sister's comments seemed to echo most people's reaction to the obvious ostentatiousness of his house. There was a bathroom on every floor, which Julian found particularly ridiculous, even if remarkably convenient at times. He'd pleaded with Wendy to have a live-in nanny so that he wouldn't feel quite as socially irresponsible taking up all that space for just one small family, but she'd chastised him as the nominal socialist he was for the idea of having 'staff' and wouldn't allow it. Besides, Wendy wanted to be a 'real' mother – although she didn't balk at employing a cleaner three full days a week.

Julian hated the red bricks and the tiny garden and the fact that theirs was the only house in the entire street that hadn't been chopped up into flats – it made him feel like he'd paid half a million pounds to live in bedsitterland. Wendy had chosen the house, and furnished it, and decorated it. Julian had merely paid for it – and he felt like a lodger.

Though at that moment he was enormously relieved to see it – it meant that he was back in the real world, that he knew where he was, and that he almost knew what was happening.

'Two out of three isn't bad,' he murmured to himself, and felt in his pockets for his cigarettes.

He lit one, slumped against the gatepost which led to the steps up to the front door and slowly slid to the ground. The smoke filled him with a sense of calm and the world became more ordered with each puff. The sun had come out since the morning and the wind had dropped and Julian shrugged his jacket off and clumsily threw it up onto the wrought-iron railings of the gate.

Resting back against the gatepost he stretched his legs out along the bottom step, and lifted his face towards the sun to let the warm rays relax the bruised feeling around his eyes.

He was reminded of Indian summers at school and recalled the days when smoking and sitting on walls had seemed to be his chief occupations, and how happy he'd been then. He remembered girlfriends who smiled and uncomplicated sex, and a sense of fun and freedom that pervaded everything he did. He wondered glumly why being thirty-eight and married to a manic interior decorator necessarily required an automatic surrender of those instinctive freedoms, and whether he could buy himself a ticket back to those days.

There must have been moments of misery and depression in his youth, but in his memory even they had been emotions to be enjoyed – so different from the numbing melancholy of the present. In his school-days his bouts of petulant unhappiness had been necessary to bolster the image he'd tried to project of himself as the tortured romantic poet, out to live and love before an early and tragic death, much mourned by his many admirers (predominantly nubile, with Pre-Raphaelite hair and full, teasing lips).

He remembered Clare, his first real love, and her tight

smooth skin, her growing breasts, and downy pubic hair. It seemed they'd had sex wherever and whenever they'd wanted, great sex, imaginative sex, exciting, uninhibited sex, sex outside, on buses, in parents' beds and in the school library. He wondered why she'd seemed so pedestrian and provincial when she'd come to visit him during his first year in London. Perhaps she hadn't been sophisticated enough for his pretentious new life-style. All she'd done was smile and have sex. She'd been sunny and uncomplicated and had always worn white, whilst the girls at the drama school had been pale and brooding and had always worn black. He wondered how his life would be now if Clare and he had fulfilled their teenage promises to each other and eloped to live in a gypsy caravan. They'd probably be having sex right now, he thought, and his cock stirred in his trousers. He lifted his knees, slipped his hand in his trouser pocket and gently rubbed himself.

The front door next to his opened and two men in bright green cotton trousers and jackets ambled out and disappeared round the back of the van. Julian sat up and looked round. He could see their monkey boots and the bright green of their trousers beneath the tailgate of the van and he sighed.

'Ordinaries,' he muttered softly.

He enjoyed recognition on the whole, but there were certain types who made it difficult, and working-class British males were the most troublesome – they would heckle and cajole and tell him dull jokes, then feel aggrieved if he didn't give them an impromptu performance of his greatest hits right there on the spot.

Julian decided to avoid these particular ordinaries by darting into the porch of his house and flattening himself against the party wall so that they wouldn't see him. He couldn't remember whether he had a door key or not but he thought it would be safer to check once he'd gained the safety of his hideaway rather than risk them finding him where he was. Thus resolved, he quickly got to his feet, made a dash up the steps towards the front porch and suddenly realised he was still completely drunk. He spun dizzily out of control and fell awkwardly over the railings dividing the two houses, landing flat on his back and leaving himself very badly winded. He looked up into the glowering face of one of the men, who was carrying a large, primitive clay sculpture.

'What's your game? Come on, mate, out the way,' said the man. 'Hey! Hang on. It is, isn't it? Here, Nigel, look, it's that Julian Mann, isn't it! Did you see him fall over the railings? He went a real cracker – didn't you?'

Julian couldn't have answered if he'd wanted to, he was still fighting the persistent thought that his lungs might never re-flate. He felt as if a ten-ton truck had been parked on his chest.

The man called Nigel emerged behind the first man. He was older than his associate, with a rocker's quiff and greying temples, and didn't sport his friend's regulation earring and razored hair.

'It's Julian Mann, you know. With the funny eye – look.

'What's he done to his nose?' asked Nigel.

Julian couldn't believe they hadn't run off to call an ambulance, and began to worry that they might continue their inane chatter through the actual moment of his imminent death. He hated their swagger and familiarity, and their football-thug looks. It was all so different from the day-dream he'd just had ... Where were the Pre-Raphaelite nymphs in their flimsy cotton slips with their soothing hands and giggly adoration?

'He's a lot fatter than he looks on the telly, isn't he?' remarked the first man.

At that moment a valve seemed to clear and Julian felt himself sucking in air. His lungs inflated steadily with one long, slow breath, the muscles of his diaphragm extending to increase the capacity.

'And he's getting even fatter as we speak,' sniggered Nigel.

Julian was incensed. As soon as he'd vacuumed in a sufficient volume of air he flailed around desperately with his arms and tried to get to his feet. The two men grabbed hold of an arm each to help him.

'Whoever he is, he's pissed, isn't he?' said Nigel, as they sat Julian on the top step where he doubled over, breathing as deeply and steadily as he could. He'd just wait until he'd recovered some composure, he thought to himself, then he'd stand up quickly, taking them by surprise, and he'd land one right on Nigel's nose.

'Hello? Can somebody move these?' came an old woman's angry voice from the other side of the van. 'Hello . . . help!' The two men went round the back of the van to investigate.

'Bastards,' muttered Julian to himself, cursing them for moving away when he'd just about worked up the courage to execute his plan – but he was glad of the extra recovery time and was beginning to feel more human with every breath.

He became aware of the sculpture standing directly in front of him. He wasn't quite sure what it was – a primitive human figure about three or four feet high, in terracotta. The legs were short stumps, more like bulbous hips with the beginnings of feet beneath, the buttocks very pronounced and provocative. He could discern a definite bosom behind a crudely designed pair of arms folded across her chest, and looking back down between her 'legs' he could now see a definite slit for a vagina which he'd missed before. He wondered why she was being so coy about her breasts when the contents of her pants were on full show. The head was very odd. There was no neck, no chin, no nose, no ears, just a simple column with two slits for the eyes. Julian chuckled as it dawned on him that it was a female figure with a phallus for a head, the slits for the eyes representing the retracted foreskin.

'Move them now!'

Julian was brought back to the real world with a jolt by the apoplectic shrieking of the old woman across the street. The situation was complex and depressingly urgent: he was dizzyingly drunk and winded; he was in a ghastly conversation with some ordinaries who kept making disparaging remarks about

44

his appearance; and he was determined to plant one on the git called Nigel.

He looked at the clay figure for inspiration and decided to shelve the planned fight and make a quick escape instead. He rose carefully to his feet to avoid a repetition of his earlier fall, and supporting himself on the gatepost he swung round onto his own steps, picked his jacket off the gate, and set off as stealthily as he could in the direction of the pub. As he cleared the end of the van – the end of his cover – he quickened his step, but was immediately spotted by the git Nigel on the other side of the street.

'Here, Julian! This is your stuff, isn't it?' shouted Nigel, pointing at the boxes which were blocking the way of the cross old woman trailing a shopping basket on wheels. Julian thought of running on and pretending he hadn't been seen but realised it wasn't on – they could easily out-run him in the state he was in. He stopped and peered across at Nigel.

'What?'

'This is your stuff, isn't it?'

'No.'

'Yes it is.'

'All right – yes it is.'

'Well, you'd better move them,' spluttered the old woman through flecks of rage-induced spittle. 'I can't get past! I've got to feed my cats!'

Julian reached clumsily for his wallet in his inside jacket pocket, opened it, and took out a fifty-pound note. He looked Nigel right in the eye with the kind of superiority he knew money could buy.

'Look, you, whatever your name is, here's fifty quid,' he said, lifting a windscreen wiper blade on the van and letting it snap back on the note. 'Do us a favour and bung those boxes by my front door, would you?' He waved loosely at his front door, gave them a kind of military nod, as if to say 'Carry on chaps', then set out again down the street with as steady and purposeful a stride as he could muster.

45

Half-way down the street he dared to look back and see if they'd accepted his instructions. They had. Each of them was carrying a box and the old woman was continuing along the pavement in the opposite direction, shaking her head in the over-exaggerated way of the slightly inconvenienced.

They were all so insignificant – just ordinary people, getting in the way. The only real importance any of them had was as people who watched his TV shows.

He found his way to Gloucester Road but instead of dropping into the Hereford Arms as he'd originally planned he headed for Parker's, an expensive little restaurant where he'd come to know the owner, and where the prices kept out the ordinaries. Without taking his seat he ordered pan-fried calf's liver with 'a selection of vegetables', a side order of mashed potatoes, and a bottle of Château Margaux Margaux, then he nipped out to buy something to read whilst they set his table. Julian wasn't a wine buff but he'd discovered Château Margaux Margaux by chance one day, liked the taste, and was comforted by the thought that its sixty-pound price tag must guarantee some sort of quality. He also enjoyed the appreciative murmurs of fellow diners every time he ordered it.

In the newsagent's, looking at the racks of newspapers and magazines, he dimly remembered Elaine saying that there was a favourable article about him in the *Telegraph* and he bought a copy. Rummaging through his pockets for loose change at the counter he happened upon his house keys, and felt happy that his next few hours were fairly pleasurably set. He would eat his favourite lunch on his own at his usual table, study the account of his genius in the paper, polish off a bottle of Margaux, and then saunter home for a little lie-down in front of the telly.

6

When Wendy arrived home at four o'clock with the twins she was annoyed, though not particularly surprised, to find the front door wide open, and puzzled by the boxes of papers blocking the entrance hall – boxes that on casual inspection seemed to contain the kind of material normally kept by Paul.

'Is Daddy home?' shouted Sean.

'Yeah, because he's not dead, is he?' shouted Jamie.

'No, he's not dead, I told you that,' Wendy replied.

'Is he home then?'

'Yeah, is he home?'

'Yes, I think so,' said Wendy.

'Yippee!' they screamed, clambering over the boxes and planting their dusty footprints all over the top layer of documents as they began a whirlwind search of the house, rushing into the front drawing room, through the double doors into the dining room, back into the hall and then into what Wendy liked to call her boudoir at the back of the house, overlooking the garden.

'Not in there!' shouted Wendy. The boudoir was *her* room, a lacy sanctuary of frills, embroidery and delicate china ornaments, the one room in the house that was off-limits to the twins. They bundled out, laughing and giggling, wrenched open the door to the ground-floor bathroom and stuck their heads in.

'Daddy, where are you? Come out!' shouted Jamie.

'Yeah, because we know you're not dead,' added Sean. They hurtled down the stairs into the basement towards the sound of a blaring television coming from the family room at the back of the house.

'Daddy!' they shouted as they ran in and saw him lying unconscious on a sofa. They jumped on top of his inert body and started landing playful punches.

Wendy followed after them into the least fussily decorated room of the house – just two enormous sofas with big throw-over blankets from Arizona, an old armoire that served as a toy cupboard, a Persian rug, and an Indian coffee table, with a TV and hi-fi system in the corner – and stood watching as they sank their fists into Julian's soft belly and kneed him in the ribs. Julian didn't stir. A bubbly mass of spit had formed at one corner of his mouth where his heavy breathing had found an escape route from his anaesthetised face. Sean and Jamie chuckled excitedly and bracing themselves against the back of the sofa they stuck their feet into Julian and pushed him onto the floor. He fell heavily, his skull hitting the ground with such force that the polished floorboard beneath the rug sang like a low-pitched tuning fork – but he still didn't waken.

'Are you sure he's not dead?' Sean asked his mother.

'No, look, he's breathing,' said Jamie. 'He's just had too much special tea, hasn't he, Mummy?'

'Has he, Mummy?' asked Sean.

'No, I think he's just tired,' said Wendy.

'Come on then, let's wake him up!' shouted Jamie.

'Yeeaah!' screamed Sean, collecting a plastic axe from a wicker basket behind the sofa and chopping at Julian with it mercilessly. Jamie picked up a Masters of the Universe sword and took to stabbing at Julian's genitals.

'Right, that's enough now, boys,' Wendy intervened. 'Come and get a biscuit, then you can go upstairs and play for a while.'

'What's Daddy done to his nose?' asked Jamie, bending down and getting his face right up close to Julian's nose. Sean got down to have a good look as well, casually prodding at it with the end of his axe. Julian instantly recoiled, spluttering and slavering, but still failed to regain consciousness. Wendy walked over and had a look.

'I don't know. Looks like he's hurt it, hasn't he?' she said.

'Yeah,' said Sean.

'Yeah,' echoed Jamie. 'Is that where they thought he'd killed himself?'

'You can't die from a nose cut can you, Mummy?' asked Sean.

'No, it was just a silly made-up story that they put in the newspapers for a bit of fun. Because Daddy's funny, isn't he?'

'Yeah, Daddy's funny,' chorused the boys.

'Let's leave him to have a bit more sleep,' said Wendy, ushering the boys towards the door. 'Come and have your biscuits and a glass of milk, then you can have a little play, and then you'll have to do your homework. What is it today?'

'It's the two times table!' they shouted together as they ran out through the door and careered off towards the kitchen at the front of the house, pulling at each other's jumpers on the way and bouncing each other off the walls. Wendy showed no outward emotion but winced inwardly as their plastic weapons scuffed against her delicate pink-and-cream wallpaper.

'Can you get the milk on your own?' Wendy asked after them, still standing at the door.

'Yes, I can,' shouted Jamie.

'No, I can,' shouted Sean.

'No, I am.'

'No, I can.'

'You can get the biscuits, Sean,' intervened Wendy.

'All right, Mummy,' shouted Sean, and he slammed the kitchen door behind him.

Wendy was secretly proud of the way she always managed to appear nonchalant in front of the boys on occasions such as this. She held the view that if she could appear calm and relatively unconcerned about Julian's bad behaviour, then the boys wouldn't worry about it either, and in consequence wouldn't suffer too much long-term damage.

49

She sighed and went back into the family room, crouching down to have a closer look at Julian's nose. The thin scab had been broken by Sean's injudicious hit, and a section of it had been folded back onto the unhurt part of his nose. Wendy carefully teased the errant flap with her fingernail and flipped it back into its rightful place. It looked a lot worse than it was, she thought, and sank back into one of the sofas with another sigh.

It had been a trying forty-eight hours for Wendy. There had been the embarrassment at the BAFTAs where she had had to sit looking quietly on as Julian and the man from LWT had grappled each other to the floor, taking two place settings of crockery and glasses with them before being separated by a group of equally drunken comics and light-entertainment executives, with a head of current affairs thrown in for good measure. She'd actually agreed with everything Julian had said, and if she'd had the nerve she would have been in there giving Julian a hand. What she'd really hated was the embarrassed murmurings of the other wives at the table, their pitying looks and patronising concern, their automatic assumption that she must be mortified, and how belittling that had felt.

The 'suicide' hysteria of the night before and the objection-able, persistent and frankly terrifying attention of the press on her doorstep had left her feeling tired and angry. The family had never suffered such abuse from the tabloid press before, even when Julian had very publicly refused to shake Margaret Thatcher's hand backstage after a charity gala in '88.

While leafing through their address book at half past three in the morning, looking for people who might have a clue as to Julian's whereabouts, Wendy had realised how few friends they actually had.

She had realised that she herself had made no new friends since she'd stepped onto Julian's tour bus eight years before in Bristol, and of the four 'friends' of Julian that she'd tried to ring, three had moved without sending them change of address cards, and the fourth hadn't seen Julian for more than eighteen months.

Slumped there on the sofa watching the rise and fall of Julian's chest and listening to his grumbling snore above the white noise of the television, it occurred to Wendy that she was almost completely alone. Being so much on the periphery of Julian's world she had been unable to make anything more than acquaintances through his work. She couldn't count mothers of other children at the twins' school; they were normally pleasant and chatty enough – though this morning after being splashed across the front pages she thought some of them had seemed noticeably cooler – but they could never be counted as real friends.

She had been more or less cut off by her own parents for marrying Julian, and for doing so so impetuously in Gretna Green, without them, and now their doom-laden visits to see the grandchildren were becoming gradually more infrequent. Though Julian's sister seemed to provoke a battle of literary references every time she and Wendy met (in an effort to prove that computer programmers were as sentient and as intellectually stimulating as erudite English scholars), his parents were perfectly affable, and had welcomed Wendy into the family with polite enthusiasm. It was Julian who had more or less cut them off for he seemed to feel he could never live up to the aspirations he imagined they had for him, could not keep up the image of the diligent and embattled little fighter of a perfect son he had pretended to be as a boy.

It struck Wendy that the only friend she had was Tom, who had been her best friend since her first term at university.

Except for Carly perhaps, she thought, reminded by two empty cups standing on the coffee table in front of her that Carly had popped in just before lunch to sympathise and offer help after seeing the newspapers. Carly had only moved into the street four months before but perhaps she and Wendy were 'friends' – though it seemed odd to have a 'neighbour' as a real friend in London. Wendy had never known it to happen before.

Carly had more or less picked Wendy up in the butcher's shop just after she'd moved into the area. She had helped Wendy carry some heavy shopping bags and held Sean's hand to stop him from running into the road. By the time they'd walked the short distance from Gloucester Road to the house Carly had told Wendy practically her whole life story. She had seemed so good-humoured and easy in conversation – the most instantly amiable person Wendy had ever met.

And Wendy found Carly's life story fascinating: her miserable childhood; her mother who had died when she was six; her father who had never taken an interest in her but had simply sent a cheque every month; how she'd moved from boarding school to finishing school to fashion school and then briefly to a sanatorium; how she had never had to hold down a real job but had ended up teaching the Alexander Technique at the East/West Centre . . . Wendy found it so fascinating that she had even wondered idly about trying to write it out as a novel.

Carly was such a voluble soul and the unexpected twists and turns in her conversation stimulated Wendy's intellect. It was Carly, that morning, who had asked Wendy where she imagined Julian had been all night. There had been nothing malicious or prurient in her tone, indeed Wendy had come to fancy that talking things over with Carly was like half an hour's free therapy with an incredibly friendly analyst.

Wendy had explained that Julian sometimes stayed out all night, but that she didn't feel threatened because that was his playtime. She realised it must seem odd to someone not involved, but the show-business world he lived in was one that she could neither really join in on, nor one that she could, or would want, to deny him. She'd seen it on the first tour with him, the need to go wild after the nerves of performing – no matter how sure of his own brilliance, he was always nervous, so nervous that he actually used to throw up before every single performance – it was like a drug, or coming down from a drug, and she had never wanted to interfere.

But Wendy wasn't stupid and she knew what Carly had been asking about – whether Julian slept around or not – and she had countered with 'Well, you know Julian. Do *you* think he sleeps around?' She'd been shocked and surprised to find that Carly had never actually met him. But on reflection it only served to emphasise their different lives: Julian's show-business life that she felt excluded from, and Wendy's domestic life that he had no interest in.

Carly had said that wives were always the last to find out because no one would ever tell – only a jealous friend or a psycho.

Wendy was returned to the present by a loud crash from the kitchen and went to investigate.

Sean and Jamie had done relatively well in their milk-and-biscuit-getting operation. The fridge door was hanging open but the bottle had been replaced, and the biscuit barrel was back on the breakfast bar, although it evidently had been the subject of the crash she'd heard as it now bore a huge dent at one corner. The boys were presently engaged in chomping up as much biscuit as they could, inflating their cheeks with air, then punching them with their fists to see how far the spray of crumbs would go.

'That's enough of that, thank you,' said Wendy calmly. 'Now go on upstairs and have a play while I make a phone call.'

The boys swung out into the hall, giggling giddily, and clomped their way up the two flights of stairs to their playroom. Wendy picked up the kitchen phone and pushed the memory button marked 'P.M.A.'.

'Paul Morrison Associates,' came Elaine's voice.

'Hi, it's Wendy, can I speak to Paul please?'

'Oh, hello Wendy. It's Elaine. Did he get home all right?'

'Well, he's home.'

'Oh it's an awful business.'

There was an unfamiliar nervousness in Elaine's voice that Wendy found disconcerting.

'Is Paul there?' asked Wendy.

'No, he had to go home.'

'Has something happened?'

'He was very upset.'

'What are all these boxes doing here?'

'Didn't Julian tell you?'

'He's sleeping at the moment.'

'Oh, I don't know if I should say, really.'

'Just tell me what's happened, Elaine.'

'I think you ought to speak to Paul.'

'But Paul's not in?'

'No.'

'Come on Elaine, just tell me what's happened,' said Wendy, an uncharacteristic hectoring tone entering her voice. She spent most of her life being reasonable to the point of stupidity, indeed she often helped herself along by imagining herself as a saint – it gave her some status in her own mind in the face of humiliation or distress. In fact that morning's *Independent* – which had cleverly absolved itself from harassment by reporting on the media circus outside Wendy's house and not actually shouting through the letter box – had reflected on the saintliness of Julian's wife 'Winnie' (sic). But now 'Winnie' was becoming impatient. 'Come on Elaine, just tell me!'

She listened to Elaine summoning up the courage to speak.

'Paul's decided he can't represent Julian any more,' said Elaine falteringly.

They listened to each other's silence for a moment.

'Thank you,' said Wendy, and she replaced the receiver. She felt a worrying sense of chaos. Paul went back with Julian further than she did; he was a friend; he'd been on holiday with them; he was the twins' godfather for God's sake!

She stared at the phone for a moment, then reached into her shoulder bag for her cigarettes. She lit one, breathed out, then pulled on it deeply, drawing surely and steadily until it seemed as though her whole body had been emptied of flesh and blood and filled with billowing smoke. She felt the nicotine hit – the numbing sensation in her head that briefly switched off her brain's capacity to feel stress – then exhaled, almost snorting, the grey smoke galloping through her nostrils as though it were alive, then slowing to a canter, through to a trot, and finally stumbling to a halt. On her next pull she sensed her shoulders droop as her head lolled back and she felt a pleasant dizziness and closed her eyes. She swayed like a young tree in the breeze and had to hold out her hand to steady herself against the big pine dresser.

Her head filled with the vision of a Jamaican beach. She was lying under a blazing sun on silky, white sand while Sean and Jamie splashed happily in the shallows. They'd become so brown after six months in the tropics that they didn't need sun-tan lotion any more, in fact they hardly needed looking after at all. They got fed by the cook and seemed happy to amuse themselves all day, only turning to her for love and affection. She rolled her head back in the sand and looked up behind her at the villa perched on the rocks above their private cove: 'Golden Eye', Noël Coward's old villa. It was an inspiring location. She had just finished correcting the proofs of her first novel, a novel that had made history by selling its film rights, pre-publication, for the most astronomical figure ever, a novel based on Carly's life story, a story of abuse, neglect and mental instability being transformed into a healing force for the world.

Back in her SW7 kitchen Wendy looked down at her cigarette just in time to see a huge cylinder of ash fall from it and break onto her shoe. She flicked it onto the pile of old newspapers, heaped by the side of the dresser, that Julian was supposed to have taken to the recycling bin – it was his *only* domestic chore and she had determined not to give in and do it for him – and castigated herself for having such a pathetic day-dream. Not just for the tweeness of it all – the smell of a Jackie Collins TV mini-series (in the past the dream had had a much more bohemian flavour) – but for the fanciful notion of presuming herself to be a writer. She wasn't a writer. *If she were a writer she'd have written something.*

Wendy had never written anything from the moment she stepped on the tour bus. She'd occasionally spent a happy hour in a stationer's shop buying new notebooks and pencils but they were never used, except for phone messages and shopping lists. Julian had bought her expensive Mont Blanc pens and sheets of vellum paper on which simply making a mark was a sensory adventure in itself, but she still hadn't felt encouraged to write. Julian had embarrassed himself with the PR and newspaper people he'd come into contact with, getting her introductions and promises to read whatever she produced – short stories, articles, film reviews, anything – but she never wrote. All she did was read. She read voraciously – classic novels, pulp fiction, popular biography, history, art, junk sociology – and the more she read, and the more she learned, the less adequate and competent she felt to write herself, until she stopped buying notebooks and pencils altogether and accepted that writing was just a day-dream that crept into her head occasionally when she felt particularly stressed and anxious and wanted to get away from it all.

The phone conversation with Elaine made her feel like getting away from it all. Not that Julian being dumped by his agent was any more trying than past calamities had been, but it was a surprise, a twist in the saga, and even though she'd learned to expect the unexpected it could still provoke a brief flurry of panic. Despite living with Julian for eight years she could still be shocked and unnerved by things that seemed more or less inevitable after five minutes' reflection.

In the first few months of their relationship Julian's sometimes erratic behaviour had excited her. His foot-stomping petulance and violent mood swings, his propensity to have it out with people who annoyed him, his extraordinary drinking habits – these were all things that enthralled her and made him more attractive to her. She'd happily deemed his excesses to be in direct proportion to his exuberant talent for making life feel continually spontaneous and 'fun'. And although that spontaneity still enthralled her on occasion – like when she would suddenly find herself transported to the Gritti Palace Hotel in Venice, or discover a diamond ring in her cornflakes – the 'fun' surprises were nowadays outnumbered by the more wearisome ones by at least twenty-five to one.

She still loved Julian, or loved an idea of him that only showed itself infrequently now, yet an inertia had set in during their courtship – an inertia that stopped her from writing, that seemed to fence her in. Her life had seemed an ever-broadening canvas until the moment she met Julian, and thereafter she'd felt her options and aspirations slowly fade until a dull languor prevailed in which she couldn't really tell whether she was unhappy or not.

She stubbed her cigarette out in an enormous, pink, shell-shaped ashtray copied from the 'Birth of Venus', carefully folding the unused portion over on itself and pressing firmly on the long, hard, glowing embers with the filter. She got a dustpan and brush from the utility room, swept up the biscuit crumbs, emptied the pan into the big aluminium swing-top bin, and set about preparing supper for the twins.

7

By six o'clock Sean and Jamie had been fed, bathed and put in their pyjamas, and were sitting on their father's prostrate form watching television and waiting for their babysitter to arrive. Wendy finished tidying their bathroom and their bedroom and laid out her clothes for the evening – a black velvet trouser suit and cream silk chemise – a style she wore to most of the functions they attended. It was fashionable without being loud, 'classic' was the word she liked to use, and its elegant anonymity was good for both impressing important people and for melting into the background if the situation demanded it – show-business functions could be very intimidating if Julian forgot about her, which he often did.

As she came out of the shower there was a ring at the front door. She put on her dressing gown and went down to answer it. It was Sally, a sunny-faced and uncomplicated young Australian – one of their regular sitters. Sally was familiar with Julian's drinking habits, but all the same Wendy liked to pretend it was a private matter and she called the twins up from the family room and sent them to their bedroom to read books and play games with Sally. Then she went down to the family room to wake Julian. He was lying with his head on a cushion from the sofa – so he'd obviously had a brief moment of consciousness since she'd last looked in on him. She kneeled down beside him and shook his shoulder. Getting no response she gently patted his face and he opened his eyes.

'It's about quarter past six,' she said.

There was a pause. Julian looked around the room. Through

the window he could see nothing but a dull, grey gloom. The television was showing an episode of the sixties *Batman* series.

'Is that morning or afternoon?' he asked.

Wendy smiled. Here was a man who really didn't know if it was night or day and objectively that was rather disarming, even attractive.

'It's the evening,' she said. 'It's a quarter past six on Tuesday evening, the sixteenth of September 1994.'

Julian smiled. 'Thought so.'

'You've hurt your nose,' said Wendy.

'Have I?' He put his hand to his nose and immediately regretted it, snatching his head back from the hot, stinging sensation. It felt like his nose was on fire. 'How did I do that?'

'I don't know.'

'Oh.'

'It's not too bad though, you've just got to try and let it scab.'

'Right,' he said, mimicking her general practitioner's tones. 'Just got to let it scab, right.'

Wendy smiled. Julian smiled back. He liked her in this mood – unquestioning and ready to be amused. It reminded him of the heady days before the cheating began. She'd always been on the edge of hysteria in those days, laughing at every joke he made, and he'd been beguiled by the poetic breadth of her knowledge, and by her beautiful arse. He'd joked about her being his 'quality fuck', his 'intellectual sex pixie' and his 'jugged-up professor', and she had seen through all the horrors of political incorrectness, and had appreciated his ironic turn of phrase and had realised that here was a man who found her very intellect a sexual turn-on.

He stretched out an arm and dragged her down towards him as he imagined Clark Gable would have done, and recoiled in agony as his nose crashed into her cheek. Wendy laughed. Julian tried to smile through the pain.

'We haven't got time for that anyway,' she said, straightening

59

up. 'It's Tom's first night tonight remember? We've got to be up and out of here in twenty minutes, all right?'

Julian sighed and looked away. An ugly snarl flickered across his face. Wendy chose to ignore it. She knew it wasn't her refusal to play sexy that had provoked Julian's sudden flash of menace, it was her mention of Tom.

'Oh come on,' said Julian, fighting back the sullen beast within himself and letting his cock take over. He pulled at her dressing gown and groped inside for her breasts.

'No, look, we've got to go. I promised Tom and he'd be very upset if we didn't show. Come on, you can come as you are, just have a bit of a wash,' she said, patting him on the hip as if to imply that everything was agreed, and heading for the door. 'I've just got to wipe this blood off my face and put my make-up on,' she said, and disappeared.

Julian folded his hands together behind his head and looked up at the ridiculously ornate crystal chandelier hanging from the equally over-the-top ceiling rose. It was all far too rococo and out of place in the low-ceilinged basement room and he hated it – but not as much as he hated Tom Bailey.

He felt a slight tightening across his chest and made an effort to breathe more regularly and more deeply, inhaling, counting to four, then exhaling.

Tom had been in the same year at Bristol as Wendy, reading English too. After each spending their first terms in hateful college accommodation they'd shared a house together with some other students – not as lovers, they'd had separate rooms – but they'd managed the house very much as a married couple for the next two and a half years, indeed until the day Julian arrived on his tour. The succession of students who had shared the house with them had variously dubbed them 'Mr and Mrs' or 'Ma and Pa', and it wasn't until Tom's famed marriage to an American lesbian student to obviate her visa requirements that the assumption that Tom and Wendy would eventually get it together and make it official was finally scotched.

They had been known throughout the university as the

60

couple that didn't sleep together. 'Too pretentiously intelligent to fuck,' had been the opinion of many, but an over-cerebral fear of the sexual act on Wendy's part was closer to the truth.

In Julian's dressing room on the day she'd interviewed him Wendy had been mesmerised by his very flesh: the way he'd constantly rubbed and fingered at his face; the oozing dampness of his lips; the way his hair had needed to be continually swept back from his broad, flat forehead; the intoxicating smell of peat in his sweat; and the incandescent shimmer of his bright blue, blind eye. He'd lain back on the thin chaise-longue like some great, pagan, elemental earth god – almost growing out of the ground – laughing infectiously and ingenuously laying himself bare to any criticism she might want to level at him. His hands had seemed so large and carnal, hyper-organic in the way they had roamed his pockets for his lighter, the way they had come forward towards her and cupped the flame as she'd lit the cigarette he'd offered her. It had felt like a primeval struggle between empiric rationality and the unruly forces of nature, but finally Wendy had managed to ignore the cries of reason from within herself and had reached out to steady his cupped hands. The sensual abandon that action had engendered had seemed like a biblical revelation and she had known immediately that she loved Julian and desired him and would never leave his side.

Tom had caught up with Wendy on Julian's tour bus a fortnight after and had tried to persuade her to go back and take her finals, but Wendy had thrown Tom's middle-class anxiety back in his face. She had felt that she was being given the keys to some kind of liberating native spirit within herself and she had no intention of giving it up for some anally retentive examination board. Standing on the stage of the Sunderland Empire during the late-afternoon sound check she had publicly declared her undying and passionate love for Julian in front of Tom, Julian and the whole stage crew, and had made it sound as though 'staying on the bus' was a metaphor for freeing her soul.

After their whirlwind marriage in Gretna Green between gigs in Glasgow and Preston, Wendy had enjoyed their honeymoon, romantically trekking round the UK with Julian's show like a couple of rock'n'roll gypsies. But that had naturally come to an end as the tour had done, and she hadn't been able to let two and a half years of living in and out of Tom's pockets go for nought. A rapprochement had been made after she had read Tom's degree result in the paper (a first, of course) and rang to congratulate him.

She had been blissfully happy with Julian and in awe of the concupiscent being he had unearthed within her, but she had also welcomed the familiar intellectual stimulation Tom's increasingly frequent visits provided.

It was only when Tom had decided to take a post-graduate course at the Bristol Old Vic Theatre School, with a view to becoming an actor, that Julian had begun to feel threatened by Tom. It seemed to Julian that Tom had taken that course of action simply to take him on at his own game and to try to compete for Wendy's esteem and affection.

Julian had tried to have it out with Wendy but she had refused to dump Tom as a friend on the grounds of Julian's unjustified jealousy. She'd lived with Tom for two and a half years and never slept with the man, what more proof could Julian want?

Yet there existed a private language between Tom and Wendy, a shared history that went back further than Julian and Wendy's. They enjoyed something that excluded him. It wasn't an affair – Julian was sure of that – but he sensed a kind of intellectual collusion that seemed to sneer at him in his Light Entertainment world.

Julian knew that Tom was 'in love' with Wendy, even if Wendy didn't recognise it as such. He knew that Tom despised him; that Tom was scornful of him and his behaviour; that Tom thought he wasn't good enough for Wendy. Tom always made him feel as if he'd sold out, as if he'd prostituted himself. It had all been all right in the early days while Tom was just a little git feeding off small parts on the fringe or even at the Royal Court. Julian had been able to handle that – he had ostentatiously paid for meals in restaurants and casually let slip the daily rate for his latest commercial, the repeat fees for his last series, or the residuals for a sale to Norway or Canada. He'd been able to mention a critic's award here, a popular people's vote there, or an article in one of the Sundays that had delved into the more fascinating socio-political observations of television comedy.

But tonight Tom was opening as Hamlet at the National Theatre. It was such a cliché, and so hard to do down, so hard to sneer at. It wasn't Lear or Othello or Macbeth even, it was Hamlet – the absolute number one part in show business, the pinnacle.

And at the National!

Julian hated subsidised theatre: the élitism, the cosseting, the intellectual snobbery, the protection from the real commercial world where performers only worked if the punters wanted to see them – but he would have killed to play there, just to be asked to play there. It wouldn't even matter what the critics might say about him, he'd be safe in the knowledge that he'd actually been asked – that would be approval enough.

He staggered to his feet and made his way to the basement bathroom which looked like the room in a museum dedicated to Victorian childhood, with clockwork toys and old games, none of which anyone was allowed to play with, filling every available piece of shelf space. He peered into the mirror. He looked dreadful, the whites of his eyes were heavily bloodshot, his face looked pallid and waxy, and he had an alarming, partially open wound on the end of his nose. Yet there was a kind of roguish, self-abused aspect that he found quite attractive, and he decided then how he'd play Tom's first-night party – he'd be the raffish, misunderstood, embattled television entertainer with the burden of great genius on his back and the bottle of scotch in his pocket – and the thought made him feel much better, even heroic.

63

Julian was constantly inventing unusual and interesting events for his own biography, and was disappointed that he didn't have a Boswell to keep a record of such things. Still, he thought, the 'suicide attempt' should make a healthily enigmatic chapter. It didn't have to be denied, and it was well documented with three front pages to reproduce in the photographic section.

He took in a lungful of air, sank his head into a basin of cold water, and felt it ease the heat at the end of his nose. Scooping a couple of handfuls of water through his hair, he lifted his head and pressed a towel, hot from the Victorian towel rail, onto either side of his face, remembering to leave a loop of material for his nose. He was invigorated and soothed all at once. He brushed his teeth with one of the twins' toothbrushes and some strawberry-flavoured children's toothpaste, combed his hair back rakishly from his forehead with the nailbrush and leered at himself in the mirror. He liked what he saw. He couldn't wait to frighten the intellectuals and their wives. Maybe he could scare one of them into a shag, he thought, a quick poke in a toilet cubicle. He felt his cock begin to harden and was wondering about having a quick wank when there was a knock on the bathroom door.

'Are you ready?' came Wendy's voice.

'Yes, I'm ready.' Julian zipped up his flies and opened the bathroom door.

'The cab's here,' said Wendy. 'Do you want to pop upstairs and say good-night while I write down the emergency numbers for Sally.' He looked at her. 'Go on,' she said, 'you haven't seen them for two days.'

She disappeared into the kitchen and Julian turned and trudged sullenly up the stairs. The speed with which moods and circumstances changed never ceased to surprise him. It seemed only seconds since he'd felt the delicious coolness of the water on his face, the soothing warmth of the hot towel and his cock stirring in his underpants at the prospect of adventure, and now he'd been cruelly shaken from his good humour by being made to feel guilty about his kids.

As he reached the next flight of stairs he heard Sally's high-pitched laugh from above and scowled. He screamed silently at the banisters around him, mouthing vulgar obscenities so angrily that he could hear pockets of air in his mouth pop as his jaws yawed this way and that. How many times had he hinted that they shouldn't use Sally any more? How many times had he carefully schooled Sean and Jamie to lie and invent misdeeds about her? How much more could he do to stop Wendy admitting one of his past conquests into the house all the time? Short of telling the truth, of course.

He fought to jettison the images of having sex with Sally that came flooding into his mind. It had been right there on the steps where he now stood. She had been so young, so pliable, so timid, so eager to be dominated.

Wendy skipped up into the entrance hall, coming to a sudden stop when she noticed Julian's hunched figure on the stairs. She could make out the snarling demeanour of his expression behind the hands clasped to his face.

'You all right?' she asked casually. Not too flippant, not too concerned. She had learned how to handle Julian's silent tempers – all he needed was a single note of admonition and he'd have something to aim at. So she held her tongue and watched Julian gradually release the grip on his face and look down at her through the banisters.

'Look, I'm not in a fit state to say good-night, am I?' he said. 'I'll see them in the morning.'

Wendy's expression stayed neutral, she remained perfectly still, her eyes fixed on him. Julian understood completely.

'Yes I *will* get up in the morning,' he chanted petulantly, then turned, grabbed his overcoat from the Shaker coat stand at the bottom of the stairs and staggered out of the front door.

8

'So who are you going to get as your new agent then?' asked Wendy in the back of the cab on the way to the National.

Julian looked at her quizzically. *She was coming from way out of left field now.* His mind raced to find a possible subtext to the question. He was still smarting from the guilt she'd heaped upon him for not saying good-night to the boys. He gave her a malevolent stare but she gazed impassively back – Wendy was never frightened by his black looks and knew that if she simply remained reasonable and rational and didn't agitate unnecessarily she would eventually win.

'What?' Julian spat, after a couple of minutes' sighing and staring.

'I gather you and Paul have come to a parting of the ways.'

Julian was reminded of the dressing-downs his father had given him as a boy. The calmness and reasonableness, the emotional control, the riddling non sequiturs that clearly hinted at something bigger to come. It was obvious Wendy had the upper hand, so why didn't she just finish him off?

He looked at her in her sexless trouser suit and wondered blackly why he had ever committed himself to her in the first place. Why not to any of the other girls before or since? He'd 'lived' with Tilly straight after drama school but only in the sense of going back to shag her every night – as soon as the sex had grown stale he'd been up and out. He'd hardly ever unpacked his bags in his first few years of independence and growing fame – even when he'd been in his own flat.

Looking out of the cab window as they drove through the back streets of Victoria it struck him that if they didn't have children he might summon up the nerve just to stop the cab and disappear into the dingily lit back allies where 'adventure' seemed to beckon from every doorway.

'I spoke to Elaine today,' said Wendy, crashing into Julian's day-dream. 'She told me that Paul's decided not to represent you any more.'

'Why are you talking bollocks to me? Are you just trying to make me cross or what?' he growled through clenched teeth, but Wendy kept up her look of cool-headed repose. It was the same technique his father had used – feeding in titbits to work Julian up into a sweat, then holding back from the promise of a fight and letting his very control compound the agony. Julian's only way out of the excruciating lack of argument was to understand what Wendy was talking about and reason with her.

He searched desperately for memories of Paul's office. He knew he'd been there, he remembered that. It was an immense struggle to marshal the events of the day into any kind of order – his brain felt like a dirty sponge – then, at last, he began to filter images of Elaine's blouse and the see-through panels, the lacy bodice, her breasts, hurting his nose, the gin, losing the film! – *Christ, what was he going to do now? He'd cleared the decks for that fucking film* – falling down the stairs, Leon. And then it struck him, falling into place like the lost piece of a jigsaw that he'd had in his hand all the time: *That's what Paul had been saying.*

The look of miserable persecution on Julian's face suddenly lifted and he threw back his head in a sudden violent roar of laughter. A huge wave of merriment began to wash through his body, his teeth glinting in the glare of the headlamps of oncoming traffic as his mouth grew ever wider, his head rocking back and forth like a laughing policeman's in a seaside arcade.

He looked across at Wendy and her blank expression made him laugh even more. The laughter was exhilarated and giddy – a release from the torment he'd just endured – and Wendy found it hard not to be infected by such obvious joy and smiled fleetingly.

'What is it?' she asked.

Julian tried to stop laughing in order to tell her of Paul's trouser-wetting routine but he couldn't, and his inability to stop made him laugh all the more. Wendy's smile broadened.

By the time they were crossing Westminster Bridge Wendy had begun to laugh, even though she didn't know what she was laughing at, and as they were turning left towards the South Bank complex and Julian finally managed to stop laughing for long enough to relate Paul's impression of 'Thunderbird's puppet meets the *Exorcist*', she too erupted and rolled from side to side, their joint hilarity feeding upon itself until they had to hold onto each other in the back of the cab, cackling and hooting with abandoned glee.

The pack of first-night press photographers waiting at the entrance of the National were surprised to see Julian at all and very pleased to see the two of them so obviously legless, helpless with laughter, and finding it rather difficult to get out of the cab. The pictures would make great follow-ups to that morning's shots of Julian being loaded into the ambulance.

A reporter from the *Daily Mail* asked Julian when he'd come back from France and whether he was feeling any happier today, but Julian could only squeeze at his aching sides with one hand as he gallantly shielded Wendy's helpless form from the rabble and tried to ease a way through the crush. Flash bulbs popped frenziedly to pick it all up and produced a stroboscopic effect that made them appear to be moving in slow motion, and the lesser and more highbrow celebrities already within the foyer craned their necks to see who it was and winced to see Julian grabbing the next day's headlines with such a cheap publicity trick.

Once within the safety of the foyer Wendy pulled some tissues from her bag and they mopped their tear-streaked faces.

'I haven't laughed like that for months,' said Julian, still suffering occasional fits, and he pulled Wendy towards him and gave her a loving hug. They kissed briefly, then Wendy repaired her make-up and they decided to make their way up to the Olivier Bar on the second floor where they imagined the free champagne would be flowing.

As they crowded into a lift someone called Julian's name.

'Hi Jools.'

It was Rob Halford, the plump, sweaty and genial half of Halford and Dixon – Julian's principal writing team since the first episode of *Mann of the Moment* – with Carol, his wife. Julian had always enjoyed Rob's company, and if it hadn't been for the master/servant relationship that underscored their professional life they might have been real friends. Their shared sense of humour was so acutely tuned that they could make each other laugh with a single word. The two couples kissed and hugged, Julian throwing an arm around Rob's obese shoulders and squeezing him warmly.

'Rob! It's great to see you, how are you, you rancid old goat?'

They'd always delighted in casually insulting each other, not because they disliked each other, but simply for the way it subverted normal behaviour so effortlessly.

'I'm fine, you steaming great twat, yeah. More to the point – how are you?' asked Rob.

Julian looked blank.

'He means the suicide story,' said Wendy.

'Oh that? That's just a complete load of bollocks. You know what newspapers are like – I was just having a little kip on the side of the pool and the fitness Nazis immediately called the ambulance.'

Rob and Carol laughed.

'As soon as you stop jumping up and down in these new fitness centres they instantly presume you're dead,' Julian continued.

'Tell me about it,' said Rob in his feyest voice, indicating his vast bulk.

Julian laughed back.

The doors closed and the lift started to ascend. 'I tell you what though, I have got some great news,' Julian said, pulling

Rob closer to him conspiratorially and lowering his voice. 'I've decided to do *Save Our Souls* after all! Fantastic news, heh? I had a big think about it and I've decided to dump the film and concentrate on the telly, because, let's face it, that's what I do best. I mean it's my home, isn't it? And this is going to be the big one, I know it. We're going to break the ten-million barrier on this one. Just look at the title – any programme that can get the continuity announcer to say "arseholes" on television has got to be good.'

Rob's cheerfully chubby, designer-stubbled face creased into a confused grin. Julian caught the concerned look and was just about to question Rob further when a bright young turk with an Oxbridge accent spoke up from the back of the lift.

'I take it rumours of your death were greatly exaggerated,' he quipped.

Julian turned and fixed the fresh-faced youth with a venomous look. He hated Oxbridge graduates for their superciliousness anyway, but hated them all the more when they presumed their education gave them an automatic entrée into the world of comedy.

'Ha . . . fucking . . . ha,' he said with slow deliberation.

The atmosphere in the lift froze, the young turk blushed, Wendy looked at the floor. Only Rob smiled. Julian noticed and gave him an approving wink.

As the doors opened the occupants fell over themselves in an effort to get away from the malicious atmosphere. Julian stuck close to Rob as he was jostled out and pulled him to one side for a chat. Wendy and Carol understood the privacy of the moment and stood some way off trying to sound interested in each other's children.

'What's wrong, Rob?'

'What do you mean?'

'There's something bugging you about the show.'

Rob looked uncomfortable; the permanent damp glow of sweat on his forehead grew to a bright sheen.

'What is it?' asked Julian. 'Come on, you can tell me.'

'Well, I might be speaking out of turn,' said Rob, 'but I was under the impression you said no a couple of months back, and . . .'

'And what?'

'Well, we've been having script meetings with someone else – trying to make it into a vehicle for him. But, you know, we writers are always the last to know, so maybe I'm wrong.'

'Who?'

'Who what?'

'Who are you rewriting it for?'

Rob steeled himself. 'Tom Bailey.'

'*Tom Bailey?*'

'Yeah.'

There was a pause. Julian tried hard to make sense of what he'd just heard. He couldn't believe it.

'Why else do you think I'm here?' added Rob. 'Not many laughs in *Hamlet*, are there?'

'You're writing a sitcom for Tom Bailey?' Julian was staggered. 'He's a poncy actor, what's he doing a sitcom for?'

'Search me. He's not as good as you though.'

'Well, of course not.'

'Keeps jabbering on about character development and cutting out all the gags.' Rob laughed uneasily.

Julian stared at Rob, peered into his piggy little eyes set deep within the too solid flesh of his face, and he began to smile. Tentatively at first, but then his smile broke into a grin and he pushed at Rob's shoulder jovially.

'You little bugger. You shithead,' he laughed. 'Christ, you nearly had me there.'

Rob couldn't help smiling back. He loved to see Julian laughing, it was always a source of great joy, so infectious, so warm – one of the things that had made Rob's job so worthwhile.

'That was a great one, that was,' Julian said.

Rob had to concentrate hard to wipe the smile off his face.

'No, look, I know what you're thinking, but it's true . . . it's not a joke.'

Julian looked hard into Rob's eyes and understood he was telling the truth. Normally he would have brushed aside a defeat like this without a second thought, he would have turned it round in a split second and made it look like a victory – made it look like part of his master plan. But it was harder with Rob. A shared sense of humour could be so revealing in that it exposed the way your mind worked, and Julian had shared more laughs with Rob over the last fourteen years than with anyone else.

Rob's face looked deeply saddened as he repeated, 'It's not a joke.'

Julian forced a confident-looking smile. 'Yeah, you're right, it's not overwhelmingly amusing, is it?' he said. He realised that Wendy was at his elbow.

'I think we ought to go in now,' she said.

Julian looked round to see that the upper foyer had almost cleared. He was glad of the opportunity to get away from Rob without signalling any kind of surrender. He turned to him. 'We'd better go in – maybe catch you in the interval?'

'Yeah, sure, one of them – they're doing the five-hour full monty version with all the boring bits that most people cut out, so there's probably about fifteen intervals,' Rob replied, trying to lighten the mood and giving Julian a friendly slap on the back.

The two couples parted and Julian and Wendy went through into the theatre and found their seats in the stalls, five rows from the front. They had to squeeze past a line of well-heeled first-nighters and endure the usual tuttings and murmurings of the corporate intelligentsia torn between excited recognition and having to keep up the pretence of finding Julian's TV show too lowbrow. Their heavy sighs and pantomimed discomfort infuriated Julian so much that by the time he reached his seat he'd swallowed several gulps of air, and as he slumped heavily into it he let out a long, controlled burp. There were several exaggerated gasps of disgust from the people round about which played straight into Julian's hands. He burped again, smiled broadly and settled back as the lights dimmed, ready to enjoy a good hour's unalloyed contempt.

9

Julian was awoken by Wendy at the second interval and discovered he'd fallen asleep even before the ghost had appeared.

'What was Tom like?' he asked, bleary-eyed.

'He's just brilliant,' said Wendy. 'It's an absolutely staggering performance, real bravura stuff. Intelligent and yet so passionate.'

'Good,' said Julian, fighting the urge to punch her in the face. 'I am glad. Shall we get a drink?'

As they battled their way through the throng towards the bar Julian spotted Rob across the room, standing on tiptoe, obviously looking for him. He hunched down and turned to Wendy.

'I've just got to go to the lav, back in a minute.'

'What do you want to drink?'

'I'll have a bottle of Pils,' Julian said, and disappeared into the crowd, keeping his knees bent as he went. He found the stairs and hurried down two flights to the Lyttelton Bar where the bar staff – a middle-aged Chinaman and a youngish-looking girl with spiky hair – were just closing the grilles. He rushed to the counter and spoke to the girl on the off-chance that she'd recognise him, perhaps might even fancy him, and that he'd therefore stand a better chance of getting served.

'You couldn't just give me two large scotches before you close, could you?' he asked with a patronising wink.

'No, I'm sorry, we're closed already.'

'Oh, go on. I'm desperate.'

'No, I'm sorry, I can't.'

'Here,' said Julian, fumbling for his wallet. 'Here's a twenty-quid note, just give me a quick scotch and you can keep the change.'

'No, I'm sorry, I've told you – we're closed.'

'Do you know who I am?' asked Julian, playing his joker.

'Yes,' came the dauntingly impassive reply.

'Well?' he struggled on.

'Well what?'

Julian held his breath as he tried to come up with a witty and cutting response, but failed and in despair blurted, 'Oh God, this is useless, just give me a drink, you stupid bitch!'

'Steve!' shouted the girl, snapping the padlock on the grille between them and looking anxiously to the open door behind the bar into which her cohort had disappeared.

'Oh, all right, all right, I'm off,' said Julian, and he started out for the main exit. He stopped after a few paces and turned back to the girl. 'Look, I'm sorry, I didn't mean to shout at you, and I know you can't give me a drink, and I am very sorry, really – but could you please just tell me where the nearest pub is?'

'The Olivier Bar's open upstairs you know.'

'Yeah, I know, but I don't like it in there. Please, just tell me where the nearest pub is.'

'Well, there's one just opposite the LWT building – but you'd better hurry, it's nearly five to eleven.'

'What? How can it be? There's still an act to go.'

'Yeah, well *Hamlet*'s a long play, isn't it?' said the girl, and disappeared into the back room.

Julian shook his watch to check that she wasn't winding him up and realised she was right. He ran out of the bar area towards the huge glass doors that led out of the foyer, but as he approached them he suddenly stopped dead in his tracks and darted behind a large concrete pillar, flattening himself against it in panic. Gingerly poking his head out, he peered through the doors and confirmed what he thought he'd seen: it was the psycho fan, hovering about at the bottom of the steps outside. Julian pulled his head back out of view and cursed. *How the fuck did she always know where he was going to be? It was as if she had access to his diary!*

When the psycho had first appeared Julian had found her devotion and her ability to seek him out at the most unlikely locations very flattering, and had always made a point of paying special attention to her whenever she was there. This wasn't a particular disposition towards generosity on his part – beyond enjoying what he liked to think was confirmation of his genius and the fact that he was adored, there was a warped commercial motive behind Julian's stage-door kindnesses. He believed that if he looked after his fan base – especially the more ardent ones, those who actively sought him out and suffered in the cold to wait for him – then the rest of the populace would stay behind him and he'd have a job for life. If there ever came a time when no fans turned up at the stage door, no matter how psychotic, then he would know that he'd lost his hold on the general public. It was a similar principle to looking after the pennies and letting the pounds look after themselves. To this end Julian had given the psycho fan tickets to his shows, rehearsal scripts from his television programmes, posters, photographs, small props from the set, call sheets, BBC paper cups, and any other odd little mementoes he'd found lying around that he thought might please her.

However, she'd been his number one fan now for eight years and the grinding banality of her unrelenting adoration was wearing him down. Standing there against the cool concrete of the pillar, Julian calculated how many hours she'd sucked out of his life: two fifteen-minute interceptions a week added up to half an hour; multiplied by fifty-two equalled roughly twenty-five hours a year; multiplied by eight came to two hundred hours . . . Julian couldn't take the maths any further but he knew that that had to be over a week. *He'd been with the psycho fan for a full week of his life, without sleep or stopping for meals!*

He sneaked another look round the edge of the pillar to see if she'd gone but there she was looking straight at him through the doors. She smiled and tapped on the glass. Julian ludicrously pretended not to have seen her and quickly withdrew his head, flattening himself back against the pillar.

Two hundred hours!

He'd read of other celebrities taking out injunctions against annoyingly persistent fans, but what could he prove? She never hung around directly outside his house – in fact he'd had trouble convincing Wendy that she existed at all as she always melted into the background whenever Wendy appeared. He'd told Wendy about her from very early on, not about the passionate kisses, but about her obsessive nature, and they'd shared a joke about the Mark Chapmanesque death Julian would inevitably meet, changing the name of John Lennon's killer to Charlie Chaplin instead, and imagining Julian being stalked by the comical tramp who would bungle every assassination attempt.

But over the years Julian had become nervous of the two women in his life meeting. The sheer longevity of his association with the psycho suggested a relationship far deeper than the casual fucks he enjoyed with other women from time to time, and his very inability to dump her had begun to suggest a bond between them. He'd eventually stopped talking about her to Wendy and had started to feel a kind of guilt.

The fact that she disappeared whenever Wendy was in the vicinity seemed to confirm some kind of collusion between Julian and the psycho, some kind of acceptance. He figured that he must be practically her sole reason for living and he worried that someday that dependency might lead her to exact a terrible revenge for some real or even imagined slight. His other conquests were easy enough. None of them would ever approach Wendy out of the blue and say 'By the way I slept with your husband last night', it would be too unnecessarily cruel and embarrassing. But though he had never slept with the psycho fan there was something alarming about the possibility of her coming face to face with Wendy.

He heard the first interval bell ring and looking at his watch he saw that last orders had already been called and that he only had two minutes before time was called at the pub. In desperation he fell onto the floor and dragged himself, commando-like, across to a line of seats, then, using the seats as cover, crawled along to where they came to an end, scrambled to his feet and sprinted into the farther part of the foyer. He could see another smaller exit door at the far end and rushed to it. Pulling hard without effect he discovered that it was locked.

'Fucking hell!' he shouted.

A wizened security guard with grey hair and a peaked hat peered out from beneath an uncompromisingly modern concrete staircase thirty feet or so to Julian's right.

'Are you wanting to get out?' he asked.

'Yes, yes, I am,' spluttered Julian. 'I am very much wanting to get out.'

'Right you are, sir,' said the little old man, and bustled towards Julian and the door, looking as if he was travelling at speed but in reality making very slow progress. Julian fretted and fidgeted and pushed pointlessly at the door.

'I recognise you, sir, yes, I recognise you – you're Mr Mann, aren't you, sir? From the television?'

'Yes, that's right, quick as you like, mate.'

The little old man seemed for all the world not to be getting any closer at all.

'Look, do you want some help?' asked Julian, rushing over to him, taking hold of an arm and half-dragging him to the door. The old man let out an exhilarated cry and the medals on his chest clinked together as Julian deposited him at the door. Then he fumbled with his keys, trying to find the right one for the lock, chattering away as he did so.

'My daughter and I have watched you on the television many times, sir. Oh yes, we laugh and laugh at you, sir.'

'That's very kind . . .'

'Oh yes, very funny programmes you make, sir . . .'

'Look, I'm sorry, but I'm in a dreadful hurry.'

'Much better than all the arty-farty things they have on here, sir, oh yes.'

Julian was surprised by this remark, it relaxed him in some way and he allowed himself a chuckle.

'Oh yes, they put on some awful rubbish here, sir,' continued the old man, finding the right key and slotting it into the lock. 'You should come here and show them how to do a bit of real entertaining.'

And so saying he turned the lock and opened the door, through which drifted the sound of Big Ben across the river chiming eleven o'clock. Julian smiled benignly at the old man with a mixture of resignation and genuine amusement. The old man held open the door and dragged his right hand up to the peak of his cap in a shaky salute.

'Been a pleasure to meet you, sir.'

Julian laughed, all sense of urgency gone. The old man smiled back. Julian looked at his watch to confirm what he already knew, beamed at the old man and shrugged his shoulders.

'Trying to get to the pub before closing time, sir?' ventured the old soldier.

'Yes, that's right, but I'm afraid I've missed it now.'

'Had enough of the play, sir?'

'Well, to be honest, I only caught the opening minute . . . but that was enough for me.'

'It can get very tedious, sir, yes. I prefer my Shakespeare a lot shorter, sir, *Macbeth* for instance – not too long and plenty of action.'

'Really?'

'Oh yes, that Hamlet takes far too long making up his mind in my opinion, sir.'

'Yes,' said Julian, feeling that the conversation had now gone on too long. He looked wistfully at the bar in the distance where the Chinaman had switched off the lights and was disappearing through the door at the back. The little old man followed his gaze.

'You'll find the Olivier Bar is still open, sir.'

'Yes, I know, it's just there's some people up there I'd rather avoid.'

'I know what you mean, sir. Some of them can get very pretentious.'

'Yes,' said Julian hesitantly.

The second interval bell rang and the old man said. 'If I may make so bold, I do have a small supply of alcoholic beverages in the guard room, and I would be most honoured if you would allow me to raise a glass with you, sir.'

In the Olivier Bar upstairs Wendy was standing with Rob and Carol, a glass of white wine in one hand and Julian's forsaken Pils in the other, as people started to drift back into the auditorium.

Rob was feeling uneasy. He had spotted at least two of Julian's previous conquests milling around the bar and he was afraid lest one of them should come up and ask him about Julian's whereabouts without realising that Wendy was Julian's wife. For all he knew Julian might already be forging a new union elsewhere in the building.

Rob was an enormous fan of Julian's rubber-faced talent to amuse, in the way only a real cognoscente could be, and though that admiration couldn't help but become a kind of love for Julian the man, he actually hated Julian's moral duplicity and the way it compromised his friends. Why should they be made to feel nervous by having to protect Wendy from Julian's treachery?

On one of the rare occasions Rob had been invited back to Julian's house with the rest of the cast of *Richard the Nerd* they had become involved in a late-night drunken truth game and the woman who played Julian's wife, Lady Anne – who was Julian's sometime lover – had asked Rob whether he thought Julian had ever had an affair since his marriage to Wendy. Rob had been flabbergasted by Julian's casually sincere insistence that he should tell the truth, thereby compounding the lie he had had to tell in front of Wendy by saying 'No'. But on reflection he'd realised that if Julian had either stayed silent or strenuously denied the claim he would have been damned, whereas by earnestly forcing Rob to lie on his behalf he had successfully defused the whole question.

'Hi, Wendy. Hi, Rob, Caroline.' It was Mitch Duncan, a second-hand car salesman of a producer who'd been involved in the production of *Charley's Aunt* that had launched Julian's career. He was tall and thin with the over-eagerness of a successful member of Alcoholics Anonymous. 'Did I see Julian in the theatre?'

'No, he's not here,' said Rob, lying automatically, much to the consternation of the rest of the group, then tried to get himself out of it, 'I mean to say he's not here with us now.'

'Do you know where he is?' asked Mitch.

'He went to the toilet,' said Wendy, and they all looked at her charitably.

10

Julian had weighed up the advantages of getting his lips round the neck of a whisky bottle against the increasingly unbearable friendliness of his new acquaintance, the old security guard. His brain had said 'No', but he'd heard his mouth say 'Yes'.

And so he'd found himself trailing along behind the infuriatingly slow old man, worrying about this new disease of saying things he hadn't meant to say. The little old man had unlocked a heavy grey door and led Julian out of the vast open spaces of the foyer through to a perplexing maze of low-ceilinged, grey-painted breeze-block corridors.

Now, as his guide shuffled along in front, turning left, then right, then left again, and down a flight of metal stairs onto a floor exactly the same as the one they had just left, Julian looked at each door they passed and wondered whose dressing rooms they might be. He was filled with a deep jealousy. He hated the architecture, the echoes of school buildings and the pervading sense of overwhelming bureaucracy that filled the place, but at the same time he desperately wanted to be part of it. For a second he foolishly imagined he might even be happy as a spear carrier in such a place.

As they turned right again into a long, wide corridor, the tannoy erupted into life and gave a Mr Jennings and a Ms Wanamaker their calls. It was very loud. It would have to be turned down before he came to work here, thought Julian.

He looked at the doddering old man in front of him, and despaired as to whether he was ever going to get a drink at all. What if his 'alcoholic beverages' turned out to be a bottle of advocaat and a barley wine? The old man didn't look like a serious drinker – maybe he just had a couple of miniatures. The whole enterprise grew duller and duller in Julian's mind. The long trek seemed to be tiring his intrepid trailblazer out, so much so that he didn't have the breath to talk any more. Julian was just giving thanks for this small mercy when he noticed an attractive girl in her early twenties walking towards them from the other end of the corridor. She was small with short black hair and she was carrying a plastic laundry basket full of neatly pressed clothes.

As soon as their eyes met Julian knew she had recognised him and that she was an ardent fan, a proper fan, the best sort of fan – one that idolised him from a distance, that couldn't imagine meeting him face to face. Her whole body seemed to weaken momentarily as they drew closer to each other. Julian's gaze trawled her jean-covered legs, took in her trim waist and then settled on her breasts which pressed pleasantly outwards against her thin T-shirt. He could make out the shape of her bra through the T-shirt, and the impression of her nipples through her bra. He looked up to her face. They were about ten paces apart now. He knew that she knew he'd been admiring her figure, and he gave her his broadest smile. She blushed, but didn't look away. Julian raised both eyebrows in a gesture of amusement and her bright green eyes giggled back as she passed him.

Julian stopped walking, turned silently, and watched her go. He was in love with her immediately. She must be a Celt, he thought, because of the green, laughing eyes, the dark hair and the fire he imagined within her. His brain raced with images of Irish misty mountains, Atlantic-swept beaches, a crofter's cottage, peat fires, Guinness, wolfhounds, the company of good friends and his fiery, smiling earth-mother of a wife nurturing their brood of seven children, whilst effortlessly keeping the looks which drove every man in the village to distraction.

He turned back in the direction of the little old man and saw that he was almost half-way to the end of the corridor: he knew the old man hadn't noticed him stop. Then he turned back to see his laughing, green-eyed goddess disappearing round the opposite end of the corridor. Taking his jacket pockets firmly in his hands to prevent his loose change from jingling about, he ran noiselessly after her.

As he rounded the corner he saw she'd disappeared. The passage was empty. He retraced a couple of steps and sneaked a look back down the main corridor – the little old man had gone too.

'Probably completely lost,' Julian muttered to himself. 'Might never be seen again.'

Julian amused himself briefly by mulling over the idea of a half-hour comedy based on an old codger of a security guard who couldn't find the way out of his own building, but then immediately dismissed it as an idea that 'didn't have legs'.

He looked around, up the main corridor and up and down the shorter passage, and reflected on how odd it was to be so totally alone in a building that must have had at least two thousand souls in it at that very moment.

Just then one of the dressing-room doors in the shorter passage opened and the green-eyed goddess reappeared. She came out backwards in order to negotiate the awkwardly shaped basket through the door, which had a strong return spring on it. As she turned her head Julian was mesmerised by her hair which brushed softly across the caramel-coloured skin of her shoulder where it was exposed by the wide neck of her T-shirt. He wanted to brush his lips against that same patch of skin and bury his nose in her hair.

As she saw him she giggled and her eyes shimmered play-fully. Her chuckling lips drew back over her porcelain-white teeth and Julian could see her moist, pink tongue glistening behind.

'Are you following me?' she half-joked.

Her County Cork accent sent a tingling sensation through Julian's body – he could feel the wind whipping the sand off the dunes and stinging his eyes, could taste the Blackbush whisky warming his throat as the banshees whistled round the chimney stack. He placed a hand against the door jamb behind her so that his face came to within a foot of hers and drank in the smell of her, the honey aroma of her hair, the light perfume of her body, the scent of expensive soap mixed with the crispness of the freshly pressed linen in her basket. He looked deep into her eyes.

'I want to marry you,' he said.

She laughed.

'I want to fuck with you until I'm so shagged out I need hospital treatment, and then I want to marry you,' he carried on.

She barely had time to blush before he pushed his face down into hers. Her lips opened and their tongues met and danced. He was aware of the fragile wound on the end of his nose, but it had either healed sufficiently for it not to hurt any longer, or the adrenalin rush was numbing the pain. His lips trembled as he nibbled and sucked and chewed. He gently pushed at her basket until she had to let it drop and they fell into a passionate, groping embrace. He pressed his body hard against hers as she leaned back against the door and dug her fingertips deep into the muscles at the back of his neck. Julian's large, open hands feverishly explored the contours of her body and sneaked up into her T-shirt. He fondled one of her perfectly formed breasts through the silky material of her bra and then, after pausing briefly to stroke her midriff with the back of his hand, he drove it down the front of her jeans.

'No,' she said, and stopped kissing him.

Julian withdrew his hand. She kissed him again. They resumed the struggle but without the same passion.

'Where can we go?' asked Julian.

'We can't, I'm working.'

'You don't have to work, I'm going to marry you.'

She laughed. 'You're incorrigible.'

'No, I'm in the corridor.'

She looked at him questioningly.

85

'Yes, sorry,' he said. 'I always make incredibly bad jokes when I fall in love.'

'Do you fall in love all the time, then?'

Julian grimaced comically. 'Look, do you mind if I just don't talk at all? I seem to be digging myself into a hole. I'm much better at expressing myself physically.'

She laughed again.

'You're funny,' she said, taking his head in both her hands and kissing him gently. He responded by rubbing his body against hers. He enjoyed the soft yet hard sensation of her breasts across his chest and thought he could feel her nipples harden. He pulled away from her kiss.

'I want to fuck you,' he said, and then regretted it as he felt her body shrink away from him.

'I've got to get on, I'm sorry,' she answered, gently fending him off to make more room for herself, and bending to pick up her basket.

'I really do want to marry you,' Julian said, squatting down to help her pick up the laundry which had spilled onto the floor. Their heads were close together. She looked up at him with her laughing green eyes.

'You don't even know my name.'

'That's not important. I know who you are, I know you as a person. Look, I know it sounds incredible, but it's true – I have fallen completely in love with you and I want to marry you. Honestly.'

He looked into her eyes with great intensity, pleading and begging, almost whimpering in his desperation. She gazed back at him mischievously.

'What about the fuck?' she asked, rising with precipitate speed and moving off down the passage with her basket.

Julian shot to his feet and scampered after her.

'What *is* your name?'

'Catriona,' she said as she opened another dressing-room door. He followed her through and the door sprang shut behind him.

The room was unexpectedly colourful after the drabness of the corridors. A window at the end of the low-ceilinged room had been loosely covered with a large cloth printed with primary-coloured Indian symbols – a series of vivid red and white triangles spreading out from the centre surrounded by circular, petal-like rings, in turn enclosed by a square with bright yellow and blue compartments. The geometric patterns were overlayed with hundreds of tiny, intricate figures of Indian divinities in garishly coloured costumes. The whole effect was rather startling. There was a day-bed in front of the window, onto which Catriona was carefully placing freshly pressed articles of clothing.

Along one side of the room a large make-up mirror framed with light bulbs was festooned with gaily patterned good-luck cards and telemessages. Huge bouquets of flowers fought for attention from all sides, and a further collection of horticultural good wishes filled the sink. Julian's eye was drawn to one of the cards on the mirror. He couldn't tell what had drawn him to it at first, but then he noticed that it was in Wendy's handwriting. She had written 'Darling Tom, break every bone in your body and give 'em hell. I know you can do it! Love Wendy'. After her own name and several kisses she had written 'and Julian' in brackets.

Julian realised with mingled disgust and delight that he must be in Tom Bailey's dressing room. He reread Wendy's card but barely had time to consider what treachery might be implicit within the pair of brackets before he was aware of Catriona behind him. She was holding the basket on her hip with one hand and the door open with the other.

'Come on, I can't leave you in here,' she said.

The world seemed to pause on its axis as they stood and looked at each other. Nothing was said. Julian held himself as still as he could for fear that any movement on his part might break the spell. The ends of his fingers tingled with the deliciousness of it all. He was unaware of moving or even deciding to move but suddenly found himself across the room and wrapped in Catriona's arms, pressing his open lips against hers and feeling her tongue wantonly exploring his mouth. Catriona let go of the door and let her basket fall for a second time. Her fingers snaked up into the hair on the back of his head as he pushed her roughly against the wall, and then slid downwards, slipped inside his jacket, and dropped to the waistband of his trousers, searching for the buckle of his belt.

'We'll have to be quick,' she whispered.

Julian was unable to resist the joke.

'Oh, there shouldn't be any worries on that score,' he said.

11

As Tom Bailey sank, dead, into Horatio's arms a self-satisfied smile tugged at the corners of his mouth. He was glad of Fortinbras's entrance as it meant Horatio would lay him down in order to greet the newcomer and he could roll his long body upstage and relax. Tom was happily exhausted after surviving the four-and-a-half-hour marathon of nerves that was the first night, and physically drained after the exertions of his duel with Laertes. He could feel that his thin cotton chemise was now plastered to his back, and his leather breeches felt hot and clammy round his groin.

As Fortinbras rumbled on Tom allowed himself a barely audible death-rattle and, relaxing his muscles completely, let his body sink into the stage. He knew he had been triumphant. He knew he had handled the mood swings from misery and despair through to impassioned madness with a poetic deftness unseen for more than a decade. He was confident that he'd exuded a measure of sexual intelligence that must have driven the girls wild without him seeming forward or cheap. *He had cried real tears for God's sake!* Managed to force them out. It was a trick that had eluded him all through rehearsals.

At last Fortinbras bid the soldiers shoot and the lights faded to black as a peal of ordnance echoed around the theatre. Tom sprang nimbly to his feet during the black-out and hurried into the wings to be hugged, kissed and communed with by his ecstatic fellow thespians. The lights came up on the stage for the curtain call, and the other actors left him one by one to take their bows until finally he was left alone in the wings, the last to go on. He waited five seconds, then another five seconds, then an outrageous further five seconds, allowing the sense of anticipation within the audience to build. The deputy stage manager on the other side of the stage made frantic gestures for him to go on. Members of the cast on stage craned their necks round to see what was amiss. An assistant stage manager rushed round from the back of the set towards him.

'Tom, you've got to get out there, now! You've got to go now!'

Tom fixed her with venomous eyes and stuck his middle finger in the air, and she retreated, shaken and hurt. Then he coughed, shook himself out and strode onto the stage – manfully but with an overwhelming air of modesty and humility, affecting the pose of an artisan having simply done his job, workmanlike, and silently repeating to himself, 'I must not appear conceited, I know I've been fucking fantastic but I must not appear conceited. Be humble. Be humble. Be humble,' like a mantra.

The audience swallowed it hook, line and sinker, and after three curtain-calls Tom managed to wrest a standing ovation from a good three-quarters of the house. He shook his head in a self-effacing gesture of disbelief and finally stepped back with the rest of the ensemble, bowing and acknowledging the tumult with a deprecating wave of his hand.

Once finally off the stage Tom sprinted lithely back to his dressing room through the grim, grey backstage corridors, which were now filled with back-slapping actors and crew sharing noisy anecdotes and plaudits and laughing the manic laugh that only a great release of tension can produce.

Entering his room he saw that his Shri Yantra had fallen from the window onto the day-bed in an unruly heap. He moved to hang it back up over the window when the phone rang – it was the Stage Door telling him he'd got a visitor.

'Yeah, thanks, send her up. I'm expecting quite a few people actually, but just hold the rest of them back for a few minutes would you?' he asked, and replaced the handset.

He quickly pulled the chemise over his head and stepped

out of his breeches. He whipped off his stockings and jockstrap, filled the washbasin with water, sluiced himself, dried himself cursorily and then wrapped a towel round his waist. He looked at his face in the mirror and frowned. He dipped his hand into the water in the basin and splashed his forehead a little so that the drops of water resembled beads of sweat, stared at his reflection once more, and was better pleased this time. He stood back to admire himself more fully. He was at the peak of physical condition, he thought to himself – *all this and a brain with it!* He unwrapped and rewrapped the towel a little lower down his waist to achieve a more casual look.

There came a knock at the door.

'Moment!' he shouted, and quickly studied his face closely in the mirror again. He splashed a little more water on his forehead, nodded knowingly to himself, then set his face with a neurotically distressed expression. He untucked his towel so that he had to hold it with one hand to keep it up and opened the door with the other. It was Wendy.

'Wendy! Darling, look I'm sorry, I'm just so absolutely shattered – I'm afraid I just haven't had the strength to change yet,' he said, allowing a slight tremulousness to enter into his voice.

'Oh I'm sorry, yes, you must be. I'll come back later.'

'No, no, don't. Look, just come in. I'm sorry, I just can't think straight. Come in, come in.'

He ushered Wendy in and let the door close behind her, casually letting his hand brush over the latch and silently squeeze it to the locked position.

'Are you sure you don't want a few minutes on your own first?' asked Wendy, and she turned to him and saw his bottom lip begin to quiver.

'No, I could do with the company really. To be frank I just feel emotionally rather overwhelmed,' he said, letting his face drop and beginning to sob. *Real tears again.*

'Oh Tom, you poor, poor thing. You were just magnificent, I can't tell you,' said Wendy, and she dumped her handbag

91

and moved forward to embrace him. Tom was a good foot taller than Wendy and she couldn't help but rest her cheek against his bare, hairless chest. 'I could see you were living it. It must have been torture. You were just so brilliant, so passionate.'

'You really think so?' sniffed Tom, letting his chest heave against her face. He wrapped his arms around her and let his towel fall to the floor. He knew Wendy must have heard the towel drop as he felt her ears prick up, and he could sense her looking into the mirror to her left and seeing his taught, tanned, naked behind. He clasped her tight and couldn't feel her struggle. There was another knock at the door, and someone rattled the door handle.

'Tom!' cried a male voice outside the door. Tom cursed silently. 'Tom, it's Vic, can I come in?'

'Moment!' shouted Tom. He took half a step back to hold Wendy at arm's length, dipping his head to look into her eyes. He glanced down at his own nakedness, then back up to Wendy to gauge her reaction. Her mouth was fixed in a doubtful smile and Tom thought he felt her shoulders stiffen beneath his hands. He waited for a second in the hope of a more demonstrative reaction, then smiled what he hoped was an enigmatic smile, turned, and stepped swiftly into a loose-fitting jersey track suit.

'Yes Vic! Come in!' he shouted, deftly unlocking and opening the door with one movement of his wrist, and in came Vic, a tall man with greying, curly, black hair and ostentatiously old-fashioned glasses. He had a face like the dregs of a wine bottle. He paused and stood stock still, and he and Tom beamed knowingly at each other for a moment.

'Sensational,' said Vic, breaking the pause.

Tom shrugged. 'It was all down to your direction, Vic. You are the master.'

'That's utter bollocks, Tom, and you know it. I only ever said one thing – that truth is art, and art is truth – and that if we worked to that premise we couldn't fail. And I think I've been proved right, don't you?' said Vic, turning suddenly and addressing this last question to Wendy. She was surprised at her sudden inclusion into the conversation but picked up the ball almost instantly.

'Yes, yes, I think I know what you mean. Aren't you confusing it with Keats though? "*Beauty* is truth, truth *beauty*"? "Ode on a Grecian Urn"?' she said unpretentiously, innocently correcting for the sake of knowledge itself. Vic looked at her unblinkingly, and Tom stepped in.

'Sorry, Vic this is Wendy. Wendy Mann. Wendy, this is Victor Blake, our glorious leader.'

Vic held his silent gaze on Wendy for a few seconds more, then said, 'Pleased to meet you.' Wendy held out her hand, but Vic ignored it and turned to Tom. 'Look, I must get on and congratulate the rest of them. I'll see you at the party,' he said, retreating out of the door like a tortoise pulling its head back into its shell.

'Sorry about that,' said Tom, as the door clicked shut. 'He's a bit of a misogynist.'

'A *bit*?'

'Yes, I am sorry,' Tom leaned forward and cupped Wendy's elbows in his hands. 'Now, where were we?'

'I don't think we were anywhere, Tom.'

'Weren't we?'

'No.'

'Oh, I thought we were.'

'No.'

Tom paused statue-like for a moment, then sat back on the counter. He scratched his head and stared at the floor. He was pleased to see the shape of his penis clearly defined through the thin jersey of his track-suit bottoms.

'This is ridiculous, you know.' He sighed, looking up at Wendy beseechingly as she leaned back against the wall opposite and fidgeted with one of her jacket buttons. She looked like a schoolgirl being challenged over some petty misdemeanour. 'You know I've always been in love with you.'

93

'Don't make it up, Tom.'

'But I have.'

'No you haven't. We've always been very special friends – best friends – soul mates – but . . .'

'But what?'

'I don't know . . . you're confusing me – I wish you'd put some underpants on.'

They fell silent again. Tom sidled over to Wendy and leaned with his back against the wall alongside her. Unintimidating, he thought to himself, the gesture of a perfectly adjusted modern man; tender and considerate, scrupulously equitable and rather attractive.

'Look, why don't we just take it gently, one day at a time, just to let the idea develop. There's no need to rush it,' he said.

'Oh Tom, I'm flattered, really. Really, I'm very flattered . . . but it's just too late.'

'Too late for what?'

'I'm where I am, I can't move. I don't want to move,' she said. Then in a rush, 'Oh, this is all too difficult.'

'Oh, but it's not, it just seems that way. Everything'll sort itself out – I mean we are two highly intelligent people, we can make it work out.'

He turned his head to look directly into her eyes. Wendy couldn't meet his stare. Her eyes were bright with the first hint of tears and she kept them resolutely fixed on the wall opposite. Tom could see her fighting within herself to let the rational hold sway over the emotional. He watched her scratch at the hard patch of skin below the first knuckle of her little finger – he'd first seen her scratch it as they waited to go in to their first-year exams at Bristol.

'We have so much fun the way we are, why can't we just carry on?' she said. 'Why do you want to risk what we already have?'

Tom sighed.

'I just can't stand the way you have to go back and sleep

with that complete arsehole every night. The idea of it drives me insane,' he said.

'You're not jealous of Julian!'

'Well of course I'm jealous.'

'But he's hardly ever there, and when he is he's usually unconscious.'

'Exactly, it's no life for you, you're too attractive for that. You're too intelligent for that. You need an emotional life,' he added, turning his body towards her and resting his hands on her shoulders. 'You need a sensual life . . .'

'I need a cigarette,' said Wendy, moving to the counter. She grabbed her handbag, wrenched it open and fished out two packets of Marlboros and her old Ronson lighter. Tom watched her extract a cigarette from the open packet and light it. There was a violence to the way she did it, nothing suave or sophisticated, no anticipation of pleasure to come, just a mechanical desperation. He watched her shoulders draw up towards her ears as she pulled deeply. There was a pause as she reached the limit of her lung capacity, then she exhaled heavily, the smoke rebounding off the mirror in front of her and filling her hair. 'I'm sure people would go to the theatre a lot more if they were allowed to smoke in them, you know.'

Tom smiled and tried to think of a reply, but was interrupted by a commotion of people outside in the corridor. His door suddenly swung open and a whole gang of first-night guests and friends burst into the room. Whatever moment Tom was building up to was washed away by the flood of homage and praise that the intruders poured upon him. He snapped back into the role of the diffident artisan, the jobbing actor who cared more about the welfare of his guests than their acclaim for his performance.

'Look, there's a couple of bottles of wine here, and there's a half-bottle of scotch somewhere. Will you open the wine André? You know me, I don't drink, so I can't vouch for its quality I'm afraid. Rob – hello – good to see you – how are the rewrites coming along? There's glasses under the sink.'

Tom rushed about tidying things off chairs and making more room for the dozen or so people that were crowding into his tiny dressing room. He whipped the Shri Yantra off the day-bed to hang it back over the window and was horrified to reveal the sleeping form of Julian beneath, clutching the now empty half-bottle of scotch.

'Julian!' he screamed in alarm, throwing a panicked look at Wendy. The whole room stopped as if in suspended animation and stared at Julian and Tom.

Wendy's jaw dropped as she spotted Julian's supine figure through the throng of people. Tom watched her turn and draw on her cigarette as she moved to the other end of the room in order to avoid being part of any embarrassment that might ensue. He turned back to Julian and shook him by the shoulder until he awoke, yawning and blinking. The whole room stayed silent as it watched the unfolding drama – no one could quite understand what was going on, but they understood the note of panic in Tom's voice.

'What are you doing here?' asked Tom.

Julian grimaced and ran his tongue over his teeth. He yawned again and stretched his arms out to either side rather exaggeratedly, then he smiled up at Tom.

'I just wanted to be the first to congratulate you on a marvellous performance,' he said.

Tom held the very concerned look on his face, pleased that he could mask his real anxiety with a show of consideration for Julian's state of health.

'How long have you been here?' he asked.

'Oh I didn't miss much,' said Julian. 'I saw it up to where The Krankies came on. They were marvellous, weren't they? Such good value for money.'

There was a big laugh from Rob Halford at the back of the crowd, and a couple of the other revellers tittered. Tom laughed too, trying hard not to sound too condescending.

'Ha, ha, ha, Julian you old bugger. I don't know how you get away with it,' he chuckled, trying not to clench his teeth.

'No, seriously Tom, I didn't see any of your performance myself but I am reliably informed that you were very brainy and very sexy. So come on, let's celebrate with a little drinky!'

With Tom's help Julian hoisted himself to his feet and pushed his way through the gathering towards Rob and the wine. The crowd took this action to signal the end of the festivities and they resumed their fawning approbation of Tom's performance.

Julian punched Rob playfully in the stomach and poured himself a glass of wine. 'How was it then, you great fat tub of lard?'

'All the better for not having you in it, you big bag of shite,' Rob replied. Julian looked momentarily hurt. Rob leaned towards him and whispered sincerely in his ear. 'Because you would have shown them up something rotten, mate, I tell you. That gravediggers' scene'd be a steal in the right hands. Perfect job for you as well – he doesn't come on till the fifth act, then he fucks off with all the laughs.'

Julian grinned and gave Rob a heartfelt hug.

'Julian!' interrupted Mitch Duncan, striding into the room and shaking Julian warmly by the hand. 'My dear fellow, how are you? It's been ages.'

'Mitch,' Julian answered. 'Haven't seen you since . . . some other time, you know, when we were in the same room together. How are you keeping?'

'Not bad, not bad at all.'

'Good.'

'No, what am I saying, that's a complete lie. Got a little crisis on at the moment – something you might be able to help me out with actually.'

'Is this business, Mitch?'

'It could be very good business, yes. I'm doing this revival of *The Importance of Being Earnest*, it's got the perfect part for you – Algy – very funny.'

'Look, you know me, if it's business you have to talk to Paul.'

97

'Paul?' Mitch looked puzzled. 'But Wendy told me you weren't with Paul any more.'

'Oh shit, yes, sorry . . . forgot about that . . . er . . . makes it a bit tricky, doesn't it?' Julian's face creased in honest amusement.

'Just a bit, yes,' said Mitch, appreciating the humour of the situation. 'Have you got a new agent yet?'

'Not yet.'

'Are you getting one?'

'Um . . . I don't know.'

'Maybe I should talk to someone else – have you got a cleaner, or a chauffeur or something?'

Rob laughed.

'All right, you'll have to talk to me,' said Julian, 'but not here, OK? Ring me in the morning.'

'Ring *you*?' asked Mitch incredulously, and the three of them laughed. 'In that case we might as well forget the whole thing right now.'

'All right, all right, let's do it . . . er . . . now.'

'Great.'

'But not in here. Come on, let's find a quiet corridor somewhere.'

'Ooh, you'll be lucky to find a corridor in this place,' sniggered Rob, as the pair of them left the room.

In the far corner of the room Tom was relieved to see them go. Though he'd been deeply involved with his other guests, he'd been watching Julian intently. It had been as if he'd suddenly had two sets of senses – making cogent denials of his great genius to a group of flatterers with one set, whilst keenly following Julian's every move with the other and listening for the slightest indication that Julian hadn't been asleep.

Now that Julian had left Tom tried desperately to catch Wendy's eye, but she was having none of it. He talked his way up and down the room trying to get next to her so that they could share a conspiratorial moment, but she kept one step ahead of him all the time. Tom was becoming increasingly annoyed – his evening, his moment of glory, was being completely spoilt, and he was unable to enjoy fully the adulation of his guests because of his fear that Julian had heard his attempted seduction of Wendy; he'd even exposed himself to the object of his desire without response – which was an insult to his vanity; and though the notion that they were both involved in a plot seemed to make them an item in his mind – a pair of guilty lovers – even that idea was fading fast as Wendy kept up her game of musical conversations.

Just as Tom finally manœuvred Wendy into a corner of the room and blocked her escape route with his arm against the wall, Julian came back in with Mitch. They were shaking hands and slapping each other on the back.

'Who needs fucking agents, heh?' Julian was saying.

'Yeah, it's great, man, it's going to be great – it's a dream cast,' said Mitch.

Wendy dodged under Tom's extended arm, gathered up her handbag and programme, and made her way towards Julian.

'I think I've had enough – you don't fancy going home, do you?' she said. 'I don't mind going on my own if you want to stay.'

'What about the party? There's a party, isn't there?' asked Julian, including Rob in the conversation.

'Oh yes,' said Rob. 'Most definitely. Why do you think I'm here?'

'Yes, there is,' said Wendy. 'But I'm very tired. It's late already, and there's school tomorrow.'

'Well, if you want to.'

'Are you coming? I don't mind.'

'Where's the party?'

'Joe Allen's.'

Tom watched Julian pause, watched his head drop as he considered his options. He looked very, very tired. There were purplish bags under his eyes and his cheeks were blotched and puffy. For the first time Tom noticed the scab on the end of Julian's nose. How had he missed it before? It was enormous.

He must have been concentrating on his eyes too much to notice. Julian sighed and Tom wondered what factors were being debated inside his head, or whether he was able to summon up a debate at all. Julian had a particularly vacant expression on his face, as if he had fallen into unconsciousness standing up with his eyes wide open. Finally he drew himself up and took Wendy's hand.

'Do you know, I think I will come home. I've had quite a big day really.'

For the first time since they'd been alone in the room together Wendy looked in Tom's direction. She mouthed a 'goodbye'. Tom rushed over – goodbyes were in the public domain, he could bid her goodbye without provoking suspicion.

'Thanks Wendy,' he said, kissing her on both cheeks and giving her a platonic hug. 'Thanks for coming, and thanks for all the things you said,' he continued, unable to prevent himself from letting a slightly ambiguous tone into his last remark. Knowing that Julian was directly behind him Tom widened his eyes as if to suggest some greater import to his words but Wendy looked away.

'Come on, Julian,' she said.

Julian drained a full glass of unclaimed wine he'd found. 'Yep, I'm ready. Night Tom. Wonderful show – think it'll transfer?'

Tom laughed politely.

'I imagine you'll be doing panto next year, after the success of your new sitcom,' Julian continued, nodding in Rob Halford's direction.

'Oh yes. You've heard about that, have you?'

'Yes. But you never know, I might be wrong – after all,' said Julian, suddenly pitching forward and whispering furtively into Tom's ear, his breath hot and moist, 'I am a complete arsehole.'

Tom barely had time to furrow his brow before Julian pulled back, smiled broadly, took Wendy's arm in his and escorted her from the room. Tom felt paralysed – he didn't know if

Julian's words meant that he'd been awake or whether he was just casually insulting him as usual. His heart fought against his ribs and he was sure everyone in the room must be looking at him; must have heard what Julian had said; must have understood the dire implications of his words. He could feel the residue of Julian's breath in his ear and, repulsed, he raised his hand and wiped it out. Inspecting the results he found an orange glow on the end of his finger. It felt as if he was looking at the physical form of Julian's words – as if he'd been handed the black spot. He rushed to the basin to wash it off, a hot wave of panic surfing up his spine.

Out in the main corridor Catriona backed out of Rosencrantz and Guildenstern's dressing room and turned in the direction of Osric's to collect his damp tights. She instantly spotted Julian and Wendy coming towards her, picking their way through the overspills from other dressing rooms. She leaned casually against the wall and waited, ready to trade a shifty wink or a wry smile – perhaps even to enjoy a brief communion of souls. She knew Julian must have seen her and was excited at the prospect of sharing their secret in such a public place – with his wife in tow as well! As they came closer her heart raced as she looked for the furtive acknowledgement. She was then filled with gall as he walked straight past as if she wasn't there.

Julian had seen her of course, but he felt no compunction to acknowledge her. His love for her had died at the moment of ejaculation. He *had* loved her, momentarily – or rather he'd loved the *idea* of her – but once the conquest had been made he'd felt nothing more. If she wanted to sleep with him in the future he might consider it, but it would depend on the circumstances of the moment – he couldn't entertain organising a relationship with her.

He could feel Catriona's eyes boring into the back of his neck but it didn't worry him. She wasn't out of pocket, he thought to himself; she'd had the honour of sleeping with a star; had had the pleasure of his imaginative love-making; he felt no compunction for her. Yet as he turned the corner at the end of the corridor and descended the stairs to the stage door his heartbeat quickened in response to a rising panic – the psycho fan! She'd be waiting outside the door. *Why did he feel this rush of guilt? After all he'd just passed Catriona without the slightest pang.*

'Are there any cabs out there?' Wendy asked the stage doorman.

'Yes, just down to your right, dear,' he replied.

'Or is there another way out?' asked Julian, looking nervously through the door at a mob of thirty or forty autograph hunters, some of whom had spotted him and were already popping away at him with their instamatics. No one had been expecting Julian and a wave of excitement rippled through the crowd.

'Oh, Mr Mann, there you are – I thought I'd lost you, sir,' came the voice of the little old man from behind them. 'Not the first time, I'm afraid – did you find a drink, sir?'

'Yes, thanks.'

'Oh good. Back way out is it you're looking for, sir? If you'd just like to follow me,' he said, dragging out his huge set of keys and setting off back up the stairs.

Julian looked out through the exit door at the throng of autograph hunters. He couldn't see the psycho fan.

'Quick,' he shouted, grabbing Wendy by the elbow, and they swung out into the crowd and pushed their way briskly through a phalanx of outstretched autograph books and pens towards a line of cabs.

'Sorry, I haven't got time, got to get home, one of my children is very sick,' he muttered as he barged through the crush holding a protective arm around Wendy's shoulders and pushing people out of the way with the other. They climbed into the first cab and squeezed the door shut against the press of arms and faces.

'Gloucester Road, please,' said Julian, keeping his head bowed to the floor of the cab in case the psycho fan was still around.

12

Three weeks later Julian found himself sitting at the back of the American Church on Tottenham Court Road, a boxy modern building that reminded him of his old school assembly hall. He was watching Arabella Frye and Lindsay Barraclough rehearse the meeting between the Hon. Gwendolen Fairfax and Cecily Cardew in *The Importance Of Being Earnest*.

The production was to go on a five-month tour of one- and two-week stands at provincial theatres, working the rich seam of middle-class, middle-brow theatre-goers eager to watch a couple of TV names in a classic play (that was out of copyright). The minor celebrity Mitch had hired to play Algy had gone down with hepatitis the week before rehearsals had been due to start. Julian had agreed to take the part over during his chat with Mitch backstage at the National. It had been a gesture of petulant defiance – a 'fuck you' to Paul – who needed an agent? – and also a desperate grabbing at straws in the drunken paranoiac fear that, as he had no work at all lined up for the future, he might never work again. But sitting in the church now he knew that he didn't want to be there.

Arabella was the better actress, but Julian preferred Lindsay. She was slimmer with louder make-up and a peroxide-streaked mane, and anything with a lip-line and dyed hair was obviously game in Julian's book.

'I like you already more than I can say. My first impressions of people are never wrong,' said Arabella as Gwendolen, on being introduced to Cecily.

'How nice of you to like me so much after we have known

103

each other for such a comparatively short time,' replied Lindsay as Cecily.

Julian exploded into boisterous laughter and rocked in his metal-framed, canvas-covered chair, which creaked loudly. Andy, the director, who'd made it obvious that he would have preferred someone less 'Light Entertainment' than Julian to play Algy, looked round from his seat half-way down the hall and smiled a patronising smile that implied he'd rather Julian didn't cheapen the rehearsal process by laughing, then turned back to the action. Julian scowled. The divergent sense of fun he'd had watching Lindsay perform, and the casual day-dream of inviting her into his dressing room and unwrapping her that had kept him amused for the last twenty minutes, receded like the tide and left him stranded on the rocks of tedium.

His eyes watered – not with self-pitying tears, but with the mind-numbing frustration of it all. He was sober, unutterably bored, and getting increasingly annoyed with himself for having taken the job on.

He looked round at his fellow thespians who lined the back wall of the hall alongside him. Sam, who was playing Jack, was all right he supposed. He was younger than Julian and supposedly a 'rising new talent', but he was in his early thirties already and Julian knew he'd missed the stardom boat long ago. He certainly didn't feel there was any threat that people would be looking at Sam instead of at him. Vernon and Tim had screened themselves off in the corner behind some upturned tables and were pouring over the *Daily Telegraph* crossword. They were amiable enough, a couple of harmless, oldish, jobbing actors, perfectly competent but hardly likely to set the world on fire. Daphne – who was playing Miss Prism – was a delight, like some great-aunt Julian wished he'd had. And then there was Bronwyn – Julian hated Bronwyn already – a late-middle-aged harridan who'd spent thirty years treading the boards for the RSC and had recently made her mark as a player of late-middle-aged harridans in TV sitcoms and consequently thought she knew it all.

'Oh comedy's easy,' she kept on saying, 'you just have to play it straight – that's all you have to do.'

It infuriated Julian. The notion that there was a *method* in comedy; the idea that *anyone* could do it; the gall of someone believing that that was *all* you had to do. *All!!* His comedy was a mixture of poetry and magic, taking the relationship with the audience to that dangerous point between giddy success and alarming failure – because that's where the excitement was, and doing comedy wasn't about just being *funny*, it was about *excitement*.

What was he doing here? he thought to himself. He didn't want to go on a five-month tour of the provinces with a slight chance of coming into the West End at the end of it. No one in their right mind wanted to go on a five-month tour of the provinces. And the hopes of the West End were *very* remote, he thought, looking round at the B-list cast in the rehearsal room – only Bronwyn and he had had any real television exposure, and she was *crap*.

It was the tax demands of course, he thought, kicking himself. He had to work to pay off the tax demands. He'd cleared the decks to do *Blood Train*, even cancelled Halford and Dixon's new sitcom – virtually divorced them as his writers, and now they'd already forgotten him and jumped into bed with Tom – he had no agent, nothing else to do, and two tax demands for nearly sixty thousand pounds. *It was all the government's fault – forcing him take on this worthless piece of shit. He would have to stay for a week at a time in shitholes like Nottingham, Derby and Wolverhampton so that the government could spend his hard-earned money on a new airport for the Falklands or a few more nuclear reactors to flog off to their friends on the cheap.*

Julian had to stand, he was so furious. He rammed his hands deep into his jacket pockets and shuffled his weight from foot to foot, his blood-gorged face bent to the floor mouthing silent obscenities, until he could curb his growing rage no longer and he turned and kicked the metal-framed chair with all his might. It looped six feet into the air and crashed down onto the bare wooden floor with a huge, echoing clatter, bouncing several times before it came to rest.

Julian looked up to see the rest of the room staring at him – except for Andy, whose thin, angry body was already half-way towards the swing doors at the opposite corner of the hall. All eyes turned to the director as he barged through the doors which swung wildly to and fro making their distinctive whoomphing noise. They could all hear his leather-soled shoes mincing furiously down the corridor and passing into the production office, followed by the slam of the production-office door. And they all knew that rehearsals wouldn't resume until Andy had phoned Mitch and had asked him to 'sort Julian out'.

An hour later Julian was sitting across the table from Mitch in a small, steamy, formica-covered sandwich bar round the corner from the church. It was late morning and the place was still almost empty.

Julian watched Mitch slowly sprinkle a thin layer of sugar on the top of his cappuccino. He'd already managed to scatter two small teaspoonsful on top of the froth without it collapsing under the strain, but the third was too much, the froth caved in at the middle and the sugar from round the edges slowly toppled into the hole. Mitch looked up at Julian and smiled broadly. Other people might have thought his smile ironic but Julian knew otherwise. He understood that Mitch was genuinely amused by the situation. He knew that Mitch was an extremely hard-headed businessman who hated the sort of problems Julian was creating, but that there was a pragmatic side to him that wouldn't allow these things to bring him down with an ulcer. Maintaining a jolly tone was Mitch's answer to stress.

They hadn't spoken for nearly five minutes now, but Julian recognised this as just another of Mitch's ploys – letting the other party do all the negotiating. Julian remembered Mitch explaining this practice to him towards the end of the run of

Charley's Aunt, when Julian had been in the process of trying to buy his first flat and had asked Mitch how to get a good deal on it. Mitch had told him simply to state the price he was willing to pay at the outset of the negotiations then keep silent and just look at the floor until the other party slowly bargained their way towards it. The longer he could hold his tongue the lower the price would fall. Julian had been too chicken to do this himself but he had coached Tilly, his girl-friend at the time, and had made her do the deal instead. It had worked exactly as Mitch had said it would and Julian had been so impressed that he'd never forgotten it. He'd never used the technique himself, because as an artist he couldn't be expected to soil his hands with sordid business, but had always taken pains to encourage his agents and representatives to use it on his behalf.

Now that he was his own agent he found that he was surprisingly good at it – he'd hardly said a word since they'd met, besides exchanging a few pleasantries, and Julian believed he had the upper hand because he was so dejected that he didn't even *feel* like talking. He held his tongue and day-dreamed about getting completely plastered. Another three minutes passed in idle tinkering and watching people walk by.

'Well, look . . . It's going to cost me a heap of money, but if it's what you really want . . . we can replace Andy,' said Mitch. Then, having caved in first, he sprawled back in his chair and waited for Julian's reaction.

Julian took a sip of his espresso, and finding it was now only luke-warm drained the cup slowly, stalling for time and trying to work out what his next move should be. If he'd still had Paul as his agent he'd have simply rung up and said 'Get me out of it' and that would have been that – he might have had to express extreme regret or remorse, but it would only have been to Paul, and so it wouldn't have counted in the grand scheme of things.

Why didn't he have an agent? Why hadn't he got a new one? He'd had three weeks, hadn't he? It wasn't as if it was difficult;

he'd had approaches from five already, all he had to do was meet them and decide which he liked best. And it wasn't as if Wendy had let him forget it either. Not that she'd been 'nagging' as such. Wendy never nagged. 'Nagging' implied some sort of pettiness or selfishness. Wendy merely stated obvious truths that could only improve his life, and only stated them very occasionally, but Julian still perceived it as nagging. It was just intelligent nagging. If she'd advised him to get off the road because an out-of-control juggernaut was headed his way Julian would still have thought that she was nagging.

Everybody nagged him, he thought, everybody wanted him to do something, wanted to put him under some kind of obligation. His wife was an obligation, his children were too. He had a mortgage and had to pay taxes. He was obliged to work, obliged to suffer all the less talented people he had to work with, obliged to be polite. He had to meet people and read scripts and make decisions. *Why did his life have to be so full of decisions?* What to wear, what to drink, where to go, what to think, which path to take, who to see . . . *Why couldn't he live in a bachelor penthouse being urbane, witty and successful, drinking and shagging his life away, having all his decisions made for him in a way that he would perfectly condone if he could be bothered to do the thinking for himself?* He wanted to surf on life but felt he couldn't even get up on his board for all the people holding him back in the water.

Mitch's chair scraped along the floor as he tried to manœuvre himself into a position where his long legs would fit more comfortably under the short table. Julian found he couldn't look him in the eye and stared down again at his empty cup.

'I'm sorry Mitch, but the thing is . . .' he felt his breathing stop as he summoned up all his courage, ' . . . I want to be out of the show altogether.'

Even without looking he could sense the shock and dismay on Mitch's face. He could picture the smile on Mitch's face freezing and hanging there out of context. He felt Mitch's feet shuffle as he sat up straighter in his chair.

108

'I'm sorry,' Julian repeated, remembering to try to sound contrite.

'Oh, no way, man, no way,' said Mitch, suddenly more forceful. 'No, you can't do that. Look, I'm offering to replace the director. I don't have to do that. Do you know how much that's going to cost me?'

'I just can't do it, Mitch. It's too . . .'

'Too what?'

'Too crap.'

'Hey, this is easy money for you – you know that? Of course you do. You knew you had me over a barrel when we struck the deal and I accepted that. I'm paying you way over the odds. If we sell out you're on six grand a week, maybe more.'

Julian looked up at Mitch with dead eyes. Malevolence was welling up inside him. He wanted a drink – needed one – either to encourage the bile to the surface or to suppress it and make him forget.

'Besides, look, I hate to get heavy,' Mitch continued, 'but we've got a signed contract and I can't let you out of it. There's a whole heap of commitments tied up in something like this, you know: theatre rents, production costs, advertising.'

'Yeah, I know, and I've said I'm sorry, Mitch, but I want out.'

'Well I can't let you out. Unless you come down with hepatitis or something like that, you're in.'

Julian looked out of the window at the pub opposite.

'What about cirrhosis of the liver? I could probably get that before late-afternoon.'

Mitch laughed and shook his head exaggeratedly in a 'you kill me' kind of gesture, then adjusted his chair and leaned forward with his elbows on the table, getting his face as close to Julian's as he could.

'So,' said Mitch, reverting to his fixed smile, 'do you want me to replace Andy or not?'

Julian sighed heavily. He could feel the beginnings of chest pains nagging behind his lower ribs on the left-hand side. *He even had obligations to his body!* He sat up straight and breathed in deeply, holding the breath for four seconds, then letting it out as slowly as he could.

'Well?' persisted Mitch.

'I've got to go for a piss,' Julian rose from his seat and headed for the flight of stairs that led to the basement. He found the toilets at the rear of the building at the end of a short passage, pushed the door to the gents open with his foot, then locked it behind him. The pain across his chest was refusing to go away and as he stood leaning against the door a violent spasm suddenly gripped him like a vice and he bent forward, wrapping his arms around himself. It wasn't his heart, it was the stress, he knew that – and if he followed Dr Sachs's instructions he knew he could beat off the attack. He closed his eyes and concentrated on his breathing until the pain subsided to an acceptable level.

As he opened his eyes again he noticed a small window high up in the back wall, and climbing up on the toilet seat he peered through it into the back yard of the sandwich bar. It was full of boxes of tomatoes and crates of fizzy drinks, dust-bins and old chill cabinets. There was a door set into the back wall which looked like it might lead into an alley.

Julian crept out of the toilet and back up the stairs. At the top he stopped and peeked round into the sandwich bar, and seeing Mitch was looking out into the street he darted away towards the back of the building, pushed through a door and found himself outside in the yard. He ran to the door in the back wall, turned the handle and pulled – it was locked.

'Mr Mann – what you doing?' came a voice from behind; a voice with a thick Italian accent.

Julian turned to see one of the men who worked behind the counter in the sandwich bar.

'Mr Mann? Yes? I know you from television. Very good,' the man continued, beaming through his moustache and wiping his hands gleefully on his apron. 'You go the wrong way. Like

110

in your television show, yes?' said the man, hardly able to contain his mirth. 'This not the café – not tables!'

Julian smiled back ingratiatingly.

'I show you the way back,' the man continued, holding his arm out to indicate it more precisely.

'Well, to be honest,' said Julian, moving over to the man and lowering his voice to a more confidential tone, 'the thing is, I want to play a joke on my friend in there. You see, he thinks I've gone to the toilets, yes?'

The man laughed loudly.

'No, that's not the joke,' said Julian.

The man laughed even more.

'No, listen, listen,' said Julian, 'I haven't said anything funny yet. You see, I thought it would be a good joke if I went out the back way, then walked past the front of the café and pretended to be surprised to see my friend . . . in the café . . . yes?'

The man stopped laughing. Julian imagined it must be the language barrier.

'Look, I'm a comedian, trust me, it's funny,' said Julian. 'Now have you got the key?' he carried on, rattling the handle of the door in the back wall.

'No, no key,' said the man, sadly shaking his head.

'No, it is funny, I promise you.'

'No, no key,' repeated the man.

'I swear by my BAFTAs – it's *funny*,' snapped Julian.

The man struggled to muster as great a command of the English language as he could. 'There . . . are . . . no . . . key.'

'There *isn't* a key?'

'No.'

'Shit,' said Julian, looking round at the high back wall and noticing two strands of rusty barbed wire held up on crooked metal struts. 'Look, give me a leg up, would you?'

He clambered onto one of the disused chill cabinets and the man climbed up with him, only too pleased to help and starting to laugh again. Julian soon found himself crouched on top of

111

the back wall, hanging onto the barbed wire which jutted out a good couple of feet into the alley. It was a treacherous-looking jump – he had to clear two feet up and out into the alley, then drop another eight or ten feet down to the cobbles below.

'Is very funny,' the man giggled.

'Yes, fucking hilarious, isn't it?' Julian scoffed back.

'I get my camera,' he said, climbing off the chill cabinet and heading back to the sandwich bar.

'Yes, why don't you do that? – I haven't been on the front page for a couple of weeks,' he shouted after him as he disappeared. 'And this certainly looks like a suicide attempt,' he muttered to himself, taking a closer look at the barbed wire.

He thought of Mitch sitting in the café with his contract and his 'deal' and his obligations and knew that he would be getting increasingly concerned by now – that was enough of a spur. In a kind of reflex reaction Julian suddenly coiled up his legs and launched himself as far as he could into the air. His jacket caught on one of the barbs as he went over the top and he heard an enormous rip as he fell heavily onto the stony ground below, then he scrambled to his feet and hobbled off through an arch towards the street beyond as fast as his jarred knees and ankles would carry him. Pausing briefly to check that the coast was clear he limped out into the street and struggled a couple of blocks away, intending to hail the first cab he saw and put some distance between himself and Mitch. But he found himself unable to make it past the second pub he came across.

'A pint of Kronenbourg and a large Jack Daniel's, please,' said Julian as he entered the pub and scanned the row of spirits. 'Oh no, hang on, you've got Wild Turkey – I'll have that.'

The barman nodded as he placed a glass under the Kronenbourg tap and pushed the button, and with joyful anticipation Julian craned over the bar to watch the lager as it streamed out of the spout. It was so deliciously cold that condensation formed on the glass as it filled, and as soon as the barman placed it on the counter Julian lifted it rapturously to his mouth and took several healthy swallows.

'That'll be four pounds fifty-five, thank you,' said the barman, returning with his Wild Turkey.

Julian gave him a fiver.

'Keep the change.'

'Thanks very much. Hey, you don't mind me asking do you – but aren't you Julian Mann?' asked the barman.

'That's right,' spat Julian. Then yielding slightly, 'Look, here's ten quid. Do us a favour and don't talk to me.'

The barman hesitated momentarily, then accepted the deal with tacit good grace. Julian deftly knocked back the Turkey and raised the lager to his mouth again. There was something majestic and inspiring about the clean crispness of it as it slid effortlessly down, and Julian felt relaxed and comforted as his nerve-endings relayed the presence of alcohol to his brain – no alarm bells, just a friendly telegram to say that daddy was coming home. The residue of pain in his chest seemed to vanish like morning mist. He drained the glass in three passes and enjoyed the slight heat it induced behind his eyeballs.

'Same again,' he said to the barman, slapping another fiver on the bar, and walked briskly off to the gents. When he returned he was glad to see the fresh round of drinks waiting for him on the bar with his change neatly piled up next to it. The few shafts of light filtering through the stained-glass windows of the pub seemed to illuminate only the lager and to imbue it with a religious significance which pleased Julian greatly – he had no religion except superstition and was glad of anything that could be interpreted as a good omen. He pushed the change back across the bar and the barman smiled and touched a finger to his forehead in acknowledgement, declining even to say 'thank you'. Things were getting better by the minute, thought Julian. He pulled his wallet out of his pocket and placed it on the bar in a line with his drinks.

13

Rehearsal Room 603 on the sixth floor of the BBC rehearsal block in Acton was a vast barn of a room eighty feet long by forty feet wide, and the autumn sun streaming in through the windows was making it as uncomfortable as a coach trip in high summer. The mirrors along one wall dimly reflected a solemn group of figures sitting disconsolately round a small table in a 'V' of shade at the far end of the room: Tom Bailey, Rob Halford, his writing partner Peter Harris Dixon or the 'Doctor' as he was known (short for 'Ph.D.'), and Charlie Nesbitt, a vacuous tweed jacket of a producer who had no interest in discussing the content of *Save Our Souls* and was privately running over ideas for the end-of-series party instead.

Tom had asked for the rehearsal room in case he should feel the urge to 'walk through' some of the material they were discussing, but as this was the second day of discussion and he hadn't yet left his chair once, he was becoming more and more guiltily aware that the presence of four grown men sitting quietly at one end of the room was barely sufficient to cause even the smallest eddy in the massive aircraft hangar of a space.

The huge stillness, the blinding sunlight and Tom's apparent lack of enthusiasm for the rewrites combined to produce an atmosphere of the most stultifying ennui.

'I don't quite understand,' said the Doctor, breaking another long silence. He was the bespectacled professor of the writing partnership. 'You're saying it's not witty enough, yet on the other hand you're saying it's too . . .' he searched hard for the right word.

'Funny,' prompted Rob, his plump face creasing into a smile that squeezed small flash floods of perspiration from the dimples in his greasy, stubbled cheeks.

Tom looked hard into Rob's face and tried to concentrate on what he wanted to say but he couldn't erase what he'd learned about Julian the day before from his mind. *He'd fucked Catriona in his, Tom's, dressing room, on Tom's first night?* It was unbelievable, but it was *the* gossip backstage at the moment. In *his* dressing room?! Did that mean there was a residue of Julian's semen somewhere? On his day-bed? On his chair? On the carpet somewhere? He was filled with loathing and disgust and seething indignation that he had been the last to be told. On the very night – *possibly within minutes* – and in the same room where he'd had to suffer Wendy's belittling rebuff.

In the rehearsal room the Doctor coughed deliberately and Tom looked up.

'Suppose we workshopped it?' said Tom, dragging himself back into the debate.

'Workshopped it?' queried Rob.

'You mean, improvising, playing games – that sort of thing?' asked the Doctor, taking a drag on his small cigar.

'Yes,' said Tom. 'You know, get a few actors in, knock it about a bit. Search for the truth of the piece.'

'Hmmn,' said the Doctor, turning his attention back to a small ball of pocket fluff that had attached itself to his match-box. He and Rob had been professional writers for seventeen years – they still sweated over every line, every nuance – and he marvelled at Tom's arrogant assumption that a roomful of vain, self-centred actors could somehow unlock hidden meanings which he, the Doctor, hadn't already made completely obvious.

'You know – find out what it's really about,' said Tom, pursuing the point as his only real contribution to the forum.

'How much more do you think there is to find out?' asked Rob. 'It's quite simple as we see it – it's about an overbearingly optimistic DIY enthusiast shipwrecked on a desert island with a suicidally depressed entertainments officer and an old Jap who doesn't know that the war is over.'

'Yes, but where's the humour in that?' Tom shook his head despairingly, then let it drop into his hands. He couldn't stop himself thinking about Wendy – still couldn't believe that his plan hadn't worked after so many years of summoning up the courage to confront her with his more worldly desires. He had plotted his dressing-room exposure months before – it had seemed to him the only way of introducing the idea of physical love into their relationship. Sure, there had been plenty of occasions when they had been on their own together but their relationship had such a long, platonic and intellectual base that the very idea of discussing a sexual dimension might have come across as a sordid betrayal. A sudden and seemingly accidental exposure during a moment of high sensibility, minutes after the most astonishing performance of his life, at his seemingly most vulnerable after four and a half hours of emotional wrestling with Hamlet's tortured soul, his body tuned to perfection after months of careful preparation in the gym (not too muscular, just lean and supple), the ugly white band of flesh his swimming trunks had left carefully tanned away in the solarium . . . it had seemed the perfect plan.

'Well, the humour is in the situation,' said the Doctor, scraping his chair back across the floor and bringing Tom back into the fold once more, 'and we try to exploit that with "jokes" and "funny lines".'

'Yes,' said Tom, trying hard to concentrate, 'but if the scripts are just a collection of jokes and funny lines – what's the show actually going to *be*?'

'A comedy?' ventured Rob.

The gloomy silence returned.

'I need to go to the toilet,' said Tom, rising dispiritedly from his chair and tramping sullenly to the doors at the far end of the room. *He'd have to wash his Shri Yantra!* They must have done it on his bed and then pulled it over them. The colours were bound to run, they were third-world dyes and that meant

116

dry-cleaning. *Would it stand up to that?* Were you *supposed* to clean a Shri Yantra? Might it remove some of its metaphysical powers?

He ignored the gents, turned past the lifts and production offices and pushed through the heavy fire door at the end of the corridor into the emergency staircase beyond. The staircase was his favourite part of the rehearsal block. Whenever he was rehearsing at Acton he liked to avoid the lunchtime crowds in the canteen and bring in a sandwich to eat perched on a windowsill looking out at the rather glum industrial estate below. He could recover his thoughts in solitude and work out how to look better than everyone else in whatever show he was working on. Besides, it gave him an opportunity to look moody and interesting if any stray actresses or directors happened to pass on the stairs.

Standing there in solitude he couldn't believe that he'd been the last to be told about Julian and Catriona. Had everyone imagined that he and Julian and Wendy were such close friends that he wouldn't have been able to take it? For crying out loud, *everyone* knew that Julian was the biggest lech in town, *everyone* had a Julian Mann story: seen coming out of a toilet with . . . ; heard through the wall of a hotel bedroom with . . . ; locked in a make-up trailer with . . . ; caught with his hand up the skirt of . . . It seemed to Tom that the whole world knew about Julian's adventures – except for Wendy.

Why had he never told Wendy himself? he wondered. Why had *no one* ever told her? Because it felt curiously disloyal, that was why. No matter how much he desired Wendy, to strike at the heart of her marriage in such a peevish, snitching way seemed underhand and unattractive, and might seem an all-too-obvious ruse to try and oust his rival.

Tom pushed his back into the window frame and adopted the lotus posture, closed his eyes, and thought back to their first term at Bristol. In a group tutorial on *The Rape of Lucrece* they had read the poem aloud, Tom reading the lust-breathed Tarquin and Wendy the earthly saint, Lucrece, within whose

117

face beauty and virtue strove for ascendancy. Coming to the part where Tarquin draws aside the curtains to reveal the sleeping form of Lucrece in her bed and lays his hand upon one ivory globe, Tom had leaned forward out of his chair and gently cupped Wendy's left breast.

He remembered as if it were yesterday the terror of the instant when he'd dared to follow his instinct so recklessly; the way his jaw had frozen as he looked earnestly into her eyes; the tremble of his hand; the confirmation that she was not wearing a bra. Would she scream and slap him down? he'd thought. Would the other students intervene and wrestle him to the ground? Would his excuses about 'impetuous art' and 'breathing life into the text' work?

The answer had been 'yes', as everyone had gasped together, then held their breath like a thunderstorm waiting to break. Wendy had stared back at Tom like the defiled heroine of the poem, but had made no move to dislodge his hand, and he had felt the frenetic, quickening pulse of her heart through the thin veil of her T-shirt and the cushioning, velvety flesh of her breast. The atmosphere had grown stiller and more breathless as Tom had read on through Tarquin's foul plan to force himself upon her, and even more hushed and pregnant as Wendy had faltered through Lucrece's entreaties to leave her be with a high reedy voice, cracked with emotion. And when at last the moment of violation had come Tom had taken a step across to her chair and symbolically pressed her head into his midriff. She had burst into tears, and the other students into spontaneous applause.

Tom had relaxed his grip on her head and tilted it up towards him, looking down into her sobbing face that was framed by great sweeps of unruly, straw-coloured hair. There had been no redness or swelling, no salty streaks, just a cascade of crystalline tears that had made her look even more beautiful than he'd already thought her to be, that had made her eyes shine like pools of phosphorescent water.

'I'm sorry,' he'd said.

'It's all right, I'm just crying for Lucrece,' she'd said, smiling bravely. He had lifted her gently out of her chair and wrapped his arms around her. He remembered how young and girlish her body had felt, how tenderly frail, and how it had melded into his. He could remember the Fruit of the Loom T-shirt, her short, printed silk skirt and her leggings and the childish, leather pixie boots sprayed gold – and the *cardigan* – the fleecy, lambswool, all-enveloping shroud that had at once protected her *and* made her an exotic sweet to be unwrapped, so casual and so sexually provocative.

Perched on the windowsill in Acton, Tom dared to wonder what making love to Wendy would be like but found himself sidetracked by memories of the sex he'd had with Carly. He'd met her for the first time three weeks before, having trouble with the bouncers outside Joe Allen's at the first night bash for *Hamlet*, and he'd gallantly pretended she was his girlfriend to help her get in. He'd found her attractive enough, and after his rejection by Wendy he'd fancied the prospect of a little physical consolation. When he'd discovered that she was actually the new friend Wendy had mentioned to him, his interest in her had quadrupled. He'd bedded her that same night. Or maybe she'd bedded him, he thought on reflection. Either way, he'd taken the discovery that she had a similar interest in the Tantrika as some sort of astral signal, had been glad of the startlingly energetic sex, and perversely pleased at the prospect of throwing news of it in Wendy's face – perhaps jealousy would finally drive her into his arms.

He was awoken from his day-dream by a loud laugh from the other side of the fire door and slipped from his perch on the windowsill.

He wondered how long he had been in a trance. He'd been practising his yoga techniques so diligently of late that he was now reaching the first stage of mandala transformation almost as soon as he closed his eyes – so he could have been on a higher plain for five minutes or five hours.

Creeping gingerly to the fire door he took a quick peek

through the mesh-reinforced window into the corridor beyond where Rob and the Doctor stood chatting with Charlie the producer. Tom pulled back out of sight and pressed his ear to the heavy door to listen to their conversation.

'Fucking actors – give me a comedian any day,' he heard Rob say.

'What do you think, Charlie?' asked the Doctor, goading an opinion out of the tweed jacket purely for his own amusement.

'Simon Callow got very reasonable figures for *Chance In A Million*,' said Charlie.

'Hmmn,' said the Doctor, 'pity it wasn't very funny.'

'Yes,' said Rob, 'well, either way, it looks like our classical actor's obviously done a bunk, doesn't it?'

'Yes, might as well call it a day,' said Charlie.

'You know Julian wants to come back in on it, don't you?' asked Rob, as the lift arrived with a 'plung' sound.

Hiding behind the door Tom seethed with rage at the mention of Julian's name. All his yogic relaxation exercises went for nought as the muscles in his neck tightened into rods of steel.

'And at least with Julian you get two people for the price of one,' said Rob as they ambled into the lift. 'Which is very good value.'

'Hmmnh?' queried Charlie.

'Yes – him *and* his ego.'

The lift doors closed. Tom's heart suddenly filled with nervous excitement as a plan formed in his mind. He sneaked back down the corridor and into the rehearsal room like a thief, and left a note on the table which read: 'Where are you guys? Waited an hour and a half, then left. Comedic regards, Tom.'

He would tell Wendy about Julian and Catriona! Of course he could have told her of Julian's philandering on any number of occasions in the past, but this time it was different – this time he had actual forensic evidence in the shape of his Shri Yantra. And this hard evidence seemed to absolve him from telling

120

tales. He'd break it to her gently, with tears in his eyes, as if the ghastly truth hurt him almost as much as it hurt her and she'd fall into his arms as she had in the tutorial so long before.

He hovered by the rehearsal-room window, his stomach full of butterflies, watching to make sure all his colleagues left in their respective cars, then flitted lightly down the fire escape, out of the building and across the road towards the tube station.

14

By half past three Julian was in a fairly crapulous condition. He'd held his corner of the bar through the lunchtime rush and had defeated all the well-wishing back-slappers and autograph hunters with the impenetrable ring of steel that signalled a serious drinker. He'd drunk steadily and continuously with the measured gait of someone competing in a marathon, and had finally managed to expunge the horror of the play and Mitch's contract. The drink had given him the courage to say 'Fuck it, I'm not doing it', and his heart felt much lighter at the prospect. His tax demands had met much the same fate – after all, it was only tax – and it wasn't as if he hadn't given already. His accountant had told him he was in the top five per cent of the nation's earners so he must have built up a healthy credit balance by now – he'd probably paid for a whole regiment of mechanised infantry!

He wondered for the millionth time why he was always in debt. It staggered him that he could earn so much yet still feel he was constantly beating the wolf away from the door. *How the fuck did the ordinaries manage on fifteen or twenty grand a year?* That'd barely cover first-class return flights to Kenya for the annual family holiday, never mind the mortgage, the school fees, the Range Rover, insurance, accountancy and pension funds. And interior decoration.

As he sat on his stool, staring at his drinks on the counter, his mind raged at the endless stream of paper and correspondence that cluttered his life – VAT returns, income tax, insurance renewals, pension queries, remittance advice notes, phone bills, electricity, gas, school fees, community charge, bank statements, contracts, fan mail – and it seemed the more people he hired to take care of it all the more correspondence he got by return. *Why couldn't his accountant just sort everything out for him, pay everything off that needed paying off and send him the balance of what he was legally entitled to spend? In cash?*

Apart from the regular domestic outgoings he didn't think he was particularly profligate. He didn't have any expensive hobbies – a helicopter, or a string of polo ponies, or a collection of modern paintings – all he did was drink. *How much could Wendy be getting through?* Though she probably knew their position better than he did, and she was too rational to get them into debt on her own account. Besides, he thought, there had to be a finite amount of ruched curtaining one house could take.

He signalled to the barman to set up the same again, then tore quietly at his hair as anger at this mess of obligations overtook him. He thought of running away, of just picking up his passport, heading out to the airport, and getting on the first plane to some place where no one could find him. The barman placed fresh glasses in front of him and Julian tossed him another fiver, but tossed it rather badly, and it fell at his own feet. Instead of leaning down to pick it up he simply pulled out another from his wallet and pushed it across the counter. The barman smiled and gave his little salute. Julian smiled and saluted back. The incident made him feel slightly happier, and as his mood lightened his fantasy grew – he dismissed the idea of running away on his credit cards and thought about quickly selling the house and disappearing with the cash. Wendy would cope, he thought, and the boys wouldn't miss him. He could start again in Australia or New Zealand.

Start *what*? He was suddenly alarmed – *what* could he do? He was an actor. He couldn't *do* anything else – he'd assiduously trained himself to be incompetent in every other field of human endeavour to make himself appear all the more devoted to his art – and if he set himself up as an actor in Australia

123

he'd become famous all over again. In fact he *was* famous there already. He'd never been there but he'd seen the royalty statements pour in as they bought up series after series of *Richard the Nerd*, so Interpol would be bound to catch up with him, and then he'd have to pay back all the proceeds of the house *and* wind up in jail.

He couldn't think of a country he hadn't received royalties from: the USA, Canada, France, Spain, Italy, Greece, Australia, New Zealand, Nigeria, Morocco, Sri Lanka, Finland, Colombia, Taiwan. There didn't seem to be a single corner of the world that hadn't received the benefit of his genius (it was this kind of notoriety that made it so difficult for him to buy pornographic magazines), though what the Taiwanese thought of his idiosyncratic Plantagenet sitcom he couldn't begin to guess. It occurred to Julian that he'd never seen a statement from the Yemen Republic and at that he suddenly gave up the idea of running away altogether.

Of course, he thought to himself in the depths of his maudlin speculation, none of this would be a problem for Tom – *Tom was fucking brilliant at everything*. It annoyed Julian that Wendy never stopped singing Tom's praises. She was an intelligent woman, she must have known how it vexed him. But it seemed she could never resist mentioning how Tom had rebuilt a '50s jukebox from scratch, or had a poem printed in the *Times Literary Supplement*, or rewired his own flat, or made a brilliantly received speech on behalf of some animal rights group. No, Tom could have run away at a moment's notice and set himself up with another identity and another successful career without anyone ever being able to trace him.

The only thing it seemed Tom had never managed to do was to sleep with Wendy. Julian could hardly believe it. If *he* had lived like that with a girl for two and a half years he'd have definitely shagged her, or died in the attempt. He knew they'd even been on holiday together and had had to share the same bed, and Tom still hadn't given her one! It was almost an insult to his wife!

There had to be something more to it, thought Julian, because Tom was *always* around, even more so in the last couple of weeks since he'd started seeing Wendy's new best friend, the almost mythical Carly.

'Very, bloody, remarkably, fucking convenient,' muttered Julian to himself, wondering paranoically if this 'Carly' actually existed at all – *he'd* never seen her – or whether she might be an invention of Wendy and Tom's to explain Tom's seemingly constant presence in the vicinity. Perhaps 'Carly' was a smoke screen hiding the affair that had at long last come to fruition. Julian's mind raced with the sudden plausibility of this conspiracy theory, and searching for a friend to support him in his hour of need he grabbed at his bourbon and drained the glass. The spirit seemed to calm him down and he became more rational. Wendy could never do that to him, he thought to himself, she couldn't deceive him. Besides, she'd been so full of detail about this new girlfriend – the little orphan Annie whose mother had died and whose father had abandoned her, who'd been shunted around from institution to institution until she'd finally found herself in an asylum and had had to pull herself together and fight to prove her sanity before they'd let her out. Wendy could never have invented such a story or she'd have made it as a writer! Unless Tom had written it all down for her and she was just spouting his fiction, because Tom was probably an accomplished novelist as well, Julian thought bitterly to himself. After all, he had a first in English, it would just be another of his wonderful talents. Tom could probably run away any time he liked, to any country in the world, even the Yemen Republic, and simply write bestsellers under a pseudonym.

'Runaway, run, run, run, run, runaway,' Julian sang under his breath and took a few heavy draughts of lager.

Running away had been so much easier in his youth when he hadn't been well known and hadn't had so much to run away from: he'd run away from school, from his parents, from girlfriends who had started talking about commitment, but he'd never needed to run far, never had to rebuild his whole life. Short separations had usually been enough to avoid the embarrassment of talking things over – other people would do all the changing for him, they'd readjust to ease the pain and hurt they felt – and he'd simply swan back a few weeks later as if nothing had happened and pick up where he'd left off.

Things were so much more serious now, so much more complex. Perhaps they needed a more serious remedy, he thought. He toyed with the notion of suicide for a while, which wasn't an infrequent pastime, but one that he could never resolve – he always imagined he would miss out on something, that a better, less complicated, easier life might be waiting just round the corner. Maybe tomorrow he'd be freed of his obligations in recognition of his services to entertainment and they'd let him live out his life as a shag-happy, drink-swilling, guilt-free comedy genius. And maybe *not*.

There was no clean way, no painless route, no way of simply stopping. And what of the consequences? He didn't have enough religion to have faith in the afterlife and wasn't agnostic enough to escape fears of purgatory.

He saw his body lying in one of the large filing cabinets in the morgue, a bloodless corpse. He couldn't see how he'd died. He could have hung himself, or slit his wrists, or overdosed, or simply fallen off a bar stool and cracked his head. He thought of Wendy and imagined her hugging the boys tight as they cried inconsolably. Their sense of loss seemed immeasurable. Wendy's eyes were brimming with tears but her jaw remained strong.

He pictured a dismal funeral attended only by Wendy and the boys and a scattering of fading celebrities desperate for any press coverage they could find, even his parents waited in their car. Then he saw Tom standing at Wendy's elbow, using the foul guise of comforter to make a play for her, and Julian's hackles rose – but as he looked on he saw her spurning Tom's advances for the sake of the boys and crying bitterly into her lace pillows at night.

126

A wave of desperate sadness engulfed Julian as he sat at the bar and he suddenly couldn't see his drinks any longer through the tears that welled in his eyes. He blinked and they rolled down his cheeks, great balls of wetness that splashed onto his lap leaving large, damp circles on his jeans. He didn't sob, he streamed silently, lowering his face and lifting a hand to his forehead to mask himself. He felt sudden, complete and utter desolation and dulled by alcohol his brain searched slowly for a lifebelt in the sea of sadness in which he found himself adrift.

He knew this was one of the dangers of drinking. Of course he could drink away his worries about the inconsequential minutiae of life – contracts and paperwork, and obligations to colleagues – but once he had done so there was always the danger he would be left contemplating the things that really mattered . . . and that could often leave him staring into the void.

He didn't have anyone! he cried to himself. His parents had given up on him long ago, or maybe he'd given up on them – in any case the gulf between them was so full of disinformation and unrequited filial obligations that repairing that relationship was unthinkable. Besides, they'd transferred their deepest affections to his dully conventional sister. Not that they'd ever closed the door on him – but they'd naturally shrunk back from a relationship in which so little was gained at such high emotional cost.

It dawned on him that the only person who'd ever made a voluntary, emotional and public commitment to him was Wendy. Wendy was always there – partly through necessity of course as they lived in the same house – but always there nevertheless, and as he thought of the handful of fly-by-night, fair-weather friends he'd had, her constancy impressed him, and he felt an enormous swell of love and affection for her. He wondered how a psychiatrist would evaluate his myriad betrayals of Wendy's trust – he'd probably reel in his chair and send off an urgent communication to the *Psychiatrists' Journal*

127

announcing the discovery of a whole new field of mental cruelty!

Julian's head sank onto the bar top and his shoulders began to heave as the guilt of it all palpably squeezed at his heart. How could he ever make it up to her? How could he show her how sorry he felt? And then it came to him – a plan to show the depths of his remorse, a plan partially to redress the balance of his treachery – *he'd go back to the American Church and retrieve the antique leather briefcase she'd given him for Christmas!*

He felt a hand on his forearm and looking up made out the concerned face of the barman through his tears. Julian fought to control himself and forced a weak smile. The barman made as if to speak.

'Ssh,' said Julian, putting a finger to his lips and shaking his head.

The barman fulfilled his contractual obligation to remain silent, but looked questioningly at Julian, seeming genuinely distressed to see him in such a state. Julian used both hands and both sleeves to wipe away the mess of snot and tears from his face and, taking a deep breath, sat up straight and looked at the barman with his bloodshot eyes.

'Fucking contact lenses,' he said. The barman's frown creased into a sympathetic smile. 'I don't even need them really, I only wear them because they make me look more intelligent.'

'Perhaps you've had enough now?' said the barman.

Julian fixed the barman with a malevolent stare, angry at the broken vow of silence and the slur on his manhood.

'Same again,' he said slowly, then carefully took another fiver from his wallet and pushed it across the bar.

The barman seemed reluctant for a moment, then nodded dutifully and turned to get fresh glasses. As soon as his back was turned Julian rose unsteadily, pulled his coat off the stool, and shambled out of the bar.

'Advantage – Mann,' he said quietly to himself as he negotiated the door.

15

As Julian staggered out from the stained-glass sanctuary of the pub into the bright daylight of Charlotte Street, Wendy was driving Sean and Jamie home from school.

She'd had an unpleasant afternoon and was feeling nervous and insecure. She'd received a phone call from Mitch shortly after lunch threatening all sorts of litigation and injunctions if Julian didn't turn up for rehearsals first thing the next morning. His tone had been distressingly terse and contentious and it had driven home to Wendy a growing awareness that all of Julian's 'friends' were really just enemies in disguise.

As Wendy turned into Rosary Gardens she immediately noticed Tom perched imperiously on the top of their gatepost, and quickly veered back into Wetherby Place and sped off.

'Why aren't we going home?' shouted Jamie.

'You're going the wrong way!' shouted Sean.

'I've forgotten something.'

'What?'

'Yes, what?'

'I . . . I . . . can't remember,' she said, driving hard to get some distance between them and Tom, and trying to think of somewhere to go until he left.

'You've forgotten what you've forgotten?' shouted Sean, bursting into incredulous laughter.

The twins made several attempts at repeating the sentence but never got past the first few words without collapsing into gales of giggling hysterics. After a minute of driving wildly round the streets of SW7 with the twins rolling around helpless with laughter in the back, Wendy pulled violently into the side of the road and stopped. She meant to turn round and bawl them out, but pulled herself back from the brink just in time – they were innocent parties, she reminded herself, and though their over-excited cackling seemed to be blocking out her ability to think, she realised it would be grossly unfair to take it out on them. She slumped against her door instead, letting her head fall back against the headrest, which had much the same desired effect upon the boys who fell silent immediately and sat there looking unsettled by her unusual behaviour.

Wendy was glad of the respite and stared out of her window at the white stuccoed splendour of the houses in Tregunter Road, reflecting dolefully on how difficult Tom had become of late – how everything had changed since his clumsy attempt at seduction in the dressing room. He'd become so oily and lascivious, and she found his enthusiastic and intimate accounts of sex with Carly quite distasteful. Wendy had been getting quite close to Carly, and though she was happy for her to be enjoying a relationship, Wendy felt a nagging doubt that Tom might only be sleeping with Carly to make her jealous.

Unless it was *she*, Wendy, who was jealous? But no, Tom had had girlfriends before and she'd never been troubled by them – though perhaps they'd been troubled by her. Why was it that only she and Tom could understand the harmless nature of their relationship, that only they could understand the simple beauty of platonic love? And then she thought how now even he seemed to be faltering in his comprehension.

Or perhaps she was feeling jealous of *Tom*? After all, Carly was the first real girlfriend Wendy could remember having since schooldays. She was so easy to talk to, so warm and loving. Wendy liked to take Carly into her boudoir at the back of the house where they'd sit and chat and hold hands. It was Carly who had first leaned across and held her hand, and though Wendy had felt uncomfortable at first she'd grown used to it, and had begun to look forward to it – it was such an unthreatening, affectionate gesture. Wendy wondered briefly if she was on the brink of a lesbian affair and though she quickly concluded that she wasn't, the residue of the idea seemed to strengthen the special friendship that Tom's affair with Carly appeared to be threatening, and made his behaviour all the more sickening.

She remembered their time together at Bristol: the *Lucrece* tutorial; the friendship ring he'd given her that first Christmas; the shared house in Clifton with Vinny and Mags; the hash she'd made of directing him in *The Iceman Cometh* and how he'd said he hadn't minded, though she knew he had; his hysterical wedding to the American student to get her a British passport, at which Wendy had 'given him away' – it had kept them in stitches for weeks; how unthreatening his sexuality had been, and how *he'd* become her best girlfriend in effect. They'd done so much talking in their lives, she couldn't imagine having talked to anyone else as much – not even her mother.

'Are you all right, Mummy?' Sean asked from the back of the car.

There was an ominous lack of echo from Jamie and she turned in her seat to look at the twins. They looked nervous and vulnerable, and, apart from their girlish bobs, exactly like their father, the glum look on their faces only serving to exaggerate the likeness.

Then came a sudden, loud and violent banging on the car window.

'Uncle Tom!' Sean and Jamie shouted in unison.

'Tom!' Wendy shouted, her heart racing as she wound down the window, searching desperately for an excuse. 'What are you doing here?'

Tom was almost completely out of breath. 'I've been . . . chasing you . . . for the last . . . five blocks.'

'Whatever for?'

'I saw you . . . go by the . . . top of the street . . . you seemed to . . . swerve . . . and pull away . . . you're not trying to . . . avoid me . . . are you?'

'Good heavens, no, whatever makes you think that?'

'Well, what on earth are you doing . . . here?' he asked, indicating the lifeless residential street she had parked in.

16

The plan to recover his briefcase from the rehearsal rooms hadn't seemed much of a plan as Julian had repeated it to himself outside the pub, but at least it had been *a* plan. It was symbolic, he thought to himself, and Wendy would appreciate the symbolism: she was an educated woman, she'd read all the classics. Besides, he told himself, this plan would only be the beginning, would only be the first stepping stone out of the abyss of his loneliness. He wasn't able to imagine what the next step might be, but that didn't bother him as he lurched along Charlotte Street keeping close to the buildings in case he started to fall.

As he struggled round the corner into Goodge Street, the antique, leather briefcase began to take on the properties of the Holy Grail – if he could only get his hands on it and get it back to Wendy then the deeper mysteries of life might be revealed to him.

Hearing Wendy's name in his head brought on a fresh, chilling wave of guilt and anguish, and he began to panic and started half-running down the street, stumbling into people as he went. He quickened his pace as the tears began to flow, and even though he swiped his sleeve past his seeing eye at regular intervals, he only narrowly missed falling into the traffic as he tried to dart through the swell of pedestrians impeding his progress. The urgency of his mission overwhelmed him as he began to imagine that he had to get to the American Church with all speed before his tears blinded him for ever.

'Out of the way! Out of the way!' he screamed, galloping towards his redemption and running headlong into a cast-iron lamppost. The whole of his forward momentum was stopped in a split second and he fell heavily onto the pavement. He felt as if he'd been the target on a 'Test your strength' machine in a fairground, and wondered briefly whether he was now permanently blind in both eyes.

Murmuring voices around him brought back memories of the swimming pool and the removal men and he fought to block out the 'he's fatter than he looks on the telly' line that would inevitably come at any second. He stuck his fingers in his ears and rose unsteadily to his feet, making nonsense 'bleurgh-leurgh-leurgh' sounds with his tongue as loudly as he could to keep the comments of the crowd at bay. He blinked furiously, trying to clear his vision, and became aware of all the startled faces crowding in to look at him. Leaning out towards them he clucked and bawled like a Maori warrior and made them shrink back apprehensively. Then, spinning slowly round the retreating horde, he looked for Tottenham Court Road and the American Church, and seeing the familiar red-brick pile in the distance he lurched off towards it, still yelling, and scattering those in his path.

As he reeled round the corner into the alley at the side of the church that led to the entrance door of the rehearsal room, he prayed that the rest of the cast of *The Importance* would have disbanded, and that he'd be able just to nip in, pick up the briefcase, and nip out again, but as he approached the door he became aware of a figure in black leaning against the railings to one side. There was something familiar about it and his heartbeat quickened as he imagined it might be Arabella or Lindsay, and that he was going to have to bullshit his way through a few awkward excuses, but as he got closer he suddenly stopped with a sharp intake of breath – it was the psycho fan.

There was no way out, he was too far down the alley. Even if he turned and ran he knew that she'd catch him. His rage filled his head with blood, engorging a bump the size of an egg on his forehead which sang with sudden pain. He covered his face with his hands in an agony of despair and suffering.

Feeling an arm slip around his shoulder he glanced sideways through his fingers to see the psycho fan's face surprisingly close to his. Her expression was somewhere between that of an affectionate puppy dog and an axe-wielding psychopath. He could feel the familiar shake of her body.

'Are you OK, Julian?'

Julian didn't answer. He was too drunk and confused to stomach ten or fifteen minutes psycho-babble, but short of a plan for getting away he determined to stay silent and stall for time.

Her cheek brushed against his and he stared obliquely into her eyes. He'd never been this close to her before. They'd kissed of course, but he could never really see her when they kissed. Now it seemed that the only things in his field of vision that were in focus were her eyes: they were light blue flecked with grey, and the whites were pure and solid. As he stared he saw himself reflected in her pupils: a tiny head and shoulders looking out from the shiny black circle, the convex shape of the cornea distorting the image like a fish-eye lens and making his nose seem incredibly long and bulbous. He looked like an incredibly dishevelled, frightened little rabbit, he thought to himself.

'You've hurt yourself, haven't you?' she said, her voice thin and whining. 'You've bumped your head.'

As she spoke Julian smelled the breath of her words, as sweet and fresh as peaches. He looked down to her slightly crooked mouth. She was wearing very bright red lipstick and in a Pavlovian response his brain raced with an image of those lips wrapped around his cock.

'Oh, poor thing,' she continued, hugging him tight around his shoulder and trying to lower the large woven bag she was holding in her free hand to the ground. As she leaned forward to do this her coat opened and Julian saw she was wearing an extraordinary red velvet waistcoat affair, embroidered with gold leaves and laced up the front with leather thongs. It was cut like a basque around her breasts and had a black voile collar-piece above. She anxiously cradled Julian's head into her chest and held him tight, pulling his cheek onto the transparent black voile. He gaped into her trembling cleavage and felt a hand glide down from the top of his head to the nape of his neck where it nervously patted and tried to soothe him.

'Poor, poor thing,' she repeated, her voice tremulous and short of breath.

Julian thought of the briefcase leaning against the back wall inside the church – it had his initials set in gold leaf above the catch – then looked deep into the psycho fan's cleavage and remembered her brightly lipsticked mouth.

'I don't suppose you fancy a fuck do you?' He felt like a ventriloquist's dummy, as if his mouth were saying things it had no right to say.

'All right.'

Julian looked up. Had he heard her correctly?

'Did you hear what I said?'

'You wanted to know if I fancied a fuck,' she repeated breathlessly.

'Yeah . . . well?'

'I said yes.'

Of course she'd said yes, he thought to himself, this was the psycho fan – *where did he think he was?* It was time to pull out and make a run for it. *She was a nutter for Christ's sake!* He could see it in her eyes; he knew it from having seen her twice a week for the last eight years; *what did he think he was doing?!*

'Come on then, there's some toilets in here,' he blurted out, grabbing her by the wrist and pulling her towards the door. Holding back only to pick up her bag she followed willingly behind him and as they squeezed through the door their bodies were pressed together. Julian feverishly suckered onto her lips and felt her pelvis grinding into his hip as they spilled into the hallway.

'This way,' he said, pushing her ahead of him and sticking

137

his hand up the back of her coat to grope at her buttocks, letting his hand dart into the cleft between her legs and pulling up hard. She spun round to a stop and felt for his cock through his jeans. Their teeth clashed as they fell on each other, and Julian began tugging at the leather thongs that held her bodice together.

A door slammed in the distance and Julian looked up in alarm.

'It's just here,' he said urgently, breaking out of the clinch and propelling her another ten feet along the passage to the door of the gents. He bundled her through and into one of the cubicles, pressing her against the flimsy partition wall as he made room to close the door behind him. As he latched himself onto her mouth once more he played back images of the bright red lipstick in his mind.

'I'd really like a blow-job,' he heard himself saying.

'Sure,' she said, sinking to her knees to oblige him. Julian could hardly believe her speed. If he'd known she was this filthy he'd have given her one ages ago, he thought to himself. But either her black ski-pants were too tight or the cubicle was too small, as she couldn't get herself down into the right position.

'Stand on the toilet,' she said. It was a suggestion, not a command. Julian's mind raced with images of compliant Roman slave girls. *He should have married her!*

He had to balance carefully as there was no seat cover to the lavatory, and the seat itself was only held on by one of its hinges, but with the psycho fan's assistance he managed to stand on it and turned to face her as he started to undo his fly.

'No, let me do that.' She brushed his hands aside, and set to work on his belt.

'Why – be my guest,' said Julian, standing up straight and folding his hands behind his head. His breathing became shorter and more urgent as the psycho fan unbuckled his belt and as she teased his zip down he let out a long snort of excited anticipation. Unfortunately this unexpected hyperventilation on top of an already alcoholically challenged brain caused him to lose all sense of balance. All of a sudden he felt faint and giddy and clawed at the air for something to steady himself by. He latched on to the small china cistern fixed high on the wall behind him as his feet slipped off the precarious plastic toilet seat, and after holding his weight for roughly half a second it was wrenched from the wall with an alarming, splintering sound. The psycho fan grabbed hopelessly at Julian's legs in a forlorn attempt to steady him as he fell heavily and awkwardly into the narrow gap between the pedestal and the cubicle wall, followed by the cistern full of water which bounced off his head, leaving him bleeding and unconscious.

17

'Why did you tell Uncle Tom a lie?' asked Sean, moments after Julian's accident, as Wendy illegally parked the Range Rover in a residents' parking bay right outside Paul's office in Soho.

'I didn't tell him a lie, sweetheart. Moira does live in that street you know.'

'Yes, but you didn't leave your handbag there.'

'No, you didn't leave your handbag there.'

'Well, it's hard to explain.'

'Is it a grown-up thing?'

'Yes, it's a grown-up thing.'

'Don't you like Uncle Tom any more?'

'Of course I like him. Now come on – out of the car.'

'Why aren't we going home?'

'Yeah, why are we going here?'

'We're just going to pop in and see Uncle Paul.'

'Uncle Paul?' asked Jamie.

'You know,' said Sean, 'the man who works in Daddy's office.'

'That's right,' said Wendy.

'But it's Thursday! We'll miss *Animals of Farthing Wood*!'

'Has he got a telly?'

'Yes, I'm sure he's got a telly,' she said, and hoiked them out of the car onto the pavement.

Once the boys were ensconced with Leon in front of the television in the back room Wendy followed Paul up to his office where he flustered about like an unsettled brood hen, unsure of how many cheeks to kiss and whether to offer tea or not. He was obviously embarrassed to see her.

She understood that Paul had suffered some great humiliations over the years and that Julian had often treated him with a thinly disguised contempt that was almost actionable – but she was there as a *friend*, on her own behalf as much as Julian's. *She* was the one who'd remembered Paul's birthday every year, sent him postcards from Kenya and wrapped up little hampers of goodies from the Conran Shop every Christmas. *He was godfather to the boys for Christ's sake!* Of course Paul had never done anything much about it save for throwing a few pounds into a Post Office account, and they hadn't expected him to – everyone was aware that it was a kind of honorary title – *but all the same!*

They swapped some desultory small talk about the twins and the weather until Elaine came in with the tea and then Paul uncomfortably took his seat behind the desk and Wendy sat opposite in the big leather armchair. Being shorter than his average client Wendy sank so low in the low-slung chair that Paul found his eye drawn to the great scuff in the leather desktop which was now directly in their line of vision. The scuff had accidentally been dyed a darker shade of green than its surroundings in Leon's over-zealous attempt to fix it.

'Look,' said Wendy, 'I don't know exactly what's happened between you and Julian . . .'

'Nor does he, I'll warrant,' interrupted Paul.

'No.'

'But he can probably guess.'

'Yes.' Wendy felt suddenly nervous in the face of Paul's huffy tone. 'Well, the fact of the matter is that he's in some awful contractual trouble, and I think you may be the only one who can get him out of it.'

'But I no longer represent him.'

'It would just be this once, just to set him straight,' said Wendy, watching Paul as he started to shake his head slowly from side to side like a disappointed schoolteacher. 'I know he probably doesn't deserve it but you go back such a long way, and it's all been so sudden.'

'No,' said Paul, still shaking his head. 'I'm afraid I couldn't.'

Paul's determined response took Wendy by surprise. She'd expected the conversation to be difficult and embarrassing and for Paul to wriggle and try to slip away from her arguments like the slippery customer she knew him to be, but he seemed so aggressively resolute and self-assured.

'He's beyond my help,' continued Paul. He slowly catalogued the grievances he'd been cheated out of listing to Julian's face on the day of the unpleasantness on the stairs. 'He's too hurtful, spiteful, treacherous and dishonest, too wild and unpredictable – to be honest I'm surprised you've lasted so long with him. You stay for the kids' sakes, I suppose.'

The scale of the attack took Wendy's breath away. She felt beleaguered on all sides – by Mitch's threats, by Tom and Carly's infatuation for one another, and now by Paul.

'If not for him, then for me and the twins,' said Wendy, steadfastly sticking to the purpose of her visit in an effort to block out the unimaginable import of Paul's unexpected assault. 'Mitch was talking about suing for hundreds of thousands of pounds.' She could feel tears forming behind her eyes and couldn't quite work out whether they were part of some cheap quasi-feminine ploy or whether they signified her true emotional state. She felt confused and looked up at Paul with the shiny pleading eyes of a hungry cocker spaniel.

'To be quite honest with you,' said Paul, feeling his top lip twitch with a nervous tick that anticipated the news about him wetting himself on the stairs spreading to every corner of the entertainment business, 'I don't really care.'

18

When Julian opened his eyes again he wondered whether he had died. He was blinded by brilliant whiteness and imagined he must be in some other dimension. There were no shapes to be seen, only a sense of crispness and the smell of pine. Yet as his seeing eye became accustomed to the brightness he did begin to distinguish different planes, angles and objects. He became aware that he was lying on his back looking up at an ornate, white-painted ceiling rose from which hung a single bright bulb within a conical white muslin shade. His gaze travelled to the edge of the ceiling and followed the barely discernible cornicing round two sides of the room before he began to feel nauseous and had to close his eyes. He tried to sit up but only got onto his elbows before the feeling that he was going to throw up stopped him in his tracks. He kept his head vertical and breathed in and out carefully as he waited for the unpleasant feeling to go.

Gingerly opening his one seeing eye, he fixed his gaze onto what looked like the mantelpiece of a white-painted fireplace that emerged out of the blankness in front of him and stared at it until some sense of equilibrium was achieved.

'I'll just sit like this for a couple of . . . hours, and it'll just . . . go,' he murmured softly to himself.

But as the nausea gradually subsided it was replaced by a tight, throbbing pain in his forehead. He suddenly remembered the lamppost, and leaning all his weight carefully on one elbow he felt for the damage and was shocked to find two lumps on his forehead. Confused and panicked he sat bolt upright and was startled to see himself in a white-framed mirror above the

143

mantelpiece. Peering into it he could see two symmetrically placed, red-tinged bumps high up on his forehead.

Horns!

The previously idle notion that he had passed on suddenly took on a more concrete form and he felt a rushing urge to cry. A lifetime of experience and a minor public-school education battled bewilderingly around in his mind as he searched for some reference to explain his predicament.

A devil?

He grabbed at his 'horns' and recoiled sharply from the self-inflicted agony as he touched them. They were real all right! And obviously very new! If he wasn't a devil he was at least some sort of faun! A hugely saddening sense that a dreadful and irreversible miscarriage of justice had been perpetrated had him suddenly lifting his head heavenward and reciting what he could remember of the Lord's Prayer, but as he became hopelessly confused about whose trespasses should be forgiven and who should have the bread his entreaties were mercifully cut short by the unexpected introduction of music into the room.

Julian cocked his head the better to listen and couldn't believe his ears – it was either Pink Floyd or The Strawbs – some kind of hippie nonsense anyway, he thought. He looked around the room. Something was very seriously wrong! A growing wave of anger that he might have been duped began to rise within him. He scanned the room for evidence but couldn't find anything in the all-encompassing white-out. Everything was white: the ceiling was white; the walls were white; the bare floorboards were white; the drawn curtains, the sofa and the wooden chair were white. Looking in the mirror he could see that even the sheet that was covering him was white, and he looked down to see for the first time that he was lying on a rather high white bed.

Cloven hooves!

If he *was* a kind of devil or faun he'd have cloven hooves, he thought to himself, perhaps even a tail. After a moment's trepidation he recognised a Roger Waters vocal and instantly threw back the sheet – he was slightly taken aback to find himself completely naked but very pleasantly reassured by the complete lack of hooves. He inhaled deeply, felt his body shudder with relief and thought he could hear traffic noises in the distance and children's voices playing outside.

He began to notice things he hadn't seen before. In the alcove to the right of the fireplace was a strangely shaped table spread with a white muslin cloth which hung down to the floor. On it was a semicircular array of variously sized and shaped candles – all white – and in the middle of the semicircle of candles, giving the room its only hint of colour, a collection of about fifteen or so roughly hewn crystals, each about an inch and a half to two inches long and mostly clear, but a few having definite tinges of blue, green or orange. The single white light above his head was reflected by some of the crystals, and as he moved his head from side to side they glittered and winked at him.

The obvious serenity and peacefulness of the room calmed him, and though he knew he was definitely in an extraordinary situation he began to enjoy a sense of adventure.

Just at that moment he heard the knob of the door being turned and he instinctively pulled the sheet up to his chin and his heart began to race. The door opened slowly and in walked a strange vision, not alarming, thought Julian, but definitely something on the edge of sanity.

'You're awake,' said the vision.

The voice told Julian it was a woman, and he couldn't get out of his head the idea that she was naked, even though she was quite obviously dressed in some broadly striped pyjamas. She turned to shut the door behind her and Julian could see every curve of her body, her breasts, the cleft in her buttocks, and as she turned back to face him he looked between her legs and could make out a bush of pubic hair – and then it dawned on him that she was painted, and painted with a very rough, muddy kind of paint. The horizontal stripes alternated between a dusty burnt sienna, and a rich, organic cream, and as she drew closer he could see that it was thickly spread and that the driest parts were beginning to crack.

'Are you feeling better now?' the vision asked, stopping at the side of the bed. The bed was much higher than an ordinary bed and Julian found himself staring straight into her mud-encrusted nipples. He felt his cock automatically twitch and start to stiffen, then with a dawning sense of dread he remembered hearing her voice before, and alarm bells rang in his head – it was the psycho fan! He looked up into her face with its crooked smile and chastised himself for not noticing her braided, hennaed hair when she'd first come into the room.

'I'll just carry on, shall I?' she asked rhetorically, and pulling back the sheet from his rabbit-like grip to reveal his naked body beneath, she leaned forward and took his cock in her mouth. Although alarmed at first by the inherent danger of leaving his most precious possession between the teeth of an obvious psychopath, Julian soon felt a wave of rapturous elation creep up his spine and into his head, and after half a second's serious consideration decided to lie back and let the element of risk merely add to the enjoyment.

A luxurious dizziness overtook him as he lay back with his hands behind his head and concentrated on the sensations of almost metaphysical pleasure that seemed to spread quickly over, above and around his body like the prelude to some minor earthquake. He lifted his head slightly to look down at what she was doing but felt a seasickness nag at the back of his head and quickly lay back down again, keen to regain the sense of growing euphoria. He couldn't distinguish her fingers, lips and tongue from each other but just felt an increasingly non-specific sense of extraordinary, sexual manipulation. Whatever she was doing was taking him higher than any previous blow-job he could remember, and although his cock was the epicentre of these sensations a numbness seemed to creep over it until it no longer felt like the primary source of pleasure but more like a conduit through which the rest of his body

146

was being transported to another, more sensuous, plane. He felt like he was shooting up into a clear, blue heaven, and though the sensation was disorientating he was glad to let it take him where it would, and felt himself disappear beyond the realms of this world into an abstract where his senses had no meaning and his brain seemed to pop.

Floating gently back down to earth again some moments later he discovered that the psycho fan was climbing on top of him. She placed a knee either side of his head and lowered herself towards him until her rusty, mud-filled pubic hair brushed across his lips. Julian looked up at the rings of brown and cream paint and couldn't help finding the situation amusing.

'But I don't even know your name,' he said, unable to prevent a shameful smirk spreading from ear to ear.

'It's Lilith. You know that,' she said dispassionately, and lowered herself onto his face.

Of course he knew that, he thought to himself, remembering that she was the psycho fan. He'd written 'To Lilith' on hundreds and thousands of programmes, photos, magazines, books and scraps of paper over the last eight years. Lilith – the psycho with the crooked smile and the whining voice; the fan with the overbearing concern for the minutiae of his life; the one who sucked time from him like a leech.

The sudden crush of these boredom-laden memories, the interminable Pink Floyd instrumental break coursing through the room and the chalky taste of the mud in his mouth rendered him suddenly earthbound and all sense of sexual excitement disappeared abruptly like a bubble bursting. He wrestled his head out from under her groin.

'Look, I'm sorry, do you mind if we stop for a minute,' he said, licking bits of grit off his teeth and spitting.

'But we've only just started,' she whined, and as if to register her intention to carry on regardless she jogged forward on her knees, causing her breasts to swing and release a shower of mud particles into Julian's eyes.

147

'Fucking hell!' he shouted, and began such an upheaval in an attempt to get his hands to his eyes that Lilith reluctantly gave up the fight and climbed off onto the floor. Julian sat up quickly on the bed, clawing out wildly for the sheet with which to wipe his eyes, but the sudden movement made his stomach begin to spin like the contents of a washing machine and he felt an irresistible urge to vomit. Blinded by what felt like a shovelful of sawdust under his eyelids he spewed helplessly about himself, feeling it splash against his bare skin until he managed to deduce where the edge of the bed was and directed the flow onto the floor where it landed heavily and echoed round the bare room.

19

Back at home, while Tom was on the telephone down in the kitchen, Wendy sat in the twins' bedroom feeling red-faced and furious about Paul's stubborn refusal to take Julian back on. She had bathed the boys and washed their hair, and now seemed to be taking her frustration out on the knots in Sean's hair as she combed it through.

'Ow!' he complained.

'Sorry, darling.'

'Why are you doing it so hard?'

'I'm sorry.'

'Adam at school says our hair's too long anyway.'

'Yeah, Adam says we look like girls,' chimed in Jamie.

'That's why we had to fight him.'

'Yeah, that's why we had to push him into the holly bush.'

'Well, if you don't like it you can always get it cut!' shouted Wendy suddenly, cowing them both into a timorous silence. She felt immediately ashamed as she saw their little faces drop and their lower lips jut out, but she couldn't bring herself to deal with it right then and there as her mind was crowded with other worries.

She hadn't heard a thing from Julian since Mitch's phone call, though there was nothing unusual about that – it was only six o'clock in the evening. She knew that he would have spent the afternoon drinking and that he probably wouldn't turn up until the early hours of the next morning, wide-eyed and legless. She looked round at the twins' bedroom, at the Colefax and Fowler wallpaper, the hand-painted wardrobes and the Eritrean dowry box that served as one of their toy

149

chests and wondered if this time Julian had put it all into serious jeopardy. Perhaps Paul was right, perhaps Julian was too wild and unpredictable? She pulled herself up short. *That's how he'd been when they'd met, that's what had made him so attractive.* It was *she* who had changed, or conformed. Why should she try and impose her new-found, early-middle-aged drudgery on him? She'd seen it in other couples – the restraining, the taming, the curbing and the eventual submission.

So many women wanted to tame a bastard, she thought to herself, dragging the comb through Sean's hair, *and Julian wasn't a bastard!* A lot of those neutered men were though. She was aware of the 'other' voice those men had which she'd occasionally interrupted at first nights and parties, the traitorous, furtive, masturbatory, schoolboy voice. Julian was never afraid to say out loud how attractive other women were and she found this a positive sign of his fidelity. Why would he tell her so much if he was *doing* it – he'd sneak and skulk like the rest of them. Of course he stayed out late and drank and flirted, but he was a show-business luminary, it was part of his world and she'd have gone out with him if she didn't feel so square.

'Lost' days – periods of more than twenty-four hours in which he made no contact at all – were the only thing she allowed herself to get particularly annoyed about. Not because she felt he was out on a rampage of cheating and betrayal, but for the waste of care and anxiety they dragged out of her, watching the clock and worrying whether and when to ring round the hospitals and the police. A phone call or even a message from a third party was enough – she didn't need an excuse, he just had to say he was playing out. Not every woman's idea of a perfect marriage, she thought to herself, but then if she'd wanted a lap dog she could have married Tom, for Christ's sake!

Nevertheless she'd felt half-glad that Tom had been there on the doorstep again when she'd finally returned home with the boys after the humiliation of Paul's rejection, as she'd been able to ask him to ring *his* agent for advice on Julian's predicament. There was something worrying about Tom's assertion that he had 'something important' to say to her afterwards, though, and she hoped she wasn't going to have to fend off another advance. *Why couldn't he just be the great Tom of old he'd always been?* Why did he have to become this new, threatening Tom – the Tom with the faintly ludicrous recent interest in Tantra, the Indian Cult of Ecstasy, and his preposterous assertions about 'enlightenment through orgasm'. She wasn't a prude, but it was all so unseemly and unnecessary for a man of his background and intellect. She tried to imagine Tom and Carly making love to the point of enlightenment as though following the instructions in a car-repair manual but her train of thought was broken by the sound of whimpering, and she broke off raking the comb through Sean's hair and turned him round so that she could see his face. He was crying quietly.

'What's the matter, darling?'

'You're hurting me.'

'Oh, baby!' she cried, pulling him close and hugging him tight. 'I'm sorry, darling. I'm sorry.' She noticed Jamie across the room looking close to tears as well and opened an arm to him, too. He rushed to her and they all clung to each other. 'Mummy's sorry, boys. I didn't mean to shout at you or make you sad, I've just got a lot on my mind at the moment. I tell you what, after school tomorrow why don't we go to McDonald's?'

'Yeah!'

'Yippee!'

As the thing she denied them most, McDonald's was a treat indeed, and a measure of how guilty she felt. 'All right, now get your pyjamas on and you can play for a bit.'

'Can Uncle Tom come and read us a story?'

'Yes, can he?'

'No, he's busy on the telephone downstairs.'

'Why are we going to bed so early?'

'It's only six o'clock.'

151

'Because Uncle Tom and I have got to have a big talk. But you don't have to go to sleep right away. I said you could play, didn't I? Or you could *read*.'

'Nah!' shouted the boys.

'Well anyway, you can keep the light on till eight o'clock, OK?'

'OK!' they shouted together.

20

When Julian awoke some time later he found himself alone once again but this time he wasn't quite as surprised by his surroundings. He knew he was in the psycho fan's house, even though she wasn't with him now. He remembered her clearing up the white room; bathing his eyes and restoring his sight; calming his stomach with camomile tea; soaking him in a bath while she showered herself; then washing, drying and powdering him, dressing him in a cool white cotton robe, and coaxing him into a gentle sexual marathon right there in her front room – after which he must have fallen exhaustedly asleep on this pile of richly embroidered, ethnic-looking cushions.

It had played like one of his favourite fantasies: the stricken airman rescued from his burning plane and dragged on a sled across the frozen wastes to safety by a beautiful maiden, half-angel, half-siren, to a snow-whipped cabin warmed by the glow of a meagre fire and his rescuer's intuitive knowledge that the only thing that could keep his broken body alive was the heat of slow and constant sexual union in which she would have to take the dominant role.

Should he still think of her as the psycho fan? he asked himself. After all, she'd become part of the reality and the fantasy of his sex life. Maybe he should think of her as Lilith from now on? But the idea of acceptance suddenly alarmed him. Pretending she was as normal as the next person by giving her a name wasn't going to make her any less of a freak.

Staring at him from the mantelpiece was glaring and rather menacing evidence of her freakishness – a large statue of a gruesomely fearsome woman with her tongue sticking out, naked save for a chain of human heads worn around her neck, and a belt of human hands round her waist. She had four arms, one of which was holding a severed head by the hair, another a bloodied sword. Beneath her squatting form lay the inert body of a naked man whom Julian presumed to be dead. Her red-pupilled eyes were popping out of her head and seemed to be fixing Julian with an accusatory and threatening stare and Julian was amazed that he hadn't noticed the statue earlier, although on reflection he remembered that he'd had little chance to view anything except the psycho fan's heaving breasts and groin during their long, grinding encounter.

Glancing behind himself for something more comforting, Julian was shocked to find a primitive Indian painting that depicted another naked woman sitting on the erect penis of a supine man whilst holding her own severed head in one hand and the sword with which she had just decapitated herself in the other, and he decided to beat a hasty retreat.

He rose to his feet, crossed to the door and gingerly poked his head half-way into the hallway.

'Psyc–'

He stopped himself just in time.

'Lilith,' he murmured gently, and strained his ears for a reply. All he could hear was a faint mumbling sound which didn't seem to be directed at him. He tiptoed out into the hall and moved towards the sound. It seemed to be coming from the next room. Cocking his head to the door he heard Lilith's voice chanting in her whining, almost mid-Atlantic drawl.

'Om mani padme hum, om mani padme hum, om mani padme hum . . .'

Julian decided to leave her chanting, track down his clothes, and scarper. He crept stealthily into the room at the end of the hallway expecting it to be the bathroom, but it was a kitchen. He peered back out into the hall and saw an internal front door staring at him – he was obviously in a flat. The front door was set underneath a flight of stairs which Julian hadn't noticed before and he tiptoed back down the hallway and stole up the stairs.

He pushed his way through the first door and the scene that confronted him literally took his breath away – the room was a shrine to *him*.

Everywhere he looked he could see images of himself staring back. It was a wall-to-wall collage of cut-out photos and interview texts from the likes of the *Radio Times*, *G.Q.* and *Chat* intermingled with weird-looking symbols and indecipherable eastern-looking words painted in garish, fluorescent colours. There were blown-up photos of Lilith and himself outside the stage doors of the London Palladium, Middlesbrough City Hall and the Aberdeen Capitol. All the scripts, props and mementoes he'd ever given her were pinned to the walls or mounted on little shelves. There was a whole tray of BBC ball-point pens, a Christmas card to him from Alan Yentob, and his hump from the first series of *Richard the Nerd*, which he couldn't remember giving her. In one corner there was a television and video player with the tapes of all his programmes stacked on top next to some home-recorded tapes that were variously titled *Wogan*, *The Big Breakfast*, and even *Pebble Mill*, and were obviously recordings of his appearances on chat shows and the like. But the most startling object stood in the middle of the furthest wall – a shop mannequin crudely dressed and painted in a way Julian could see was meant to look like him, around which a small, primitive altar had been built. On it stood at least a hundred candles, all lit.

Julian fought for breath at the sight of it all. He fought against all the images that rushed into his mind from horror films of sudden stabbings, pointless murders, lunatics and the Bates Motel. Turning to leave he caught sight of one of the few family portraits he'd allowed the press to take on the back of the door, and he noticed that Lilith had very carefully cut out Wendy's face and had replaced it equally carefully with her own.

He staggered out into the hallway and fumbled his way to

the next door, letting out a sigh of relief when he discovered he had found the bathroom and his clothes neatly folded on the linen basket just inside the doorway.

He dressed quickly, silently cursing himself for his weakness in giving in to sex with an obvious lunatic in the first place and fearful of what might befall him if he didn't get out immediately. Then, becoming aware that he was making too much noise in his effort to get dressed so hurriedly, he stopped and strained to hear Lilith's chanting – it wasn't there any more. He worked out that the bathroom must be directly above the white room where she'd been mumbling away and put an ear to the ground to see if she was still in there – but he could hear nothing. A rising terror gripped him and his breathing became short and difficult.

There was no time for breathing exercises to calm the growing cramp under his ribs and holding his boots in one hand he crept as stealthily as he could over to the window, each footstep and creaking floorboard amplified tenfold in his own mind. It was a large sash window with frosted glass and the whole frame was painted over and obviously hadn't been opened for years. Julian made a couple of desperate straining attempts to push the bottom half up before acknowledging that it was well and truly jammed.

He thought momentarily of taking a running jump and smashing his way through to freedom but reminded himself that, firstly, he was in a flat and didn't know how many floors up he was, and secondly, that even *one* floor would be enough to kill him – presuming he survived the lacerations received from smashing his way through the glass in the first place.

Why couldn't life be more like television?! Where was the sugar glass? Where were the mattresses? Where was the camera to record it all and make him seem an even bigger sex god than he already was?

Giving up the window as a bad job he crept back to the bathroom door and pressed an ear up against it. *If she wasn't in the white room chanting, where was she? Maybe she was right*

156

there outside the door, maybe her head was only half an inch away from his!

He tried to stop breathing completely so that he could hear more effectively, but it only seemed to increase the volume of his thumping heart. He looked down at the keyhole for the key, thinking he could lock himself in, smash a hole in the window and shout for help, but there was no key – not even a small bolt for modesty's sake. *Damn these fucking hippies! Where was it all going to end? Open-air cubicles?*

It struck him that his chances were getting shorter the longer he stayed in her domain and, struggling to bottle up his increasing sense of dread, he gingerly squeezed the knob of the door, turned it, opened the door a crack and peered out, half-expecting Lilith to be there Jack Nicholson-like with an axe or a carving knife, but the coast was clear. With long, careful strides he reached the top of the stairs and looked down, willing his ears to pick up anything untoward as if they had extrasensory perception – still nothing. He almost floated down the stairs and his heart started banging against his chest as he passed the door to the white room – still nothing. He lengthened his stride and made the front door in one step, his hand starting to shake in anticipation of the freedom beyond, as he fumbled with the latch and opened it – only to reveal Lilith standing on the top step, holding a bottle of milk in one hand and her key in the other.

Julian jumped back in terror and slammed into the wall, an incredulous, terrified cough seizing his throat.

'You're not going?' she asked, closing the front door behind her. 'I've just put the kettle on for some tea.'

Julian tried to say 'Yes' but could only manage a strangled hawking sound.

'I've just been down to get the milk,' she continued.

The milk!

'What time is it?' shouted Julian, suddenly finding his voice at the horrifying thought of having 'lost' another day, and the truckload of guilt that would bring.

'It's about eight o'clock,' said Lilith.

'Is that morning or night?'

'Night.'

'Night?'

'Yes,' she said, making her way into the kitchen.

'What are you doing bringing the milk in at eight o'clock at night!' he shouted, following her and feeling frantic and perplexed. 'How long have I been here? Is it still the same day?'

'What day?'

'I don't know – the *same* day!'

'What – Thursday?'

'Is it the same day as the day I came here?!'

'Yes it is,' she said, calmly taking the kettle off the stove and opening the utensil drawer. 'And there's no need to shout.'

She sounded absurdly normal but as Julian watched her rummage about in the drawer among knives, skewers and apple corers, his fear of imminent death rose again, only to subside once more as she retrieved nothing more harmful than an infuser from the back of the drawer and began to fill it with tea.

Standing there in her black ski-pants and white cheesecloth smock she didn't look particularly intimidating. He could handle her, she wasn't that big, couldn't be that powerful. She was still a complete fruitcake of course and not to be trusted one inch, he thought, and though he now no longer felt nervous of impending physical attack he still felt pretty keen to leave immediately.

'Look, I think I'd better ring for a cab.'

'Oh, I don't think you'll need one of those.'

'No, I've got to go, really. I've got lots of things to do.' Then, after a pause, he threw in a titbit for his most avid admirer, the walking curriculum vitae of his career to date. 'I represent myself now – did you know that?'

'I still don't think you'll need a cab.'

She was pouring hot water into a strange vessel that looked

to be half-way between a teapot and a samovar, and her back was turned. Julian couldn't remember having seen her back before; all he'd ever had was her face thrusting towards him, pen in hand, camera at the ready.

'Right, well, I'll just walk then,' he said. 'I'll see you soon I suppose, and thanks for the . . .' A catalogue of words ran through his mind that included 'shag', 'servicing', and the rather more demure 'afternoon', but none of them seemed to fit, and as she seemed determined to keep her attention fixed on the samovar/teapot affair he left the sentence unfinished and made his way out into the hall to the front door of the flat.

'I've got it all on video tape if you ever want to have a look at it,' she said casually from the kitchen, as Julian's hand reached for the door handle.

He turned, but she made no appearance at the kitchen door, and feeling tired and so close to escape, Julian decided not to take what he presumed was bait of some sort, and slipped out quietly.

Closing the door to the flat noiselessly behind him he eagerly trotted down two flights of steps to the main door, each tread seeming to ease the burden of fear and loathing on his back so that by the time he reached the front door he felt a good two inches taller.

Breathing a grateful sigh of relief as he negotiated the front door he skipped down four steps and out onto the pavement. He hurriedly looked both ways for cabs but to no avail. It was a very quiet street of big red-brick houses with parked cars lining both kerbs. He turned to scurry towards the livelier looking end of the street when a parked Range Rover caught his eye. It looked very familiar. He peered at the licence plate but that didn't give him much of a clue because he had no idea what his own number was. *But it definitely looked like his car*. He walked up and pressed his face against the back window. *Yes!* – there were Sean and Jamie's Thunderbird's steering wheels suckered to the back of the front seats.

This seemed very odd to Julian, and he wondered in a sudden fit of paranoia whether Wendy had taken to spying on him. Had she seen him enter the psycho fan's flat? Was she waiting in the shadows summoning up the courage to leap out on him and confront him red-handed?

He spun round quickly but couldn't see anything, no twitching curtain, no shadow pulling back into a doorway.

Then it struck him like a body blow – the tall red-brick houses, the Range Rover, Shakespeare's skewered bust staring at him from the bay window in front of him – *he was in his own street! He was standing outside his own house in his own fucking street! And it was right next door to Lilith's!*

A feeling of having dug his own grave overwhelmed him – he could practically smell the soil – and he struggled to fight a way out of the collage of satanic rituals and many-limbed women with castrating knives that filled his brain. Instinctively he ducked for cover behind the Range Rover and looked warily up to the windows of the psycho fan's flat, half-expecting to see her tipping the contents of the knife drawer out onto his head. He was surprised to see the crude terracotta statue he'd met a few weeks back standing in pride of place in Lilith's front window, squinting down at him with its foreskin eyes that seemed to be quietly mocking him.

How the fuck was he going to get out of this one? What had she said about video tape? They were bound to meet – Lilith and Wendy. And she was a psycho *– she was bound to blab. Or take it out on the boys! Maybe it was blackmail!*

Caught in the headlights of a van coming down the street, Julian scuttled round to the back of his car and squatted there for a moment, resting back on his elbows against the conveniently shaped bumper of a Jaguar XJS.

He looked at the number plate on the Range Rover, D666 FRT, and kicked himself for not recognising it before, especially as he'd been the one to invent the mnemonic to remember it by: 'De devil's fart'. The memory of Wendy's disgusted chuckle at his invention brought a slight warmth

160

back into his heart, and gazing at the dirty back end of the car he felt a strange, growing sense of relief at having *got home*, whatever else. It was, after all, the only base he had, the only real bolthole available to him, discounting the Yemen Republic.

He looked up at his house and saw that the lights were still on in Sean and Jamie's bedroom and felt pleased that he'd be able to go up and see them. He couldn't remember the last time he'd been with them properly, and right now he felt a surge of genuine love for them that he was eager to share.

As he looked affectionately at his house a figure walked past a chink in the curtains of the kitchen window in the basement. He couldn't see a head but he knew it was Wendy by the shapeless brown cardigan that stretched almost to her knees. Craning his neck to get a better look, he saw Tom sitting at the far end of the kitchen table and his heart sank.

The rosy vision of reconciliation that had been forming in his head vanished like a startled cat. He'd been all ready to make his entrance like the returning prodigal son, he thought to himself, ready to run upstairs and tumble with the boys, ready to take Wendy in his arms and promise to retrieve his briefcase the following day, ready to play the all-round family man, the good husband returned from the wars, and there was Tom, fucking it all up, the slimy fifth columnist in his kitchen.

Crouched in the gutter, Julian stared wretchedly into the warm light of the kitchen through the gap in the curtains. Their conversation seemed spirited – obviously it was no idle chat – and Julian cautiously crabbed closer, eager to eavesdrop on their earnest discussion. He gently opened the small, squeaky iron gate to the basement yard and swung round onto the top step.

21

In the kitchen Tom was finding it more difficult than he'd expected to turn the conversation round to the point where he could casually drop his bombshell about Julian and Catriona, complete with forensic evidence in the shape of the Shri Yantra he had carefully wrapped up in his yoga blanket, and a personal sense of grievance that he'd been practising all afternoon. But since Wendy had come downstairs they'd spent all their time discussing Julian's contractual situation.

Tom had played along with a furrowed brow but secretly his heart had been racing at the steadily rising prospect that Julian might be branded a financial liability *and* a foul philanderer all in one evening. This would surely further his cause, he'd thought to himself.

Now, as he watched Wendy lean forward across the sink to fill the kettle, his gaze dropped to the contours of her delicate buttocks pushing against the soft wool of her cardigan. He thought of classical paintings he'd seen of Greek nymphs in swathes of clingingly revealing white muslin, drawing water from streams on the foothills of Mount Olympus. *If only he'd declared his red-blooded, physical desire for her all those years ago, before Julian had pitched up in Bristol!*

It had all seemed too poetic and eighteenth century back then as a student – the delicious, dark pleasure of unrequited love that would eventually spin into an all-consuming fireball of desire, a love affair straight from classic literature. He'd played the big platonic card for more than two years, getting nothing more than the occasional hug and a kiss. They'd even shared a bed on their jaunt round Portugal but he'd kept to the master plan and resisted – *this was the stuff great biographies were made of* – apart from that one night in Porto Corveiro when they'd both been so drunk, but in the morning he hadn't been able to work out whether they'd actually done it or not, and had eventually marked it down as a near-miss.

This was the best chance he'd had to turn the tables since then. A potentially destitute Julian could leave him playing the big provider against Julian's perfidious pauper, and fortunately Carly was in place as the perfect cover – *and a damn good lay* – in case his suit backfired.

'. . . and then, just as I was leaving, he asked how I coped with Julian sleeping around all the time,' said Wendy, turning from the sink and putting the kettle on the hob.

'What?' asked Tom, surprised into the real world.

'Paul. So I asked did he *know* that he slept around . . .'

'Who?'

'Julian.'

'And what did he say?'

'Well, he was frankly quite crude. He said he'd never actually seen it going in but that it was *pretty obvious* – I mean, honestly, *pretty obvious* – things have come to a pretty pass when people you thought were your friends suddenly turn out to have minds like tabloid journalists . . .'

'Yes, but . . .'

'Do *you* think Julian sleeps around?'

'No.'

'There you are, you see.'

Tom couldn't believe what he'd just said – after all the waiting, he'd just been offered his moment on a plate – but everything seemed to have happened so quickly – the conversation turning to the subject of Julian's fidelity; the sudden direct question. And there had been such a singsong rhetorical tone to her question, she'd obviously either wanted or expected him to say 'no'. And by the time it occurred to him that perhaps the moment was still alive and open for further discussion, the pregnant pause that hung in the air between them was suddenly interrupted by a loud clattering noise of milk bottles and dustbins out in the basement yard. He and Wendy rushed over to the window, flung back the curtains and peered out into the dark, shielding their eyes from the reflections inside, to see Julian lying among the bins at the foot of the steps. Julian waved weakly and smiled one of his pathetically ingratiating comedy smiles.

Tom clenched his teeth in anger and hatred, then suddenly the outside light was on and Wendy was out in the yard helping Julian to his feet. Tom hadn't even felt her leave the room. He wondered what Wendy could possibly see in Julian in comparison to someone as fine and noble as himself, yet there she was, dusting him off with tender, loving care. And his stomach churned as he watched Julian suck her in, playing the helpless boy and pointing to two big bumps on his forehead. *Served the fucker right!* But Wendy was comforting and caressing him like some over-familiar Florence Nightingale.

Julian suddenly broke away as he spotted something on the stairs and stumbled up to fetch it – it was a banana skin – and he brought it down to show Wendy, triumphantly, like a returning Caesar, and erupted into a fit of raucous laughter.

Wendy was not obviously amused at first, but after Julian had performed a little mime to show how he must have slipped on the banana skin her face creased into an easy grin. It was a welcome moment of light relief which seemed briefly to dispel the gloomy anxieties of her day. And as Julian repeated his mime with the greatly exaggerated movements of a Buster Keaton she caught his good humour like a disease.

Tom tapped censoriously on the window and they both stopped to look at him. He gave them a disapproving stare and they suddenly exploded into an obscene, helpless mirth that had them slapping their legs, bouncing off the bins and hanging onto each other to prevent themselves from falling. Tom winced at their physical proximity, snapped the curtains to and resumed his seat.

'What were you laughing about?' he asked, when they'd

164

finally managed to control themselves and made their way back into the kitchen, trying to camouflage his resentment by casually flicking through the arts pages of the *Independent*.

'We weren't laughing about anything,' snarled Julian, with a ferocity that shocked Tom and made him catch his breath. 'We were laughing *at* something.'

'Then what were you laughing *at*?' replied Tom, standing up to it.

'We were laughing at *you*,' spat Julian.

Tom felt his eye twitch and knew that Julian had seen it.

'No we weren't,' said Wendy. 'Well, only because you weren't in on the joke. We were laughing at the banana skin – Julian slipped on a *banana* skin!'

'Oh yes, that's right, we were laughing at a banana skin,' said Julian, fixing Tom with a shark-like meanness in his eyes.

'I mean it's a classic, isn't it? You see it in films all the time but you never see anyone *actually* slip on one, do you?' said Wendy, forcing a laugh in an obvious attempt to diffuse the hostility between them.

'No,' answered Tom, unimpressed.

'You see the thing is,' Julian carried on, 'technically, and I do mean technically, I don't want you to take this personally in any way, Tom, but *technically*, this banana skin is much funnier than *you*!' And like a school bully he thrust the banana skin right under Tom's nose and jiggled it about to taunt him.

'I've got to go,' said Tom, rising and taking his jacket from the back of his chair.

'No, Tom, please stay. I want you to stay,' said Wendy, deftly plucking the banana skin from Julian's grasp and dropping it into the big aluminium flip-top bin. The lid closed with a satisfying sucking sound that seemed to act as a coda to the whole banana-skin subject.

'Julian, we need to talk,' she said, recovering her sombre tone. 'Mitch phoned this afternoon.'

'Shouldn't you be doing your show?' Julian snapped at Tom.

'It's the National, Julian, we're in rep with *Little Shop of*

Horrors,' Tom replied with a smirk. 'I only have to do three shows a week.'

'Well, thank God they don't pay you properly then.'

'What do you mean? I'm on six-fifty a week.'

'Exactly,' said Julian.

Wendy reached out and held Julian's arm. 'Julian, please!'

Julian thought of the exotic sexual marathon the psycho fan had just taken him through barely twenty or thirty feet away from where he now stood, and tried to remind himself that he really had no excuse for feeling so hostile towards Wendy.

It was Tom! How could he be expected to lie down and play dead with Tom hanging around as a spectator? If Tom hadn't been there he'd have been pleased to let her nag him for a little while – it would have been the least he could do to atone for his afternoon.

'Yes,' he said, 'sorry. Perhaps you ought to leave us to it, Tom.'

'Tom's here because he can help.'

'What the fuck's Tom got to do with it?'

'He's got an agent!'

'So? I don't need his fucking agent! I can get a lot more than six-fucking-fifty a week on my own, thank you very much!'

Wendy sighed. Out of the corner of her eye she could see Julian's head drop as well – he obviously knew he'd gone too far. She felt sorry for him, he looked so defenceless and so stupid with those twin bumps on his head. She knew people laughed at the number of times he fell over but it seemed she alone remembered that he only had one eye, and therefore that he could only see in two dimensions, which made stairs especially tricky, even when he was sober, and he seemed sober now.

She watched him turn, heavy-limbed, and trawl his pockets for loose change, depositing his catch in the enormous glass jar they kept on the end of the kitchen counter. His sobriety struck her as a mark of how seriously he must be taking the situation and her heart swelled with pride. Normally he'd have been completely smashed by now, she thought to herself, but he'd obviously spent the afternoon in tortured reflection on his extraordinary predicament. She fancied she'd even detected the smell of soap on him. And more than that – she'd just had his constancy confirmed by *Tom*. *Tom*, the man who probably had more to gain from betraying Julian as a womaniser than anyone else in the world. In the back of her mind there had always been a tiny, nagging doubt, and she'd been rattled by Paul's casual insinuations. But Tom would have said, wouldn't he? Asked directly like that?

'So what did Mitch have to say?' asked Julian, keeping his back turned.

'In a nutshell, he said that if you walk out on the play he's going to sue you for the full capitalisation, which amounts to three hundred and fifty thousand pounds.'

'And what's that got to do with Tom?' Julian was still facing away.

'Tom's here because I asked him for some advice.'

Julian spun round on his heels, his face incandescent with rage, his arm knocking the jar of pennies perilously close to the edge of the counter. 'What? You're not doing a new sitcom as well, are you? Or are you going to steal my voice-over work instead?'

Wendy briefly questioned the efficacy of her plan but couldn't think of a clearer way of getting the full horror of the situation out into the open, and pressed on. 'I got Tom to read the contract over the phone to his agent. What did he say, Tom?'

'He said you couldn't get out of it,' said Tom.

'Well, that's a spectacularly muscular agent you've got there Tom – no wonder you're only on six-fifty a week,' said Julian.

'Julian!' shouted Wendy.

'Good-night,' said Tom through gritted teeth, standing to put on his jacket once again.

'Tom,' said Wendy, but there was no real passion in her voice, even though it was obvious he would have liked her to plead again for him to stay. She remembered the protestation of Tom's love Julian's timely arrival had forestalled and let him go. 'Well, thanks a lot anyway,' she said as Tom passed behind her. 'Good-night.'

'Good-night,' said Tom, staring hard at the back of Wendy's head, willing her to turn and face him. 'I think I'll pop in and see Carly, seeing as I'm in the neighbourhood.' He waited too long for a reaction which never came, then headed towards the door. 'I'll let myself out.' He loped out of the room and softly up the stairs, and after a brief silence they heard the front door slam behind him.

Wendy and Julian stood motionless for a while in the new-found stillness, each thinking quietly.

Wendy felt torn between her belief that if they didn't settle the business over the play now they would never settle it, leaving the family to founder on the rocks of destitution and uncertainty, and her desire to run to Julian and hug and squeeze him, partly for her own comfort, but mostly for the big, honest, faithful husband she deludedly believed him to be.

'Do you think you should see a doctor about those knocks – you might have cracked your skull,' she said at last.

'What? Oh no, that's nothing, I mean that's . . . er . . . they're from earlier actually.'

An image of the psycho fan unzipping his trousers and the cistern falling on his head flashed through Julian's mind, but the unexpected recollection didn't divert his thoughts from the problem of Mitch and his contract for long. He reflected that there wasn't much to think about, he obviously had to do the rotten, stinking, fucking play or they'd be completely wiped out. He found that he wasn't particularly upset by the reali-sation, more weary to his bones. As he pressed the heels of his hands hard into his eye sockets it struck him that three hundred and fifty thousand pounds was exactly the same amount of money their house was mortgaged for, and wondered briefly whether this was a good or bad omen, before a rising tide of anger swept over him at the stupidity of anybody lending him that much money. Couldn't they see he was a financial incompetent?

They broke the spell of immobility simultaneously – Wendy rummaged nervously through her handbag for a cigarette and Julian trudged over to the fridge, opened it and began to sift through the seemingly endless bags of celery and lettuce, tubs of cottage cheese, bowls of cling-filmed left-overs and cartons of homemade soups from Marks & Spencer.

'What are you looking for?' asked Wendy, lighting her cigarette and dragging hard.

'Found it.' Julian emerged triumphantly from the chilly recesses with a bottle of Grolsch he had a distant memory of hiding behind the phalanx of opened pickle jars that seemed to have lived in the fridge for a decade. He flipped open the china stopper and took a satisfyingly long draught. If he was going to go down he was going to go down fighting, and the only way of fighting he knew was to get completely arseholed. He opened the kitchen cupboard in which he sometimes kept a bottle of beloved Turkey, but the cupboard was bare, so he moved towards the stairs and the ground-floor sitting room, intent on chugging his way through the contents of the drinks cabinet.

'Well?' asked Wendy.

Julian stopped and took another swig of Grolsch. 'Well what?'

'What are we going to do?'

'What do you mean "What are *we* going to do"? *I'm* going to do the fucking play, aren't I?' A nightmare vision of touring Britain with Bronwyn and the rest of the B-list rose up before his eyes and he couldn't help the malevolence that welled up inside him from spilling over. 'I mean that's what you want, isn't it? You and your gang? You and Mitch and Tom. And Tom's fucking agent.'

Wendy's chest started to rise and fall more quickly.

'It's what you've all been working towards all day, isn't it? I

169

mean none of you gives a toss what I think, do you? None of you ever fucking do anything for me, do you?'

He paused, enjoying the adrenalin rush that he always felt when misbehaving.

'You never . . .'

'Does,' interrupted Wendy.

'No you fucking don't!'

'No – none of you ever fucking *does* – not *do*.'

Julian looked at her incredulously. He couldn't believe she was actually picking him up on his grammar, she was usually overcautious not to let any hint of intellectual vanity cloud their relationship. Before he could think of a response Wendy quickly stepped around him and headed up the stairs to the ground floor. Julian stood still and listened to her feet echoing loudly on the wooden floor of the hallway before heading up the next flight of stairs to the bedrooms beyond.

'Well, fuck you,' he whispered under his breath and launched himself up to the ground floor and into the sitting room and the drinks cabinet. There were two inches of bourbon in a bottle of Jim Beam which Julian polished off in one. He switched on the television, selected the channel with the least covered-up women on display and set about inventing a new cocktail with the sad remnants of the drinks cabinet – a bottle of sherry, a bottle of ginger wine, a bottle of Marsala and one of Martini.

Three hours later he was awoken by the loud and unpleasant hissing of the television after closedown. His neck felt uncomfortable and strained after falling asleep awkwardly against the arm of the sofa. He thought of spending the night there, but having got up to reach the remote control to turn the television off he decided he might as well go the whole hog and climb upstairs to bed.

As he reached the bottom of the stairs he found a note lying on the third step, with his name on it, in Wendy's handwriting.

He picked it up and had to blink hard and wipe his eye a few times before being able to read it. It read:

Dear Julian,

You are absolutely right, and there is no reason at all why you should have to do something that makes you so obviously unhappy. I feel deeply ashamed of my selfishness and for seeming to 'gang' up on you.

We can get through this, I know. The worst that can happen is that they bankrupt us (and let's face it – having nothing would give us a better credit balance than we have at present).

Things cannot go on as they are, it's not fair on any of us.

I do love you,

W. x

Julian sat down on the bottom step and read and reread it about ten times. He couldn't tell whether it seemed cryptic because he was close to unconsciousness or whether it was a heartfelt message of love and support, and hoping it to be the latter he read it again and again to find the proof until his eye misted over and he gradually fell asleep on the stairs.

22

The post thudded onto the mat at six thirty the following morning but failed to wake Julian, who had slid from the stairs onto the hall rug during the night, and had semi-consciously acquired Jamie's Dennis the Menace backpack to use as a pillow. The *Independent* which was slammed through the letter box ten minutes later similarly failed to stir him, even though it landed on his foot. It was only when Sean and Jamie crept as silently as they could down the stairs with their mother 'shushing' after them that he became aware of the world around him. He could hear the boys trying to suppress fits of giggles as the stairs creaked under their tread and he imagined Wendy following behind straining to keep them quiet with frenetic hand signals.

Julian felt too weary and ill-prepared to face Wendy after the note and the previous night's unpleasantness, and decided to remain 'asleep', happily aware that most of his face was hidden in the crook of his elbow as he lay face down on the floor.

'I'll just get the post,' he heard Wendy whisper. 'You two go on down to the kitchen.'

He felt her stride across his sprawling body, felt the hem of her ankle-length jersey skirt brush over his hip and heard her bend and pick up the mail.

'That's my Dennis the Menace bag!' said Jamie suddenly, in a loud whisper. 'He's lying on my Dennis the Menace bag!'

'It doesn't matter, come on, downstairs,' whispered Wendy.

'But it's got my pirate ship in it that I made!'

'We'll get it later, come on, off you go.'

172

'But it'll be all bashed up!'

'I'll fix it for you later.'

'But I want it now!' Jamie grabbed a shoulder strap and yanked the bag out from under Julian's surprised head, which landed with a crack on one of the painful bumps protruding from his forehead. It was only through exercising the greatest self-control that Julian managed to stop himself crying out and rolling over in agony. He felt his eyes smart and well up with tears, and was glad he was facing away from them all.

'Look – Daddy's crying in his sleep,' said Sean, surprising Julian with the proximity of his voice. Wendy strode over to him again and Julian felt her eyes staring down at him and heard the sharp intake of breath as she realised he was only pretending to be asleep.

'Right, I've had enough of this, if both of you don't get down to the kitchen this minute I'm going to have to punish you! Now get down the stairs! Come on – move!'

Julian could hear the hurt in her voice.

'But look, it's all squashed!' cried Jamie.

'I don't care! Just get down the bloody stairs!!'

The boys were stunned into silence by the ferociousness of their mother's response – Wendy hardly ever swore in front of them. Jamie sneaked another furtive look into his Dennis the Menace bag and gasped at the scale of the damage to his ship.

'But why's Daddy crying in his sleep?' whispered Sean as Wendy herded them down into the basement.

Wendy's voice of reason struggled to the fore. 'You've heard of people laughing in their sleep, haven't you? Well, sometimes people cry in their sleep, too.'

'Why?'

'Because they're having a bad dream.'

More like a fucking nightmare, thought Julian, and his tears of pain mingled with tears of self-pity. He listened to the sadly incomplete family group making its way down to the kitchen below and decided to steal upstairs and into bed rather than risk a confrontation there in the hall. He reckoned that if Wendy came back up once she'd set the boys at their breakfast and found him gone, she would realise he couldn't face her at that moment and she would leave him alone.

He dragged himself up to their eyrie on the top floor, a riot of swagged drapes and rag-rolled walls, and collapsed on the bed, trying to suppress the sudden recollection that he had to be at rehearsals by ten or they'd lose the house. Five minutes later a desire to piss overcame him and he had to stagger through into the cool Cunard chic of their *en-suite* bathroom. As soon as he'd relaxed the sphincter on his bladder he felt an urgent need to crap. Weary, hungover and self-pityingly depressed though he was, he resigned himself to this bodily obligation, sat on the toilet and starting leafing through one of the women's glossy magazines Wendy kept in a four-foot, freestanding pile beside the toilet. Finding a questionnaire entitled 'How Good Is Your Man In Bed?' he held it up to the light to see if there were any indentations left by ticks and crosses which Wendy might have subsequently rubbed out, and as he was doing so Wendy appeared at the door.

'You're up then?'

'Yes.'

She had obviously been crying but seemed quite together now, in a stoic, pulled-up-by-the-bootstraps kind of way.

'Interesting letter from Paul this morning,' she said, holding up a letter with the P.M.A. logo blazoned across the top.

Julian racked his brains in an attempt to imagine under what circumstances one of Paul's letters could ever be described as interesting. He felt suddenly vulnerable sitting there with his trousers round his ankles and quickly flicked through a clump of pages in the magazine so that Wendy couldn't see he'd been looking at the sex quiz.

'Do you want to hear what he has to say? I think you ought to.'

'Right, well I will then.'

' "Dear Julian . . ." '

174

'Well, that's a good start,' Julian said, pulling a winsome smile out of the bag like a magician.

'Yes.' She gave Julian a solemn look to signify that she wasn't about to be bounced into a good mood by any attempt to joke his way out of the situation, and once he'd adopted a suitably chastened expression she returned to the letter. ' "*Dear Julian, Picador have come back to me about* Blood Train. *If you want to get out of the play and do the film then I can fix it for you – at a price. Yours, Paul. P.S. You are an unconscionable shit.*" '

Wendy looked expectantly at Julian, who nodded sagely and then said, 'What does unconscionable mean?'

'It means having no conscience; or not being controlled by your conscience.' Wendy paused, then carried on. 'Not being in accordance with what is right or reasonable.'

'Yes, yes, I think I get the general idea.'

He looked up at her shamefacedly, but couldn't handle her statuesque impassivity and looked away, lost in a miasma of guilt and unhappiness. Hearing her sniff he looked up again and saw her face was now tight with raw emotion.

'I'm sorry about last night,' she said suddenly. 'It was tactless, I'm sorry.'

'No, I'm sorry, I was horrible to you.'

'I love Tom dearly, but he's just an old friend. I thought he might be able to help. I didn't mean to make you feel hemmed in.'

'I'm sorry I was so angry, it was . . .'

'It's all right.'

'It . . . it wasn't in accordance with what's right or reasonable. I'm sorry.'

'So am I,' she said and walked across to hug him awkwardly as he sat on the toilet. Believing that their apologies might have cleared the air he pulled her close and squeezed hard, but sensed a stiffness in her body that suggested unfinished business. He felt horribly insecure, trapped in his submissive position on the toilet, with no freedom to thrust and parry.

'I'd better see to the boys,' said Wendy, suddenly squeezing his head even tighter and kissing him on the crown before flitting out of the room without showing her face.

Like Judas? Julian thought to himself. What *did* it mean? 'Things cannot go on as they are.' For the first time in his life it dawned on Julian that *she* might be on the verge of leaving *him*. Not that Julian hadn't often day-dreamed about her leaving him in the past, but it had always been at his instigation – he would prompt her into leaving by confessing a few affairs and one-night stands – whereas now it seemed she'd taken the idea upon herself.

His mind raced through the possibilities of a loveless future without the support of his wife and children. He could see himself being made bankrupt by Mitch and his ilk but not caring a jot, arrogantly turning his back on the world and shunning them all as they'd shunned him, taking up as the broken-hearted singer with a hauntingly emotional pub band to earn his daily dram, and drinking himself to worry-free oblivion.

A muffled scrabbling from within the party wall interrupted his wistful day-dreams, and he put the noise down to mice or plumbing as usual before suddenly pulling himself up short – next door in the direction the sound had come from was the psycho fan's flat! He ran through the layout of the top floor of her apartment and worked out that the noise must have come from the shrine room. He wondered if she was watching the video tape of yesterday's encounter, but his fear of what chaos the tape could cause was quickly outweighed by the memory of the sex they'd had, and the idea of being venerated as a god, and he felt his growing erection pushing up clumsily against the rim of the lavatory.

And suddenly there she was again, the mother of his children, standing at the bathroom door, a vision of stoicism and tenderness, timid and red-eyed.

It struck him that he couldn't let her leave him because of the boys; that letting her leave him was as good as leaving her himself. In Julian's book the children were innocents, and wilfully abrogating his responsibility to them was something eighteen years of casual church attendance and school assemblies would not let him do. And of course, to complicate matters, he was in love with Wendy, or at least, in love with the *idea* of being in love with her.

'Jamie wants you to fix this,' said Wendy, holding out a loosely glued bundle of empty toilet rolls and string.

'What is it?'

'It's his pirate ship. He made it at school.'

Julian looked up into Wendy's face. 'Why don't you fix it? You're better at that sort of thing.'

'Well he'd know if I fixed it. He doesn't really think you'll be able to do it but I think he'd be pleased just to see that you'd had a go.' She laid the tangled mess on a linen chest by the door. 'I'll be taking them off to school in a minute, and I'm helping out with the cookery lesson this morning, then I'm having my hair trimmed – so I won't be back till about two.' She paused, uncertain whether to continue. 'It's good news from Paul, isn't it?'

'Yes.'

'Will you ring him?'

'Yes.'

'It would be better to do it sober,' she added quietly.

'Are you planning to leave me,' Julian heard himself say.

'Oh no, no!' She rushed to him and clasped him to her bosom. 'I'll never leave you. I love you.'

Julian didn't know whether he was crying because he was trapped for the rest of his life or because Wendy was the only person in the world who loved him.

23

'Paul Morrison Associates,' came Elaine's voice.

'Yes, hello Elaine, it's Julian.'

'Oh, hello.' Her voice sounded suddenly guarded.

'Yes, look – is Paul there?'

'I'll just see if he's in.'

Her voice was replaced by Vivaldi's *Four Seasons* which seemed far too jolly for the occasion. Julian tucked the receiver under his chin and twisted the tiny top off another miniature from the malt whisky selection his sister had given him for Christmas. It seemed to be the only booze left in the house. He'd already drunk two of them so this was his third – he was saving the remaining three for any moments of panic that might crop up during his conversation with Paul. He drained the Laphroaig in one gulp and dropped it into its own little niche in the presentation pack. It was a ridiculous amount of packaging, he thought to himself – the velveteen tray with its six compartments, the six tiny bottles each in its own miniature cardboard tube, the tartan cardboard box and the plastic wrapping – all for what amounted to less than a quarter-bottle of scotch. He took the Bowmore, Aberlour and Glengoyne out of their tubes and stood them on the box so that they would be easier to get hold of in an emergency, and noticed the gift tag for the first time. It read:

To Julian, wishing you a very merry Christmas. Not your usual size I'm sure, but they should come in handy for a trip to Brobdingnag, love Helena and Geoff. xxx

Julian pulled it off the box roughly and held it up close to check he'd read it properly. Brobdingnag? *What the fuck did*

178

that mean? He seemed to be surrounded by cryptic messages: '*unconscionable*'; '*Things cannot go on as they are*'; *Brobfucking-dingnag!* What was the point in sending a message if the person you were sending it to couldn't understand it?

'Hello, Julian?'

Paul's clipped voice took him by surprise and the phone slipped out from under his chin and dropped onto the end of the tray of miniatures which was overhanging the counter, sending them crashing across the kitchen floor with a great din. Three bottles broke on the terracotta tiles; Julian couldn't see whether they were empties or not.

'Yes? Paul? It's me. Sorry, I just dropped the phone,' said Julian, stretching the phone cord to its limit as he tried to reach the outermost spread of the debris to check for full bottles.

'Are you all right?'

'Yes, honestly, I was just . . . conducting away to Vivaldi, when you startled me and I dropped the phone.'

'You're not drunk?'

'Do I sound drunk?'

'Yes.'

'I'm not,' Julian said, stretching out his foot to hook a full miniature back to within range of his hand, but he skewed the kick and it disappeared under the fridge.

'*Blood Train*,' said Paul coldly, as if it were a chapter heading in an instruction manual.

'Yes,' said Julian, filling the pause.

'They're quite keen again. To be frank I think they'd started negotiations with someone else some time back and used the business in the papers as an excuse to dump you, but the someone else seems to have fallen through. Now they want you back.'

'That's great,' said Julian, getting a purchase on the bottle under the fridge with some salad tongs.

'Well, do you want to do the film?'

'Of course I do, but what about the bastard play? Mitch

179

says he's going to sue me.' He pulled the bottle out from under the fridge, grabbed it with his hand, and taking the top between his teeth, began to unscrew it.

'Come to my office and we'll sort that out. Shall we say two o'clock?'

'Two o'clock.' Julian spat the top away and put the bottle to his lips.

'Don't arrive drunk – if you've had a drink I don't think I'll be able to work with you.' The line clicked dead.

Julian was sitting on the floor with his back against the fridge, the telephone cord still at full stretch. He let the receiver go and it smashed into the cupboard opposite, splitting open along one side. Julian looked at the miniature in his hand – 'Bowmore, Islay, Single Malt' – he felt he could actually *see* the succour held in suspension in the golden, caramel liquid. The bottle seemed *very* small, and the glass very thick. It could only hold about a tablespoonful, he thought. He tipped back his head and poured it into his mouth from a height. The whisky splashed off his tongue all round his mouth and onto his lips with a pleasant stinging sensation.

The desire to get drunk despite or even *because* of Paul's warning was overwhelming – a synaptic impulse to obliterate everything important and fly in the face of restraining responsibility – and Julian was glad for his own sake that there was no booze in the house. His brain started performing somersaults of logic as he reasoned that there could still be two miniatures somewhere in the kitchen, and as a compromise he decided he'd have to finish them off first, just to make doubly sure that there was no drink left in the house. Then he would order a cab for one thirty, and sit and drink black coffee until it was time to go.

An hour and a half after he'd accepted the sad fate of the remaining two miniatures and swept the broken glass into a corner, he was one and a half cups into his second cafetière of black coffee. He was bored to tears and feeling very sober, and the excessive intake of coffee was giving him an unpleasant, anxious feeling. He'd tried watching *Anne and Nick* on morning television but it had made him angry so he'd had to turn it off.

He was so bored he even ventured a look into the drawer that served as their in-tray. It was so full of unanswered correspondence that letters fell down the back of the drawer and he had trouble closing it properly, wrenching it backwards and forwards a few times before giving up and leaving it a quarter open. He examined Sean's Gameboy and managed to turn it on but couldn't get passed the first few seconds of *Nemesis* without crashing head on into an enormous asteroid.

Moving through into the family room he began to experience an extraordinary sense of déjà vu. Everything looked familiar – the giant sofa, the Peruvian tableau of the nativity that they kept on display all year long, the CD player with its ugly cigarette burn on the lid that he'd unsuccessfully tried to camouflage with a black felt-tip pen – but at the same time it all seemed rather alien.

He idly ascended the stairs to the next floor and went into the sitting room. Every door and drawer of the drinks cabinet was hanging open from his earlier search for booze, and the empty bottles of sherry, ginger wine and Martini sat on the coffee table, testament to last night's drinking, and proof that he'd been here before. He could see everything with such clarity, it was as if his home had been turned into an advert. Everything looked like a pack shot or a still from some feature film – the fan-backed wicker chair, the curtaining, the empty bottle of Marsala stuck down the back of the sofa, everything screamed out 'You know me!'

Then the truth suddenly dawned on him: *he was sober!* That was why everything seemed hyper-real, why it all seemed so detailed and intricate. He'd been sober before of course – but not like this. He never drank before going to work, and on a night shoot that could mean hanging around the house sober *all* day. But on those occasions he had his work to think about

– there was a good reason for being sober. The prospect of performing was always enough to fill his day, not in the direct way of a pernickety perfectionist, but as a subconscious under-tow that gave it a purpose. On rest days and at weekends he was always at least *partly* drunk, even if he was picking the boys up from school. Indeed, one of his favourite pastimes was taking them to the park so he could sit on a bench taking illicit nips of bourbon from a hip flask, hiding it behind a paper. It made him feel like a cross between Eric Morecambe, secretly drinking from a bottle hidden only by his comically upraised arm, and a rebellious schoolboy behind a bike shed, and the rush of warm blood to his face would ameliorate the sting of the wind and make watching the boys swing endlessly to and fro slightly more amusing.

But here he was completely sober and without purpose! Even worse, he had to meet with Paul in a couple of hours to discuss one of the most momentous pieces of business of his life and he wasn't allowed a drink!

Remembering the emotional upheaval of the morning Julian wondered whether he ought make use of this moment of sobriety to consider his responsibility to Wendy and the boys, and how he might make himself a better husband and father. He wandered into Wendy's boudoir to see if he could find some clue as to how he might inveigle himself back into her deepest affections once the business with the play was sorted out and the fun was back on, but couldn't get past wondering what someone of Wendy's intellect could find interesting about the embroidery that lay half-finished on her work table. Casting his eye about for inspiration his gaze fell on a collection of Victorian thimbles and he had to leave the room quickly before a rising anger at the futility of her pastimes took hold.

He climbed the stairs to the first floor and went into the boys' bedroom. He didn't know what he was searching for really as he picked idly through the toys and knick-knacks – perhaps some key to greater understanding – but what finally caught his eye was a sheet of work that had been mounted on black card and pinned to the notice-board. It was entitled 'My Dabby by Sean'. It read:

My dabby is the funist comejun in the wrld, but sumtims he is sad.

Beneath it Sean had drawn a picture of Julian's face. The right-hand side was happy and had a smile that reached up to a big cauliflower ear, his bright blue blind eye surrounded by florid yellow eyelashes like rays of sunshine, whilst the left-hand side was woeful and sad, the smile arcing down to his chin and his brown seeing eye streaming rivers of blood-red tears.

Julian smarted at the accuracy of Sean's psychological pro-filing and traipsed up to his own bedroom on the top floor, wondering whether in the distant past he might have hidden a bottle in any of the cupboards or drawers.

'Sumtims he has to get pissed as well,' he muttered to himself as he looked through all the possible hiding places, but to no avail. He thought of running out to the off-licence and buying in a crate but by an enormous feat of will-power he managed to run into his bathroom instead and lock himself in.

He heard the phone start to ring in the bedroom and knew immediately that it was Mitch trying to find out where he was. He felt the muscles across his chest tighten into clawing knots of steel and desperately took up his breathing exercises in an effort to fight off the panic and his increasing desire to drink. He racked his brain for something to take his mind off it all. *If only he had a fucking hobby! Why didn't he have a hobby?* He dragged his hands down his face and cast his bleary eye about the room in a forlorn search for an instant diversion and it fell upon the improbable tangle of Jamie's pirate ship.

That was it – he'd mend the fucker!

How difficult could it be? he thought to himself. Of course he pretended to an ingenuous naïvety in the face of technology but that was just a pose, schoolboy proof of his artistic sens-ibility. Sticking a few toilet rolls together couldn't be that

challenging – he'd show Wendy, and Jamie, the whole world!
And it would pass the time.

An hour later in the kitchen he was beginning to wonder
whether he'd been over-ambitious or whether he just had the
wrong kind of glue. He'd decided to surprise Jamie with a ship
in a bottle – he'd seen it done on television – the secret was
to tie the masts together with a single piece of string then pull
the whole assembly up as one, once the ship was in the bottle.
Unfortunately, even though his assembly was nothing more
adventurous than a single, split toilet roll and three wooden
skewers, he'd ended up with a Wild Turkey bottle full of
cardboard, string, skewers and evo-stick. The more he'd tried
to tamp the increasingly unravelled toilet roll into position the
more glue he'd managed to smear over the glass until now he
could barely see what was going on inside the bottle at all.

In a last-ditch attempt to get something standing erect in
the bottle he batted the skewers as close into position as he
could with a pickle fork, emptied a tube of super-glue down the
neck of the bottle, and gently pulled on the string connected to
the masts. He peered anxiously through the opaque glass,
getting more and more angry and despondent as the loops of
string slipped off each mast in turn letting the skewers drop
slowly back down towards the bottom of the bottle. As the
last one fell he yanked the string out furiously, then, eager to
punish the model for being so stupidly stubborn, he grabbed
the kitchen matches, lit one and dropped it into the bottle.

There was a short, gusting explosion accompanied by a flash
of white light and a menacing lick of orange flame, and the
room began to fill with dense, black smoke.

As Julian stood, open-mouthed, watching the billowing
column of smoke fan out across the kitchen ceiling, he heard
the doorbell ring. It must be his cab! he thought to himself,
and his first impulse was to run to the front door, pull the
cabbie down the stairs and plead with him to sort things out,
but as he reached the kitchen door he was seized by the

notion that speed was of the essence in preventing a major catastrophe, and turned back. The idea flashed across his mind that this was the action of a responsible person and that therefore he wasn't the man for the job – but then a kind of religious zeal took hold of him as he realised that this was his chance to prove himself the dependable head of his own household.

He ran to the bottle and grabbed it, meaning to rush it to the sink and stick it under the tap, but had to drop it just as speedily as the white heat of the glass seared into his fingers and thumb. The bottle smashed into pieces on the kitchen tiles, each fragment carrying its own gluey inferno to a different corner of the kitchen.

The doorbell rang again.

'Help!' shouted Julian. Standing in the centre of the room surrounded by symbolic fires at all the points of the zodiac, he felt like the subject of a weird satanic ritual. 'Help!' he shouted again, his voice breaking a little with fear. He grabbed a tea towel and began to beat at one of the fires, but after a couple of swats he noticed that the tea towel itself had caught fire. The flames shot up the towel and licked at his already blistered hand. In a blind panic he flung it as far away from himself as he could and it landed on the unruly pile of newspapers that he knew with a sudden blinding recognition of his own shortcomings should have been carted off to the recycling bin weeks before. They erupted instantaneously into a six-foot sheet of flame that began to eat into the end of the great pine dresser.

The doorbell rang again, long and insistent.

'Help! Fucking help!' yelled Julian.

By now the smoke had filled the top half of the room and it was biting into his eyes and clawing at the back of his throat, and the heat was getting frighteningly intense. Through the rapidly increasing gloom he saw that two of the bottle-fragment incendiaries had managed to ignite a wickerwork wine rack and the pantry door, and abandoning all hope of controlling

185

the blaze he made a frantic dash for the basement door, bursting out into the little basement yard at the front of the house, eyes streaming and gasping for breath, just as the doorbell began to ring again.

'Stop ringing the fucking bell and call the fire brigade, you cunt!' screamed Julian, struggling to get the words past the growing lump in his throat.

A glum, balding, pot-bellied cabbie of about forty with a maroon sweater and thick glasses peered round from the front porch and down into the basement yard. 'Cab for Mr Manx?'

Julian scrambled up the steps into the street fighting for breath. 'Help! Fire! Help!' he barked, unable to get any volume into his voice. He felt as if the walls of his throat were closing together. 'My house is on fire! Someone call the fucking fire brigade, *please*!' Then his entreaties were interrupted by a coughing fit so severe he had to hang on to the railings for support. Bent double and fighting for breath he hawked up great gobs of blooded spit flecked with soot.

The cabbie sauntered round onto the pavement next to Julian and looked down at the smoke pouring out through the basement doorway below. 'You've not left the oven on, have you?'

Choking back a small stream of black mucus and blood Julian looked up at the man.

'It's too much smoke for a toaster, init?' said the cabbie.

24

'He's down this way,' said the nurse, leading Wendy towards another gleaming white corridor with a mirror-polished floor. The shocking cleanliness of the hospital and the crisp uniforms of the nurses made Wendy feel even grubbier than she was. She looked down at her hands and tried to rub more of the grime off onto her skirt. 'He's all right really, we're just keeping him in for observation. He can go home tomorrow.'

'No he bloody can't,' Wendy murmured to herself, 'he's burned the sodding thing down.' Her head swam with the nightmare vision that had greeted her at two o'clock that afternoon – of their street filled with flashing blue lights, of rounding a fire engine for her first glimpse of the smouldering, blackened, waterlogged wreckage of their home – and she had to fight hard to keep her composure.

'Here we are. Now he's on some rather strong painkillers so don't be too concerned if he seems a little confused,' said the nurse, opening a door and ushering Wendy into a rather smart two-bed ward. 'He's very lucky – he's got this to himself.'

Wendy stood stock still in the doorway looking at Julian in his bed as the nurse launched into a voluble account of his injuries and bustled around the bed checking his blood pressure and other indicators. He was sitting up with an oxygen mask sticky-taped to his face, holding up his right hand in the air, swollen, bloody and blistered, the middle finger held in a tight white bandage. At first Wendy thought he was waving at her but as she waved feebly back she noticed his wrist was held in a sling tied to a bar above his bed.

'They can be quite tricky – dislocated fingers,' the nurse

187

wittered on, 'because the ligaments are quite tight around the knuckle and it's difficult to get a good grip on the end of the finger, but they got it back in all right in the end didn't they?'

Julian nodded glumly.

Wendy walked slowly round the bed, subliminally taking in the nurse's commentary on smoke inhalation and second-degree burns, until she reached Julian's bedside. She looked into Julian's eyes and they gazed back into her's like a wounded puppy's. Taking a closer look at his hand she could see that the middle finger was held in a metal frame secured round either end of the bandage. The other fingers sported massive blisters which stood half an inch proud and seemed so over-inflated and tight that they might pop at any moment.

'He doesn't have to keep it up there all the time, but if he keeps it higher than his heart it'll reduce the pressure a little.'

The blister on his thumb obviously *had* popped, it was a sticky swollen mess of raw flesh and glistening fluids. Wendy imagined she could even see it throbbing. Looking behind at the back of his hand she saw that that was badly scorched too. She looked down at him as the nurse removed his mask. His eyes seemed sad and doleful while his mouth appeared to be fixed in a crumpled, drugged smile, and the combined effect made him look genuinely insane.

Wendy looked away, out of the window. They were on the sixth floor of St Stephen's Hospital and she had a great view of West Brompton and Fulham beyond – a vast, friendly pano-rama of autumnal trees, church spires and houses stretched as far as the eye could see. Homes, thousands and thousands of *homes*, crammed full of personal possessions, knick-knacks accrued over lifetimes, photograph albums and favourite toys, each home the sum of a myriad of individual preferences and decorating decisions.

She burst into tears and slumped into the chair at Julian's bedside, resting her folded arms on his bed and burying her face in the crook of her elbow. She could smell the stench of charred wood on her cardigan, could see again in her mind's eye the total devastation she had witnessed from the front door of the house before the fireman had pulled her back out – the huge hole in the floor, the missing internal walls, the water cascading from the stairwell above and the complete lack of anything remotely recognisable, save for a small two-foot-square patch of 'pavilion candy-stripe' wallpaper which must have been protected by the electricity meter underneath it. She remembered how she had first seen it in an American interior design magazine; her long hunt through overseas directory enquiries; the even longer wait for it to arrive and to be hung; and then how she had overheard Julian's remark to Bill Tyndall that he felt as if he was living in a 'fucking Dayvilles ice-cream parlour'.

Despair seemed to reach into her chest like a cold hand and wrench out the core of her being. An overwhelming sense of emptiness swept aside all propriety. She wept loudly and without restraint like an abandoned child, tears pouring down her cheeks, her mouth hanging open.

She felt Julian's good hand rest lightly on her head, could feel the nurse beside her wrapping a comforting arm around her shoulders and burbling words of solace – but there was no comfort to be had. She knew only that her world had crumbled round her ears and that it could never be the same again; she was drowning in an ocean of uncertainty. *What would she tell the boys? Where could they live? How long would it take to rebuild? Where did she start?*

She tried to quell the rising tide of anger welling up inside her. The rational undergraduate within told her that there was no point in getting angry, that anger wouldn't help anything. Besides, what was she angry about? she asked herself. *Julian?!* Of course she was angry with Julian, but not in a recriminatory way. She was angry because she loved him and for the anguish that caused her; for the gut-wrenching moment of panic she'd had that the boys might have to grow up without a father. She knew he was an incompetent father, but he *was* their father, and he *wanted* to be their father, and that made him a good father – and the only father they could ever have. And the boys *worshipped* him. They knew nothing else. They fought for him in the playground and gave Wendy the tightest hugs to pass on to him every time he wasn't there to wish them good-night.

She heaved herself forward and threw her arms around Julian's midriff, hanging on as if he were a lifebelt. Through her howling she heard the nurse's clipping footsteps move across the room, and the click of the door as it closed behind her.

She wailed with abandon for a good five minutes until she was surprised to feel some actual, physical benefit, as if the crying was soothing her from within. She could feel Julian's hand on her head keeping up a steady quieting beat, and felt the love that was in it. For a further ten or fifteen minutes she kept up a plaintive lament which gradually began to ease until her whole body felt numb and washed out and she fell into a sleep.

When she woke she had no idea how long she'd been asleep but she could still feel the gentle pat of Julian's hand on her head. She was facing his feet and slowly turned her head to look into his face. He was crying silently, two salt-reddened lines down either side of his face bearing testimony to the depth of his suffering.

'I'm sorry,' he said, his rasping words barely audible through his smoked vocal chords, and as he spoke his face collapsed in agonised despair sending shock waves of hacking sobs through his defenceless frame.

Now it was Wendy's turn to console and caress. She got up from her chair, sat on the edge of the bed and tried to cradle his head in her arms – but it was difficult as the arm tied to the bar above the bed got in the way. She switched sides but it was still obviously uncomfortable – there was no way of holding his head without increasing the weight on his injured arm and thereby adding to his discomfort. By the time she'd settled for simply sitting half-way down the bed and holding his good hand in hers he'd overcome the worst of his grief and even seemed to be smiling slightly – the strange quarter-smile she'd seen before when the nurse had removed his mask.

'What are you on?' she asked.

'Morphine,' croaked Julian, mopping at his tears with the sleeve of his pyjamas. 'The nurse said "beware of euphoria" – but it hasn't been a problem yet.'

He chuckled at his own wit and waited for a sign that she could still laugh at a joke, but she couldn't even force a smile. Realisation dawned on Julian's face.

'It's bad, isn't it?' he said.

She nodded.

'It hasn't all gone?'

She nodded again. His shocked intake of breath brought on a coughing attack – painful, choking coughs which seemed to halt at the base of his throat until enough pressure had built up to force them explosively past the constriction in his windpipe. Wendy could see his misery as he tried to swallow, the hesitant movement of his Adam's apple before it jigged agonisingly up and down, and the stoicism on his brow.

As he recovered panic suddenly flashed across his face and he flung his arm towards his watch on the bedside cabinet, accidentally knocking it to the floor. 'What time do the boys get out of school?!'

'It's all right – Tom's picking them up.' She tried hard not to give him a look which read 'He *is* a friend, he *is* genuinely helping us in our hour of need, and at least *he* didn't burn the fucking house down', but it was a Herculean task.

Julian winced at this fresh assault on his fatherhood, throwing his head back in despair and banging it against the metal bars of the bedhead, making his head sing.

There was a cursory knock on the door, and the same nurse ushered in two uniformed policemen.

'Mr Julian Mann?' asked the leading policeman, very young with short, ginger sideburns and freckles across the bridge of his nose. 'Bit of a stupid question really, sir. I know it's you because I've seen you on the television.'

Julian gave an ingratiating smile and indicated with a wave of his hand that he was unable to speak because of his injured throat.

The policeman smiled but carried on. 'I must say that I'm really quite a big fan of yours, sir. As is PC Austin here.' PC Austin looked over the first policeman's shoulder with a cheesy grin; he was finding it hard to keep a straight face in the presence of his comic hero. Wendy felt immediately annoyed at their flippancy, and the intrusion on their private grief.

'Look, can't you interview us tomorrow? He's really not in a fit state and I'm feeling pretty lousy myself.'

'I'm afraid we have to talk to your husband as soon as possible, Mrs Mann.'

'Look – he's in a hospital bed! He can't even talk! Our home has been burned to the ground! Just leave it till tomorrow!'

'We're not here about the fire, Mrs Mann.'

'What is it – fans outside?' croaked Julian, sending PC Austin into fits of giggles. The first policeman looked round as sternly as he could at his colleague who tried valiantly to suppress his laughter.

'No, I'm afraid it's about an incident involving a Mr Reginald Lyle outside your house earlier this afternoon.'

Julian looked nonplussed.

'A cab driver, sir,' the policeman continued.

Wendy watched Julian's eyes widen in fear and comprehension.

'He fucking deserved it!' shouted Julian, immediately paying for his vocal profligacy with another convulsive attack of coughing.

PC Austin snorted uncontrollably – a great stream of mucus flying from his nose and fanning across his chin – and thrusting his hand into his pocket for his handkerchief he struggled from the room muttering barely intelligible apologies to his partner.

'What are you talking about, what cab driver?' asked Wendy.

'Well,' said the policeman, adjusting his tie and gently clearing his throat as if about to walk onto a stage. 'In the words of Mr Mann's TV character, Richard the Nerd, it appears he gave the cabbie "a great big bunch of fives right up his hooter".'

As the policeman fought hard to rein in his pride at his impersonation, Julian fondly reran the highlight of his afternoon in his mind: his frustration with the recalcitrant cabbie; his memories of all the screen punches he had ever thrown; and then coiling himself up like a discus thrower and swinging his fist into the cabbie's face, smashing his lip into his teeth before collapsing onto the pavement.

Wendy looked away out of the window towards West Brompton and Fulham and blinked hard to stop the tears. As soon as she'd nailed down sufficient composure she turned and walked swiftly to the door, roughly elbowing the laughing policeman aside. She stumbled out into the corridor beyond and passed PC Austin – sitting on his haunches with his head buried in his hands, rocking backwards and forwards in silent hysteria.

25

Julian was extremely grateful to Paul for picking him up from the magistrates' court the next day; for arranging his bail; for organising the cab; for helping him through the pack of photographers and pushing out with his briefcase to shield his burned hand. He was even gladder to learn that Paul had squashed the play, that Mitch could claim the entire production on his insurance, and that the film was definitely back on – even though Paul's dubious plan to get an obliging doctor he knew to testify to Julian's 'nodes' had been rather more effectively superseded by Julian's real-life throat condition. More than that, Paul had sought out Wendy in her hour of need and installed the family in a smart hotel in Kensington – he had become the protector and provider for Julian's boys.

Now, as the cab drove them along past Hyde Park, Julian felt genuinely penitent. 'Look, I really appreciate all you've done for me in the last day or so Paul, and I'd like to say how ... how really, very sorry I am for the way I treated you the other week.' His voice was cracked and gravelly, the result of the smoke-inhalation rather than over-riding emotion, but meat to his cause nevertheless.

'An apology isn't necessary,' said Paul, his tone as starched as the velvet-collared, high-buttoned suit he'd bought especially for his appearance before the press cameras.

'No, but it is. I'm really *so* sorry, and deeply ashamed.'

'I've said I don't need an apology.' Paul's clipped rebuttal unsettled Julian, it suggested a sense of purpose that was unfamiliar and rather cold. 'I've talked it over with Wendy and I've decided to be your personal manager.'

'What's the difference between that and being my agent?' asked Julian, with a smile that he hoped would thaw the frost that seemed to hang in the air between them.

'Fifteen per cent.'

'You take fifteen per cent?'

'No, the *difference* is fifteen per cent, I take twenty-five per cent.'

'That's outrageous!' Julian forced a laugh.

'Yes.' Paul very coolly took a document from his briefcase and retrieved a fountain pen from his top pocket. 'I want you to sign this.'

'I can't.'

'You have to.'

'No, I mean I physically can't, I've burned my hand.'

'Use your left hand.'

'But that's stupid, Paul,' he said with a playful smile. 'It won't look anything like my signature. I could claim I'd never signed it, or that it was a forgery – it'd never stand up in court.'

'Just sign it.'

Julian signed clumsily with his good hand and tried to ignore Paul's burgeoning hostility, which wasn't difficult as he felt a profound sense of relief that someone was taking such definite control of one part of his life. 'I'm quite glad to sign, you know. I think we always needed a formal agreement – maybe that's what went wrong between us.'

Paul took the signed document and put it carefully back into his briefcase as the cab pulled into the side of the road. After an awkward pause Paul leaned across and opened Julian's door for him and sat back in his seat rather heavily to indicate that their meeting was concluded. Julian thought he caught a slight tremor in Paul's hand before it clutched onto the handle of his briefcase to steady itself.

'Is this where I live now?' asked Julian, looking out of the open door at the hotel entrance.

195

'Yes. I got quite a good deal for you – two interconnecting suites for the price of one.'

'Thank you.'

'It's all part of the service.'

Julian made as if to get out of the cab, then turned back and laid his good hand on Paul's arm. He felt genuinely humbled by recent events and wanted to make a new start with Paul – wanted his forgiveness and his love. 'Friends?' he said, his eyes glistening with moisture.

'I'm doing this for the boys, you know,' Paul said tersely. 'After all, I am their godfather. Five per cent of my fee will go into a trust fund for them.' He paused and looked out of his window at the other side of the street.

'So are we friends?' Julian persisted.

'Let's just leave it at personal manager for now, shall we?'

'OK,' said Julian, rather crestfallen, and he got out and waved the cab goodbye as it pulled out into the traffic and away down the street. Paul never looked round.

He turned to look at the Kensington Parkview Hotel. It was a modern, four-star establishment. Julian knew from the smoked glass of the entrance doors that it would be well-appointed with every amenity but wouldn't have any personality. He gazed up at the seven floors of identical tinted windows, all uniformly hiding any sign of their occupants behind swathes of net curtaining, and wondered which one hid Wendy and his sons.

He had been very pleased with his performance in the hospital – he'd felt genuinely upset, but hadn't counted on being able to cry like that. If the policeman hadn't blown it by cutting in first with the tale of the recalcitrant cabbie, Julian felt he might have been walking in now as the wounded hero rather than the cashiered traitor dragging misfortune in his wake.

He wondered whether it would ever be possible for Wendy and himself to get their relationship back on an even keel, and thought how he would gladly swap their present status for the anodyne, deceitful grind that had subsisted for the last few

196

years, then looked round with a sudden panic and wondered how long it would take the psycho fan to find out where they were holed up and move into the suite next door.

As he stood on the pavement feeling emotionally beleaguered he sensed a familiar tension in the muscles under his ribcage and realised his breathing had become so shallow as to be virtually non-existent. He struggled hard with the impulse to run away rather than face Wendy, managed to steel himself and walked nervously into the hotel. Coming out of the revolving doors into the foyer his eye was immediately drawn to the small, wooden signpost which read 'Bar This Way'.

Just one quick one, as a relaxant, he thought to himself, and headed towards the bar. But as he reached the door and saw the optics shiny and welcoming behind the bar on the opposite side of the room, he felt suddenly over-burdened with guilt about the fire and the cabbie, and with a superhuman effort he decided that he owed it to Wendy to be clean for their first confrontation. He rammed his good fist deep into his pocket with the frustration of it all and happened upon the tube of painkillers in there. Remembering the buzz they had given him, he decided to have a couple of them instead of a drink and fumbled one-handedly with the lid as he headed back towards the reception desk.

Rounding the strange four-sofas-stuck-together-cum-small-planted-tree-and-shrubbery-unit which dominated the foyer he tripped over a pair of outstretched legs and went flying, watching in despair as the pill-container hit the deck spraying his painkillers across the marble floor, and shrieking in agony as he instinctively broke his fall with his burned hand.

Almost blind with fury and pain he jumped to his feet and rounded on the owner of the legs. 'You stupid fucking cunt!'

'Hello, matelot, fancy a quick pint of the cider that's brewed that extra bit longer for that extra-satisfying taste?'

It was Bill Tyndall, thin as a rake with his Andy Capp paunch and shabby leather jacket.

197

'Bill!' Julian said, surprised. 'Oww!'

'Ooh, that looks nasty. How are you, you old bastard?'

'In pain! Quick, get me my painkillers,' Julian said, indicating the empty container on the floor.

Bill leaped into action, snatching up the container and zipping about the floor on all fours, his bony buttocks moving up and down in double time inside his ragged jeans and the resoled rubber tips of his beaten-up cowboy boots leaving a trail of black streaks across the floor.

'Here you go,' he said, returning with the container half full. He emptied a few into the palm of his own hand. 'Look, how many do you have?'

'Well, it says one every three hours but I'm going to have four.'

'Fuck it, have eight,' said Bill, tipping them into Julian's hand.

Julian poured the pills into his mouth but found he couldn't swallow.

'You need a drink to wash them down with. Come on,' said Bill, taking Julian by the arm and briskly pulling him through into the bar. 'Got any bourbon?' he shouted across the room to the barman. 'Get me a double, quick.' The barman casually took a bottle of Jack Daniel's from the shelf and reached for a glass. 'Come on! This is an emergency!'

Julian could feel the shiny coating of the pills starting to dissolve and the foul taste of rusting metal filled his head, taking his mind off the blazing throb of his hand for a second. The barman measured out a double and placed the glass on the bar-top.

'Here you go, come on,' said Bill, holding the glass up to Julian's mouth. 'It's medicinal.'

Julian took it from him and drained the glass. He felt the pills disappear as he swallowed and then reeled at the aftershock as the alcohol scorched into the raw flesh of his throat.

'Is that better?' asked Bill.

Julian couldn't speak.

'That's five pounds sixty, thank you,' said the barman.

All Julian could produce was a squeaky rush of air.

'Hang on,' said Bill, surveying the range of taps on the bar, '*I'll* have a pint of Strongbow,' he scanned the line of optics, 'and a large Macallan. And the same again for my friend.'

'Another large one?' asked the barman, taking Julian's glass.

'Oh yes. Oh very much yes,' said Bill.

Julian began to feel an anaesthetic effect from the bourbon, and as the barman placed his refilled glass on the bar-top he gladly took it and sipped cautiously. First came the fire, then an increasing numbness accompanied by a little flick of a switch inside his head as the idea of obliteration loomed welcomingly.

'That's nineteen pounds sixty, thank you.'

Julian used all his learned techniques to relax his throat as much as possible and forced a breathy whisper. 'No, put it on my room.'

'Certainly, sir, what number?'

Julian paused. 'I don't know.'

'It's three two two,' said Bill, turning to Julian, 'I was up there earlier.'

'Was Wendy there?' croaked Julian, his eyes widening apprehensively.

'She didn't look over-happy to see me. I think she feels I'm a bad influence,' Bill grinned through his yellowing teeth.

'I don't think she's particularly happy about anything at the minute,' said Julian solemnly.

'Yes, well,' said Bill, suitably corrected, 'I suppose she has just lost her house and everything she owns.'

There was a pause as both men stared pensively into their drinks. Then Bill's shoulders began to shake and after a few seconds he snorted and collapsed into a paroxysm of laughter, tears streaming from his face as he slapped helplessly at the bar.

'All ... that ... fucking ... decoration!' struggled Bill, turning to Julian, and feeling glad to see that he too was

199

suddenly laughing fit to bust, his injured throat making him bray like a donkey and causing him considerable pain which he was trying to alleviate with generous gulps of bourbon.

'Oh, it's good to see you, matey,' said Julian, wrapping his arms around Bill and slapping his back.

'Oh, you too, you soppy cunt. I can't tell you how good this film's going to be. They tried to fob me off with someone else, you know. I had to fight really hard to get you, but now that I have, I'm really very well pleased.'

They hugged and slapped, then stood back and looked at each other grinning wide, wordless smiles, before punching each other playfully on the shoulders and taking up their drinks again.

'Well, when do we start?' asked Julian hoarsely. 'I can't wait to get started – get out of London. I'll miss the boys of course, and Wendy, but, well, you can imagine there's a lot of "stuff" going on at the minute – and LA'll give me the chance I need to regroup. You know,' he said, with a knowing wink, 'on my own.'

'LA?'

'We're filming in LA, aren't we?'

'We're making it in Scotland.'

Julian's jaw dropped. 'But it's set in America!'

'Yeah, but Scotland's cheaper. And it looks like Montana.' Bill could see that Julian was not convinced. 'And the crews are better over here. And cheaper.'

Julian let out a long, disappointed, rattling sigh.

'Look, you'll still be eight hundred miles away, or something like that,' said Bill, trying to cheer Julian up. 'I tell you what – we're not starting for three weeks or so, but if you're really that keen to get away, I could get you up there in a week for "rehearsals" or something . . . "acclimatisation" . . . I don't know.'

Julian thought of Wendy sitting upstairs in their hotel suite, of the house and the insurance and the court case, of the recriminations that were bound to linger and fester for weeks to

200

come. The thought of leaving it all behind made his shoulders suddenly drop two inches. He raised his head and smiled. 'That'd be great, Bill. Thanks, I'd really appreciate that. Have another drink.'

26

When Julian stumbled into Room 322 three hours later Sean and Jamie looked round from watching the in-house cartoon channel on the TV and ran to him, whooping and hollering, and trying to jump up into his arms – which gave him a good excuse for falling onto the bed.

Wendy appeared at the door to the adjoining suite.

'Sorry, I was with Bill Tyndall in the bar,' said Julian.

'Yes, I saw you in there when I brought the boys back from school,' she said, and disappeared back into the room beyond.

'Yeah, we saw you fall off the big tall chair!' shouted Jamie.

'You bonked your head and the other man laughed!' said Sean.

'Didn't it hurt?'

'Yeah, didn't it hurt?'

'Not really,' said Julian.

'Your voice has gone funny.'

'You sound like a frog.'

'Can we look at your hand?'

'Is that the finger that was discolated?'

'Ow, don't pull it like that,' said Julian.

'Why haven't you got a bandage on the other fingers?'

'Does that mean they're not a proper hurt?'

'No, it means they need the open air to heal properly,' said Julian, struggling to keep his voice from slurring. 'Please, don't sit on my bladder like that, I'm desperate for the toilet.' He fought them off one-handed, heaved himself off the bed and staggered to the bathroom. The boys followed him in, hanging on to his jacket.

'Are you paralytic again, Daddy?'

'What?'

'Uncle Tom said you were always getting paralytic every day.'

'Oh, he did, did he?' said Julian, relieving himself.

'Yeah, he said you drink too much beer.'

'Have you had too much beer today?'

'When did he say that?' asked Julian.

'Last night.'

'Yeah, last night. Uncle Tom came to stay last night.'

Julian's mind suddenly buzzed with alarming notions of infidelity and images of Tom and Wendy naked on the bed.

'Is that the beer coming out?' asked Jamie, watching the stream of urine splash into the bowl.

'Yeah, is that the beer coming out?'

'No, that's neat bourbon,' said Julian.

'Like the biscuit?'

'Yes, like the biscuit.' He shakily zipped his fly and moved to the sink. 'So Uncle Tom stayed all night, did he?'

'Yes, he slept in Mummy's bed.'

'But he'd already got up and gone to his work when we got up in the morning.'

Out of the mouths of babes! Julian's sense of outrage at being cuckolded by Tom was immediately countered by his sudden consideration that if she was having an affair this could be it! He could be on his way! he thought to himself. He could go to Scotland, leave them behind to get on with it, leave the psycho fan to fuck herself and her tape, leave the mess of the burned-out homestead for the semen-stained adulteress to sort out, and by the time he'd finished shagging his way round the Scottish Highlands he'd have a tidy little divorce on his hands and then he could really get himself sorted out.

And be happy.

In his inebriation he couldn't imagine how he'd ever come to the conclusion that Wendy leaving him was tantamount to him leaving Wendy, and this sudden release left him speculating on life as the wronged party, licensed to find solace in an orgy of booze and young models.

'Uncle Tom said you might have to stay in prison for a long time,' said Sean.

'He said if he was the judge he'd put you in prison and throw the key in a ditch,' said Jamie.

'Yes, well, Uncle Tom's a fuck-brained half-wit with a pecker the size of a drawing pin, and the next time you see him you can tell him that from me.' The boys sniggered at Julian's use of the F-word. 'Now just get out for a minute, would you, and let me sort myself out? Go on, go and watch telly.' He pretended to growl at them like a grizzly bear and the boys ran laughing from the room.

He washed his face with his good hand and after wrestling one of the new toothbrushes Wendy had obviously bought for the boys from its packaging he gave his teeth a thorough scrub, brushing his tongue to disguise the smell of alcohol on his breath.

Moving towards the adjoining suite with the confident air of a gambler with an ace up his sleeve he passed Sean and Jamie sitting on the floor watching Daffy Duck, and felt a sudden pang of remorse – there was no way they weren't going to get wounded in the crossfire. He sank clumsily onto his knees behind them and put a paternal arm round each of them. 'Are you all right, boys?'

'Yeah, we're all right,' they said together, not looking up from the television.

'You're not feeling sad about the fire or anything like that?'

'No.'

'No.'

'Is it true life that you made the fire, Daddy?' asked Sean, his gaze fixed on the television.

'Yeah, did you in true life?'

'It was an accident,' said Julian.

'The man from the fire engine said you made a bomb,' said

Jamie, suddenly bursting into laughter as Daffy's beak was punched so hard that it spun right round his head.

'Are you sure Uncle Tom slept in Mummy and Daddy's bed last night?'

'Oh yes. He said that because you were in prison he'd sleep in your bed as a special treat,' said Sean.

Julian patted each of them on the head, heartened by their innocent resilience, and made his way unsteadily into the adjoining room. Wendy was unpacking a multitude of Marks & Spencer's carrier bags and piling all the new underwear, T-shirts, shorts, socks and jumpers onto the bed.

'I'm back on the film.'

'Yes, Paul told me. That's good news,' she said, not looking up from her work.

'Look, I'm sorry, I had to have a drink with Bill because he stuck up for me. I mean, it's only really because of him that I'm back on it at all. He said to them "No Julian Mann – no Bill Tyndall", so, you know, I owed him one.' Julian tried to lean nonchalantly against the door-frame but missed it completely and had to do some fancy footwork to prevent himself from falling onto the mini-bar.

'Yes, of course,' she said, biting into a T-shaped piece of plastic to remove the price tag from a child's vest.

'Aren't you going to ask me how I got on in court?' he said.

'Paul rang – "summary trial" or something?'

'That's good apparently, because it's just a magistrate. The solicitor says it'll only be a fine, a suspended sentence at the most.'

'Yes.'

'And it won't be till January anyway.'

Julian watched with increasing annoyance as Wendy dedicated herself to freeing more and more underwear from the swathes of noisy packaging, and attempted to damp the fuse in his head which burned ever shorter, trying to hold back the moment of truth until the time was just right. After a while he managed to speak again. 'And I've patched things up with Paul.'

205

'Yes – there seems to be no end of good news.'

Julian looked at her sharply. 'You're not angry, are you?'

'What have I got to be angry about?'

He couldn't tell whether she was being sarcastic or whether she meant it as a leading question. Did she want him to list his misdemeanours one by one? *Wendy? The base adulteress?* But he played along. 'I don't know . . . the fire?'

'Did you do it on purpose?'

'No.'

She scrunched up several cellophane wrappers and jammed them into an empty plastic bag. 'They're saying you made some sort of Molotov Cocktail.'

'Who?'

'The firemen – Tom overheard them when he went back to the house last night to see if he could find anything worth rescuing.'

'And was there?' asked Julian, taking Wendy's hushed description of Tom's brave and valiant gesture as further evidence of their treacherous conjugation.

'Anything worth rescuing? No.'

Wendy went very still and stared into space. Julian could see from the minimal rise and fall of her chest that she'd almost stopped herself breathing altogether. He felt a rising anger at this long-suffering display in the face of her perfidy and heard himself snap. 'Oh God, don't start crying again.'

Her eyes fixed themselves on the carpet. 'Don't worry, I haven't got any tears left – I've been crying all night.'

'*All* night? I thought Tom was here last night?'

Her eyes looked up into his, trusting and innocent. 'Yes?'

'Did he stay the night?'

'The boys made him promise that he would – they were very upset – but he left once he'd finally got them off to sleep. He's been a great support.'

Looking into her eyes Julian could tell this was the truth.

The bastard! What right had he got to come round to the hotel, put his kids to bed, be in a bedroom alone with his beautiful wife, and not shag her?

The confusion this sudden reversal in his position brought about made him long for escape, for somewhere to put into order all the conflicting thoughts, desires and half-truths that battled for prominence in his mind – and the idea of Scotland loomed large as his sanctuary.

'I'm afraid there's even more bad news,' he said. Wendy looked up. Staring into the deep black pupils of her eyes he could see straight into her soul and saw her heart breaking. 'I have to go to Scotland at the end of the week.'

'Scotland?'

'That's where we're making the film.'

'But I thought it was set in America?'

'Yes, it is, but they're making it in Scotland – it's cheaper. And apparently it looks like Montana. Anyway, they don't start actual filming for three weeks or so, but they need me up there early for make-up checks and rehearsals, that sort of thing. It's a bugger, I know, but I don't think I can get out of it.'

He dropped his head and watched her carefully out of the corner of his eye, wondering if he'd sounded sufficiently contrite.

'But that's fantastic news,' she said.

'Mmn?'

'We'll all come! We'll rent a cottage! Oh, it'd be wonderful. Whereabouts in Scotland?'

Julian's voice sounded strange to him. 'The Highlands, I think.'

'Oh, fantastic. That's just what we need – to get away from all of it, to find some wide open space. Get away from the smoke, get some clean air into our lungs. I mean, we can't stay here, look at it,' she said, throwing her arms wide, 'it's like living in a cupboard.'

'But what about school? You can't just take the boys out of school like that, can you?' Julian remonstrated, taking a last desperate stand.

207

'They're only six – it can't hurt them,' Wendy said recklessly, her eyes widening with a growing passion for the whole idea. '*I'll* teach them!' she shouted, and flung her arms round his neck. 'Oh, Julian . . . Julian . . . it's a godsend,' she cried with breaking voice, and burst into tears.

27

Wendy had mixed feelings as she picked up Tom and Carly from the train station at Fort William. She'd proffered the invitation at the height of the upheaval when she'd felt particularly indebted to Tom for the way he'd put himself out to help them after the fire – bouncing around like a surrogate mother, taking the boys to and from school and on outings to the zoo and the Natural History Museum, whilst Julian seemed to have shared his days equally between the outpatients' waiting room at St Stephen's and the Hereford Arms, and Wendy had been locked into a whirlwind of shopping, trying to replace their lost wardrobes. But after a restorative week alone with Julian and the boys in their wilderness hide-out up in the hills above Strontian on the west coast, Wendy had reservations about sharing their romantically meagre living conditions with Tom's newly aggressive ego and felt annoyed that he had taken it upon himself to include Carly in the invitation.

Wendy's relationship with Carly had soured daily since Tom had first broadcast the news of their affair. Wendy couldn't explain to herself why, but she felt like she had been betrayed by them both, and she was sick to the back teeth of their constant bragging about the delights of Tantrik sex. Carly seemed to have turned Tom into some kind of sexually voracious Mormon and Wendy found their patronising and embarrassing attempts to proselytise her almost obscene. She'd begun to see another side to Carly, a pushy arrogance, perhaps a sneering disdain, as if she were hiding some kind of desire for vengeance behind her seemingly permanent half-smile, and it struck Wendy that if she *had* been secretly in love with Tom, she would have thought their behaviour was a determined effort to unhinge her with jealousy.

As Tom and Carly came out through the ticket barrier Wendy was surprised to see him wearing a shabby linen jacket with a red and white spotted neckerchief over a loose jersey track suit. He looked dressed for a dance class rather than a week in the wilds of Scotland. Carly was wearing her usual rag-bag mixture of over-colourful hippy clothes topped off by a large floppy velvet hat.

'Hi!'

'Hi!'

'Hiiiiiii!' said Tom.

They all three kissed and hugged with exaggerated warmth. Wendy caught a stale smell on Tom's cheek and knew that they'd had sex on the train.

'Oh, they're so small those cabins, aren't they?' said Tom, standing on tiptoe and stretching himself in the exaggerated manner of an actor warming up, flopping forward to let his head dangle between his knees before slowly pulling himself back up to the vertical, vertebra by vertebra. 'And I don't know why they call them sleepers.' He smirked at Wendy who didn't know what reaction was expected of her and she turned to look at Carly who grinned back at her like the cat that got the cream. Tom waited until Wendy looked back his way then ostentatiously took Carly's face in his hands and planted a huge soft-lipped kiss on her mouth. 'I love you,' he said, and beamed back at Wendy.

Wendy smiled politely, picked up one of Carly's bags and headed off to the Range Rover, struggling to change the subject. 'At least the four-wheel drive's slightly more useful up here than it is in London,' she said, unlocking the back of the car and hoicking Carly's tote bag into the boot.

'Heh, hang on, let me do that,' said Tom.

She felt his long arms on either side of her helping to lift the bag and couldn't tell whether the forearm brushing across one of her breasts was accidental or not.

210

By the time they'd made the hour-long journey down through the crisp, clear, lakeside splendour of Loch Linnhe to the Corran ferry, across into the 1950s time warp of rural Scotland, and on to Strontian – the last village before the rough mountain track that climbed three miles up a deserted valley to the isolated farmhouse they'd rented – Wendy had completely tired of Tom's continuously repeated assertion that the dome-topped mountains reminded him of Carly's breasts. She screeched to a sudden stop outside the village store. 'Look, I'm sorry, there's a bit of shopping I've forgotten to do. Would you just stay with the car while I shoot off for a moment?' she asked, and rushed off without waiting for a response.

Julian was sitting in clear blue sunshine on the edge of a small corrie carved into the head of the valley high above their farmhouse. Behind him the boys were fishing in the crystal waters of a large pool. He squinted down at the grim-looking farmhouse far below and wondered why Wendy had turned down the amenity-infested house overlooking Fort William which the film company had arranged and opted for this one way out in the sticks with no electricity, gas, or central heating. A yearning for the simple life was easy to understand, but for the lack of facilities available in Gleann a'Bhuic he thought they might as well have stayed in the burned-out shell of their London home. Though, strangely, he'd come to love it, and he was dreading Tom's imminent intrusion.

It had been a fraught journey up from London in the car – two days' driving with a night in a plastic motel just off the M6 to increase the tension. As a non-driver he was always the spare grown-up stuck with the onerous task of keeping the boys entertained, fed and watered, and settling their interminable arguments. He'd bought a tape of 'Traditional Scottish Music' in Tyndrum to use as an emergency distraction should he need one on the final leg of the journey. Crossing the bleak, boggy wilderness of Rannoch Moor on the A82 the boys had started an argument about who could hold his breath the

longest – Batman or Robin. Julian had slipped the tape out of
its cellophane wrapper and slotted it into the tape deck as they
came down off the moor and entered the awesome, cathedral-
like majesty of Glen Coe. He had opened his window, taken
in the first chill mouthfuls of real mountain air and turned the
volume up high. The loud, lamenting whine of a lone piper
playing 'Amazing Grace' had filled the car, shocking the boys
into silence – its piercing sound pinning them to their seats –
the sudden trills like energetically plaintive machine-gun fire.
The second verse came round and the lone piper was joined
by a whole mass of pipes and drums in a skirling frenzy of
stirring noise and emotion. Julian had felt the top of his head
lift off with the rawness of it all – the sudden, humbling
intensity of the landscape, the wail of the pipes, the rattle of
the drums, the sheer volume which was bouncing the speakers
against their homes in the car doors; the fire; his life; the past
and the future – and hadn't known whether to shout out some
kind of war cry at the top of his voice, or cry. The hairs all
over his head had seemed to stand to attention as he'd looked
up at the almost unbelievable mass of the Three Sisters, their
tops concealed by wisps of spiralling cloud which might have
hidden the very stairway to heaven. Tears had welled in his
eyes and braving a glance towards Wendy he'd seen that her
eyes were misty and primed as well. As he'd tentatively reached
out a hand, she had taken it gladly, and had squeezed so hard
that the stone of her diamond engagement ring had cut into
the newly formed scar tissue of his fingers. Decelerating as a
car in front of them slowed to pull into a lay-by Wendy had
to pull her hand from his to change gear, and as 'Amazing
Grace' came to an end and was replaced by a jauntily second-
rate orchestra fighting its way through a medley of Scottish
dance tunes, Wendy had turned down the volume and wiped
the tears from her cheeks with the back of her hand.

'Noël Coward,' she'd said.

'No, trad. arranged,' said Julian, inspecting the listing on
the back of the cassette box, 'it's an old Scottish song.'

'No, it was Noël Coward who said something pithy about the potency of cheap music.'

She'd been right of course, but even though she'd pricked the emotional bubble of the moment, now, as he sat looking down at the slim hold of the homestead on the hard land, Julian realised it had been the first moment of a new beginning.

'I'm not going to drink until I've finished the first week's filming,' he'd said to Wendy as they'd carted their baskets round the leanly stocked shelves of the miserable local store at the start of their sojourn. It was partly a vain effort to tighten up the slack in his jowls before committing himself to celluloid, but mostly an honest attempt to give the new beginning a chance, and he knew Wendy would appreciate the scale of the gesture.

He'd been shocked by the primitiveness of the house – he imagined that the PA at the film production office must have sent Wendy the details out of spite for being so huffy about the first house – two storeys of dour grimness and unfriendly windows beneath a grey slate roof with harled walls of peeling, dirty-white paint. The sense of isolation was extreme. Their only neighbour within six hundred feet above sea level being Dougal, a filthy, grease-faced farmer who lived at the back of the house in a disintegrating caravan amongst a messy clutch of outhouses in which he was illegally breeding turkeys for the Christmas market, and who was hardly ever there – he seemed to disappear every evening on a small piece of farm machinery and come back looking even worse for wear the next afternoon to feed his birds and have a quick kip in his rank-scented hovel before setting off again in the evening – and when they did see him his accent was so thick as to be almost impenetrable.

''Twis biggid tae faur up the glen, ken. Ca' winter ye cannae git up aa doon wi'oot a tractor.'

'So . . . how do you get up and down?' Wendy had asked falteringly.

'Al hae a tractor. Ainly a wee ain.'

Julian hadn't understood the reply and since then had left

all communications to Wendy. She had tried to ingratiate herself with Dougal by ordering a turkey for Tom and Carly's first night.

The only thing Julian had liked about the house on first appreciation was that it didn't have a phone. But now, after only a week, it somehow felt like home. He could breathe better, not just in terms of feeling recovered from the effects of smoke inhalation, but in terms of not feeling the tightness across his chest any more. Maybe it was the air, not drinking, not having any work to do – the excuse of the rehearsals and make-up calls hadn't been mentioned since the first day, despite Bill's rather wordless and uneasy visit midweek – or the hard, physical labour of splitting logs and hauling them in for the stove. They were in bed by ten every night, partly through dog-tiredness and because there was no television, and partly for the fun of making love in the pitch-black and freezing cold, trying to keep their extremities beneath the covers. He felt strangely untroubled and wondered if what he felt was happiness.

The boys seemed happy – enjoying the pioneer spirit of the great outdoors and the concentrated attention of their parents. They kept asking what time it was and gleefully working out what their less fortunate classmates would be up to. *Their father had even made them some fishing poles!*

'I don't think there are any fish in this lake, Daddy,' said Sean, looking up from the big pool.

'No, I don't think so as well.'

'Yes, either that or these nails are too big,' said Julian, taking Sean's pole and examining his handiwork. The half-inch nails he'd twisted into hooks were the smallest ones he'd managed to find in Dougal's scruffy shed.

'Or they don't like cheese,' said Jamie, lifting the small lump of New Zealand cheddar from his 'hook' and popping it into his mouth.

'Don't talk nonsense – all fish like cheese.'

214

'Look, there's Mummy!' shouted Sean, pointing down into the valley.

'Look, there's Mummy!' shouted Jamie.

'Look, there's Mummy!' mimicked Julian, making them laugh.

They all watched the car battle its dusty way up the track between the felty smoothness of the steep valley walls, like a matchbox model in a railway-modeller's fantasy. The air was so hard and clean and the sun so bright that everything was in an almost dreamlike, pin-sharp focus. Julian could see way out beyond the bounds of his own green and brown mottled valley to the heavy, purple peaks of Moidart across Loch Shiel, and glancing back down at the tiny Range Rover inching along the valley floor to the matchbox house with its miniature outbuildings, he was awed by the scale of the place. He breathed in deeply and sighed contentedly.

'Come on then, I suppose we'd better get back down,' he said.

'Yes, because Uncle Tom will be there.'

'Yeah, Uncle Tom.'

'Yes – *isn't* it a treat?'

It was a half-hour walk back down to the valley floor and Julian watched with interest as the car pulled up outside the house and three ant-like figures emerged and began to carry bags inside. Sean and Jamie waved and shouted to get their attention.

'Mummy!'

'Uncle Tom!'

'Aunty Carly!'

The tiny figures stopped and looked round, shielding their eyes from the sun and scanning the mountainsides until they spotted the bright yellow jackets of the madly waving boys and waved back.

'*Aunty* Carly?' asked Julian. 'How long have you known her?'

'Uncle Tom told us to call her Aunty.'

'Yeah, Uncle Tom said.'

'Hmmn.' Julian motioned them to carry on down the slope and squinted at 'Aunty' Carly as she followed Tom and Wendy into the house. All he could make out from so far away was that she wasn't fat and that she was wearing some kind of floppy, hippy hat, and in a kind of reflex reaction he wondered whether he might be able to charm a shag out of her, then berated himself for defiling the spirit of the last week with Wendy and wondered darkly whether his desires might be some kind of a genetic disorder.

Seconds later Tom bounced back out through the door of the house, minus his jacket, and began bounding up the valley wall towards them. He loped ostentatiously up the slope, springing from incline to incline like a gazelle, and the boys skipped down as fast as they could to meet him. Julian hung back and felt the bitter poison of undisguised loathing spread through his veins. It was like watching a Hovis advert – he could hear the mournful brass band in the background and the bluff, bass, northern tones of the voice-over.

But he was glad to see that Tom had misjudged the distance – after five minutes of leaping he was still a long way off and though he reduced his athleticism to a stiff walk for a while, and untied his neckerchief to mop his face, he soon had to stop altogether and bend over double as he massaged the aching stitch in his ribs. By the time the boys got down to him Julian had caught up with them and was able to savour Tom's discomfort.

'How ... you ... doing ... guys,' said Tom, trying to smile through gritted teeth. He was dripping with sweat and clutching his side, looking positively ill, and as he bent forward to ease the pain Julian could see the beginnings of a bald spot through the lank hair plastered to the overreacher's head.

'Are you all right, Uncle Tom?'

'Yeah, you look sick.'

'No ... I'm fine ... come and give your Uncle Tom a big hug.'

216

The boys were hesitant in their willingness to hug this new, grey-faced, skull-like Uncle Tom, but shuffled towards him dutifully until they were close enough for him to wrap an arm round each of them. They looked uncomfortable cradled in his sweaty grasp, and found it hard to conceal their disgust as he squatted and pressed their fearful faces into the damp chest of his track suit. They were visibly relieved when he suddenly released them to fold his arms tight across this chest. 'Just got to get my breath back . . . it was a bit steeper than I thought.'

'Look, why don't you two stay here with Tom and help him down when he's better, and I'll go on and see Mummy,' said Julian.

'No, we want to come with you.'

'Hey guys . . .' said Tom, 'I'm fine now . . . we can all go together.' He struggled to his feet, grabbed a hand each from Sean and Jamie and began a modest descent down into the valley.

Julian was so pleased to be the twins' preferred choice of walking partner that he decided to walk down faster and leave them behind with the slightly frightening, unappealing alternative, in order to rub it in. Though he was careful not to walk too fast – he didn't want to work up even the slightest sheen of perspiration. They called out a couple of times for him to slow down but he ignored them and pressed on, and by the time he reached the house they were two or three minutes behind.

Wendy was unloading shopping bags from the car and Julian immediately ran over to help – he would prove himself the ideal father *and* husband. He was amazed at how fit and active he felt after not drinking for six days. Taking two bags in each hand he yanked them out of the boot and was surprised to hear the familiar clinking of bottles. He looked through a small gap into the bag.

'Wine? Tom doesn't drink. And I thought his girlfriend didn't either.'

'No, but I do.'

Julian weighed the bag in his hand. 'There's four or five bottles in here.'

'Yes. Well, I thought you might be ready to break your vow after a couple of hours with the sex evangelists.'

Julian looked puzzled.

'You'll see,' said Wendy, slamming the tailgate down and heading back into the house. Julian followed after her into the kitchen.

'You haven't met Carly, have you?' said Wendy, thrusting tins of beans into the cupboard beneath the primitive work surface.

Julian turned to see a figure by the door and was instantly paralysed – rooted to the spot by open-mouthed incredulity and rushing panic – it was the psycho fan!

'Pleased to meet you,' said Carly, offering her hand, her lopsided grin stretched to its meagre limits, her eyes dancing with a vicious merriment.

Julian thought he was going to faint.

'Wendy, I hate to tell you this,' said Carly, as Julian threw out a hand to steady himself against the kitchen table, 'but the truth is I've been having a love affair with your husband for the last eight years.'

Julian could feel his knees buckling beneath him. He felt as if he'd swallowed an enormous cannonball that was pressing down between his hips. Wendy stood and turned.

'With his work, I mean,' said Carly. 'I just love his sense of humour.'

28

The revelation that Carly was Lilith was the psycho fan had shocked Julian to the marrow. He felt as if his hair must have turned white, and couldn't believe that Wendy hadn't noticed his terrified reaction. He'd been glad that Tom and the boys had walked through the door a minute later – glad of the opportunity to kneel and hug Sean and Jamie, and hide the uncontrollable tremble in his knees – but it hadn't been enough to check the spine-weakening fear of imminent nemesis that seemed to hang on Carly's every word as she carried on toying with him, saying how some of his best work had given her 'actual physical pleasure'.

He'd found himself desperately trying to remember exactly what she'd said as he'd been leaving her flat. *Had she definitely said 'video tape'? Could he have misheard? Could he just deny all knowledge of her if she blabbed?* No, he knew he was trapped.

Carly's eyes were so manic, burning like small fires behind her bloodless, grinning face, yet at the same time Julian could see how Wendy might not be able to notice the madness through the masquerade of bonhomie and social pleasantries; he was struck dumb at the thought that he was in the presence of a genuine psychopath – a psychopath who seemed to hold his increasingly fragile future in her hands.

It had been as if his head were on the block, the axe man taking jokey little swings at his bared neck but pulling back just before the moment of annihilation – the moment of divulgence and exposure that could wreck his new-found happiness – and he'd kicked himself for inflicting this on Wendy

219

and himself just when they'd seemed on the verge of a new dawn.

Every nerve in his body had screamed out to flee Carly's presence as soon as he was sure he could walk without collapsing to the floor, but when the twins had insisted on showing her the turkeys – just as Tom had been disappearing up the stairs to wash and change, and Wendy had been busying herself with the lunch – Julian had felt paternally bound to go along and protect them from Carly and her poisoned mind. It had suddenly seemed imperative for him to police her every move until the fateful moment came – like a prisoner keeping watch over his executioner.

Finding Dougal amongst the scruffy outhouses had been another huge disappointment, especially as he'd made some barely intelligible noises about the turkey Wendy had ordered and had ominously taken them to the shed in which he kept the larger turkeys normally reserved for breeding, the new crop not yet having much flesh on them as it was still only October.

Since they'd left what, on reflection, seemed to Julian to be the relative safety of the kitchen, Carly's demeanour had changed. She was now slightly nervous and shaky having cut Julian out from the flock of adults, and tried to push herself up against him and nuzzle herself in under his arm, but Julian grabbed a hand each from Sean and Jamie and that seemed to stop her game – or was forcing her to take another direction, for, as they stood before the fearsome-looking turkeys in the stinking shed, she launched into a discussion with Dougal about how many females a male turkey could mate with at the same time, all the while keeping a sniggering and suggestive eye on Julian.

'Afftimes a cupple o' bubblycocks'll ficht fir up til twae hoors, just tae prove wha's top dug – an' it's ainly the top dug wha gits the queens. Ye micht find a few wee loons wha's bin jilted i' haughmagandie all's life!' Dougal McIntyre said, laughing hoarsely, his rheumy eyes glistening gleefully.

'He says that some of them will fight for nearly two hours to decide who's the best, and that the winner gets the girls – that an unsuccessful cock might spend his whole life without having any sex at all,' Carly translated, as if further to prove to Julian just how mad she was, by being the only one to understand Dougal's accent. 'What about the successful ones?' she'd asked Dougal.

'They can dee it wi' as mony as they lik. Jammy buggers,' Dougal said, throwing his head back in a roar of spit and bad breath, before opening a wire-mesh door and letting himself into the pen of turkeys. Carly gave Julian a knowing smirk, and Julian looked away uncertainly into the cage where Dougal seemed to be practising a kind of t'ai chi in readiness for pouncing on one of the birds.

There were five turkeys in the cage and Julian reflected on what strange animals they were, with their pompous demeanour and awkward, strutting gait, neither wild nor particularly tame. The ugly fleshy caruncles on their heads that made them look like they were wearing their brains on the outside, and the wattles that hung like three huge goitres at their necks had reminded him of alien life forms in *Star Trek*.

Then Dougal suddenly struck out with surprising agility and captured one of the turkeys, swiftly getting it out of the cage and slamming the door behind him, gripping its body under his arm and holding its neck in one hand. He seemed to delight in frightening the twins, breathing his beery fumes over them through bright yellow teeth, and forcing them to stroke the turkey's carunculated head and pull on its ridiculous snood.

It escaped from Dougal's grasp though, just after he carried it into the slaughtering shed next door, and as Julian flattened himself against the wall with Carly and the boys the turkey displayed a surprising turn of speed, leading Dougal in a wild turkey chase round a rusting obstacle course of abandoned farm machinery, almost causing him to fall headlong into the dangerous-looking spikes of a massive pitch-pole harrow. The turkey hollered out its startlingly loud, guttural gobble and jumped in the air, beating its crumpled wings, pecking and scratching, occasionally fanning its glistening bronze tail feathers and puffing up its chest in an attempt to intimidate but looking like nothing so much as a kind of crap peacock. If Julian hadn't been so frightened and disgusted he'd have laughed.

As Julian looked at the distraught bird hanging upside down from the giant hook on the wall where Dougal had left it, he felt a savagely sympathetic pity for its plight. It was tightly trussed with baler twine, turning its head rapidly from side to side and darting its frightened eyes in all directions – as if in full knowledge of its impending doom and hoping against hope for the sudden arrival of the seventh cavalry.

Julian was desperate to get the boys out of the corrugated-iron shack that served as Dougal's abattoir before the killing began but felt held by Carly's unspoken threat to spill the beans. He thought of Wendy and tried to imagine if there was a way of calling Carly's bluff and trying to talk his way out of it, perhaps even by coming clean about the whole affair, but all he could think of was that Wendy would never have ordered the turkey if she'd known her boys were going to have to watch it die, and it merely served to compound his guilt for letting it happen.

'Noo,' said Dougal, pushing Sean and Jamie over to a greasy metal cabinet in the corner of the shack, 'whit ain o'these d'ye reckon I use tae kill the bud?' he asked, proudly opening it to reveal an array of gruesome-looking knives, cleavers and other tools.

'What did he say, Daddy?' asked Sean.

'He's asking which one of the knives you think he'll use to kill the turkey with,' said Carly.

'Aye, 'at's it. I'd bet ye hunnerd tae ain ye'll nivver guess,' said Dougal, pulling the two boys in close to him to get a better view. The boys looked anxiously back at their father with puzzled little frowns on their faces.

'I think he wants you to pick one,' said Julian, and they turned back to the cabinet.

'That one,' said Sean, pointing to a gnarled and ancient cleaver.

'No, that one,' said Jamie, daring to touch the handle of a long, serrated carving knife.

'Ye're wrang, baith o'yers,' shouted Dougal, throwing his head back with a roar of laughter, 'es is the wee bugger!'

'The screwdriver?'

'Nae, it's a chusle!' Dougal said, brandishing the long, thin instrument dangerously close to their faces.

'What did he say?' asked the boys, turning to their father.

'I think he said it was a chisel – that's what it looks like, anyway,' said Julian.

'Aye, a bonny, sleekit chusle. Noo, awa' ye come,' he said, shoving the boys over to where the turkey was hanging from it's hook, 'ye'll be wintin' tae staan here tae git a guid luik at it.'

'Look, I'm not really sure . . .' started Julian.

'Oh don't be such a prude, Julian,' said Carly, taking her opportunity to grab Sean and Jamie's hands firmly and keep them facing the ill-fated bird. 'It's good for them to see how food's prepared. Everyone's so used to buying meat beautifully wrapped in a little polystyrene tray off some supermarket shelf – people ought to be more in touch with what they're eating and where it comes from.'

Dougal squinted at her uncomprehendingly, shook his head wearily, and carried on regardless. 'Ye grab the beak, mind,' he said, grabbing the bird's beak, 'ye prise it apen, lik' 'at, slide in the chusle – an' 'is is the tricky pairt – ye hiv tae feel fair the saft pairt i' the raif o' the bud's mou', an' 'en you stick 't in haird lik' 'is,' he said, feeling for the soft part in the roof of the bird's mouth and sticking the chisel in hard. The turkey squawked violently, its eyes flashing an all too human look of complete desperation before rolling back in on themselves. 'Gie it a quick quarter-turn,' he said, twisting the chisel, and the bird sagged lifelessly in its bindings as if its weight had suddenly increased tenfold, 'an' 'ere's it.'

'You see, it was quite painless, wasn't it?' Carly asked the boys.

'Is it dead now?' asked Sean.

'It's nae ainly deed, bit whan it's bin killid lik' 'at it's awfu' easy tae pluck,' said Dougal, ambling off to his metal cabinet to dip his chisel in a jar of filthy-looking disinfectant.

'Does that mean it's dead, Daddy?' asked Jamie.

'Yes,' said Julian, feeling rather sick.

'And it wasn't that gruesome either, was it?' Carly asked Julian, as Dougal wandered back from his corner with a long, thin, much-sharpened knife in his hands.

'All ye hef tae dee noo is let it drain,' Dougal said, deftly slipping the blade in behind the turkey's throat and pulling it down and forwards with a flick of his wrist. The turkey's neck opened up and its blood cascaded out, bouncing off the wooden table below and spattering the boys' faces.

29

At least the slaughter gave Julian legitimate cause for excusing himself from Carly's presence for a time, as he ensconced himself in the rudimentary bathroom with Wendy and the boys to scrub the blood from their tiny bodies, safe in the knowledge that none of his family could learn anything untoward about him whilst they were all locked together in the same room.

But as the day wore on Julian found himself increasingly trying to keep the whole company in the same room – forcing everyone to help Wendy in the kitchen, or factitiously cheering Tom on as he had a go at splitting logs – in the belief that there was safety in numbers. And to his relieved satisfaction, the presence of the whole gang seemed to quell the needling and dangerous spirit within Carly and make her momentarily impotent. He was sure that the respite was only fuelling her increasing desire to betray him – that she was only bottling up the bombshell for later, but felt content to hide away from immediate confrontation and glad of the opportunity to try to get his head around some solution to his predicament other than lying down on the floor and playing dead – it had worked for Basil Fawlty, he thought bitterly to himself, but this was real life.

'Have we got any more of this?' Julian asked, two dimly lit hours into the tortuous dinner that evening that seemed to have gone on for an eternity. The tallow candles Wendy had bought for 'authenticity' had filled the room with a fug of smoke that reeked of the chip-fryer in a fast-food outlet, and produced less light than a ten-watt bulb.

'More of what?' asked Wendy, peering through the cande-

225

labra which virtually obscured Julian altogether, to see him waving the third empty bottle of red in the murky glow of the candles. 'Oh yes,' she said, scraping her chair back. 'It's in the pantry.'

'The pantry!' guffawed Tom from his side of the dinner table, and he was joined by Carly's high-pitched cackle opposite. 'How very highfalutin.'

'Well, what would you call it then, Tom?' asked Wendy, her hackles rising. She'd grown tired of the evening – of Tom and Carly's superior attitude, of their constant sexually orientated hectoring, and of trying to maintain an air of politeness through the conversation that seemed to bounce endlessly back and forth from the banal to the patronising – and had got through the best part of a bottle on her own. She'd never perceived Tom as plain stupid before, as a blabbering, pretentious idiot high on self-importance with no regard for rational deduction in his argument. Remembering how sweet and loving Julian had been all week in Tom's absence, Wendy wondered whether Julian had been right all these years in his frequently repeated assertion that Tom was a 'complete wanker'.

'Well, I don't know, but I wouldn't call it the *pantry*!' sniggered Tom.

'Well *what* then? The larder? The scullery? The walk-in cupboard where we keep the food and other household necessities?' Wendy's eyes burned dark and furious in the meagre candlelight. 'It's only a room for God's sake – we have to give it a name otherwise we have to describe its whole function every time we refer to it!' The room went quiet and she started to rise.

'It's all right, I'll get it,' said Julian, moving quickly from the table, clutching his napkin to his groin and weaving towards the door.

'Maybe it's these upper-class tendencies that are repressing you sexually,' said Tom after a pause.

'Are you truly happy with your sex life?' asked Carly.

Julian closed the kitchen door on the conversation and leaned against it, thankful for the respite and the comparatively bright light of the paraffin lamp hanging from a hook in the middle of the ceiling. On the kitchen table in front of him lay Sean and Jamie's dinner plates, each wiped clean save for mounds of turkey slices that had been left untouched despite hearty mountain appetites. They'd gone to bed extremely worried that the blood would never wash out of their *Lion King* sweatshirts, and Julian had had to promise to buy replacements before they would snuggle down under their blankets.

He looked down and felt his aching erection subside – Carly had had her hand on his cock for almost the entire meal. He'd tried shifting his chair as far from her as possible but the gate-leg of the table had got in his way and her arm seemed to be six feet long. The back of his hand was scratched and streaked with blood from his attempt to move her hand away.

The constant threat of discovery, of spoiling the new beginning and laying open the past, had left him neurotically weak and mentally exhausted. He'd been slurping down red wine like Ribena to get his head out of the situation, or foster brewer's droop, and had been concentrating hard on a concocted image of his own paraplegic, piss-reeking grandmother, uncharacteristically and unflatteringly garbed in suspenders and a peek-a-boo bra, in an effort to douse his unwelcome state of sexual arousal. But Tom had gone on and on describing coital positions in explicit detail which would 'stir the lotus between the perinaeum and the anus' and awaken 'kundalini, the serpent of truth' who would climb his 'sushumna' and burst through the top of his head, providing him with a blissful insight into the 'supreme truth'. And apparently all Julian and Wendy had to do was abandon their tight-arsed western view of sexuality and yield themselves to the pursuit of positive, unconstricted pleasure and they too could use their sexually awakened energy as 'spiritual rocket-fuel' on a journey to enlightenment. And as Tom had painstakingly described the intimacy of his daily congress with Carly, she had been masturbating Julian under the table, managing to break through the final barrier of his zipper as Tom, in hushed tones, had revealed with narcissistic pride that Carly had made a shrine to him in her flat.

As memories of his own shrine and the extraordinary blow-job Carly had given him flooded into his mind, Julian dashed from the kitchen to the lavatory and masturbated furiously, coming almost immediately and feeling a post-orgasmic relief that he wouldn't be able to entertain any more thoughts of sex for at least an hour.

He flushed the toilet and made his way back through the kitchen to the pantry or larder, scanned the shelves feverishly and was astonished to find ... a bottle of Jim Beam! He couldn't believe his luck. Was this proof that Wendy was the most brilliant woman on earth? he asked himself. Mother of his children, lover, protector – he wondered who else could have anticipated his need so perfectly.

He twisted off the top, sniffed at the bottle, savouring its familiar caramel aroma, then put it to his lips and drank heavily, enjoying the satisfying fire in his belly and the promise of being wiped out.

Wendy really was the one, he thought to himself as he took another slug, and having her and one of his casual fucks sitting at the same table only served to hammer the point home. And Wendy was beautiful, he said to himself, she was it, she was strong and calm and loving. He wanted to carry her up to their freezing bedroom and make love to her, and promise never to leave her, and confess, and start over – using his confession as the proof of his love. *Fuck London, fuck work, fuck fame, they could become crofters on some faraway island, just them and the boys against the elements, in tune, in love, happy.*

He raised the bottle to his lips again and heard Wendy's voice raised in heated debate in the dining room. He knew she needed his help as he imagined her sitting there all alone against the forces of psychotic bullshit, and he realised that he was the one to help her. He would be her champion! – no matter how much cock clamping he had to endure. He lifted another bottle of red from the shelf, *for Wendy, his brave drinking companion*, and moved through into the kitchen, but reaching the dining room door he lost his impetus and stood listening to Tom's pompous pontificating for a moment.

'This reliance on logic, on "acceptable behaviour", on perceiving the visible world as the only reality is screwing everyone up – it's making people unhappy. The Tantrika says, "Fuck all that – let's rouse every single thread of emotion and pleasure within us, take them to the highest heights, and use the energy we produce to give us some knowledge about who we really are – where we've come from" – that's all I'm saying.'

'And all I'm saying,' said Wendy, 'is that if you need all this ridiculous, hippy mumbo-jumbo to get a good fuck, then fine, arouse the lotus between your perinaeum and your anus as much as you like – just don't expect the rest of us to jump up and down shouting "Wow – they really know where it's at!" because it's just the vacuous prattle of the intellectually moribund desperate for an easy fix on life. Now, if you don't mind, I'll make a start on the washing-up.'

Julian heard her chair scraping back violently across the flagstone floor, and before he had time to move, the door in front of him was open and Wendy was pushing furiously past him.

'I've got you another bottle of wine,' he offered.

'No thanks,' she said, almost throwing her pile of plates into the sink. She wrenched the tap on and squirted in the washing-up liquid as if she were wringing its neck, scraping the cutlery on the draining board into the sink with a satisfying clatter. Julian sloped up behind her and put his arms around her, still holding a bottle in each hand.

'Thanks for the Jim Beam,' he said, nuzzling her neck. He felt her shoulders relax and she rested her head back against his chest, bringing up a soap-sudded hand to caress his cheek.

'That's all right. I thought you'd need it.'

'I do love you,' said Julian, and he started to cry softly.

'I've come to help you with the washing-up,' said Carly, snaking her hand between Julian's buttocks to pull at his balls. Her sudden appearance and lewd behaviour made Julian jump and he leaped to one side, bringing up the bottles to defend himself in case of actual physical attack. 'Sorry about Tom, Wendy,' Carly carried on, nonchalantly picking up a tea towel as if nothing had just happened between Julian and herself, 'things got a bit heavy just then, didn't they?'

'Let's just forget it, shall we?'

'To tell the truth he hasn't quite understood it completely yet, he's only a novice. I've been practising for years. I could explain it to you if you'd like.'

'I'd rather not.'

'Well then, let's not. You can't learn if you're feeling unreceptive. Let me help you with the washing-up anyway. Why don't you go in and talk to Tom, Julian – he'd like that.'

Carly's assertion that Tom would enjoy a chat with him struck Julian as the absolute final proof of how barking mad she was, but he was glad of the opportunity not to be in the same room as her – he knew it had got to the point in the game where she could blurt it all out at any moment, and somehow it no longer seemed relevant whether he was in the room when it happened, or not. In fact, the stronger his feelings for Wendy grew the more he was coming round to the conclusion that he'd rather not be there to witness the hurt when the bullet hit, and he staggered gratefully through into the dining room where Tom was still at the table, sitting in his chair in the lotus position with his eyes closed. Julian sat down opposite and filled a wineglass to the brim with bourbon.

'I think it's about time you and I had a little chat,' Carly said to Wendy, closing the door to the dining room and returning to the draining board to dry some forks.

Wendy was in no mood for a 'chat' and kept her gaze fixed on the contents of the sink, industriously taking her frustrations out on the dirty crockery.

230

'Let's talk about Porto Corveiro, shall we?' said Carly, stunning Wendy into immediate stillness.

'Carly, I'm really not in the mood,' said Wendy with quiet forcefulness, feeling stung by how much of their history Tom must have shared with this arrogant young witch.

'I think the incident there stands up to some scrutiny,' said Carly, the annoying whine in her voice somehow accentuated by the analyst's intonation that she now assumed. 'Because it was in Porto Corveiro that you and Tom had sex together for the first and only time, wasn't it?'

'No!' Wendy was incensed, but felt equally keen not to fall into the trap of sanctioning Carly's argument by joining in, and refrained from saying more.

'Well, whether you did or you didn't, I was wondering whether the reason you haven't slept with him at all, or since, is that you're afraid to admit to yourself that you're a lesbian. As I see it, you've always seen Tom as essentially female – that's why you've always been drawn to him.'

Wendy more or less threw a plate onto the draining board, then pulled herself up short. She called on her reserves of forbearance and understanding, got a grip of herself, turned to Carly, and smiled condescendingly. 'Please understand that in the short time you've known me we have never had a conversation of any real depth; that whatever Tom may have chosen to tell you about my past may be erroneous or indeed complete fabrication; and that therefore you are in no position at all to make wild pronouncements upon me or my sexual orientation. And I'd really rather you didn't. Now, do you need a fresh tea towel?'

Wendy's calm, polite but firm rebuttal seemed to subdue Carly. She nodded her assent on the matter of a dry towel and the pair of them continued the washing-up in silence for a while.

'I just think it would be an awful shame,' said Carly, starting shakily but gaining in confidence as she went on, 'if you lived your whole life without being true to yourself. I think you ought to let yourself go, and that you should sleep with whoever you want to. You can sleep with me if you like. Or sleep with Tom, and I'll sleep with Julian if it would make you feel less guilty. I know Julian fancies me, I can just tell. He never looks at me and always tries to move away from me whenever he can – which is a sure sign, isn't it?'

Wendy quickly finished the pan she was holding, threw the rest into the sink to soak, dried her hands and disappeared through the back door.

In the dining room Julian was sipping peacefully at his drink but keeping a careful watch on Tom, who still had his eyes closed. He watched with disdain as Tom slowly pressed the palms of his hands together, as if in prayer, then lifted them up and rested them on the crown of his head.

'Ommmm,' Tom chanted, letting the sound reverberate around his skull.

'Oh, shut up,' spat Julian in disgust at Tom's pretentiousness.

Tom opened his eyes and feigned surprise to see Julian there at all. 'Sorry, didn't see you there,' he said, taking his hands down from his head, 'must have been in a trance.'

'Don't give me that,' said Julian. 'I may not have a degree but I can spot a complete wanker when I see one.'

Tom flinched at the ferocity of Julian's attack, but then recovered, smiling broadly to himself as he leaned back in his chair. 'Is Bill Tyndall still the director on your film?' he asked.

Julian looked bemused and didn't reply.

'Yes, I liked him,' said Tom, grinning conceitedly. 'I'm sorry I couldn't do the film – for his sake really.'

Julian tried to hide his utter fury and paranoia that Tom had had anything to do with the film by burying his nose in his bourbon, but lifted the glass too quickly and spilt some down the front of his jumper.

'Oh, didn't you know?' Tom carried on. 'Sorry, I thought you must have known – you're playing the part I turned down.' He grinned triumphantly, baring his teeth in self-satisfaction.

'Well, I only had a six-week break before *Hamlet* went back into the repertory, and I thought, "Too much like hard work", you know. Besides which, I didn't really think the script was very good.'

Julian could hardly believe it. It seemed that Tom was calmly taking over his professional life completely. His mind reeled with the imagined treachery of Bill Tyndall. *So he'd preferred Tom had he? But Tom had turned him down, so he'd come crawling back to Julian with stories of fighting for him tooth and nail!* It occurred to Julian that the only thing he had left that Tom didn't have a hand in was Wendy, and that Tom's spiteful girlfriend, Julian's very own ex-one-night-stand, was with Wendy in kitchen as he sat there, and could be about to obliterate his marriage at any moment.

Or was Tom calling his bluff?

'What do you mean, the script isn't good enough? It was written by Steve Martin's writers!' he said, taking a huge draught of bourbon and immediately cursing himself for taking the bait.

Tom laughed condescendingly. 'It was written by two guys who once wrote about three lines of a sketch for Steve Martin on *Saturday Night Live*. Wise up, Julian – it's not like you to be quite so stupid – why do you think you're making it in Scotland?'

'Because it looks like Montana!'

'Montana looks like Montana – why not do it there?'

'Because it's cheaper here.'

'The whole film is cheap, Julian – it's an ex-Hollywood, small time, Channel 4-funded, very "British" film.'

'What about Curt Redwood?'

'Curt who?'

'He's the bright young bastard, the hottest new thing.'

'Ever heard of him before?'

'No, but . . .'

'I rest my case.'

Julian held back from answering as Carly appeared to clear

the table. As she leaned over towards him to reach for the cheese board, her face screened from Tom's view, she pushed her tongue into her cheek in the promise of oral sex and winked a mischievous eye. Then she rose and headed back to the kitchen with her full load, and as she did so Tom slapped her playfully on the behind.

'She's a fantastic-looking woman, isn't she?' he asked Julian as she left the room, then leaned forward confidentially. 'And she gives the best blow-jobs in the world.'

Julian refilled his wineglass with bourbon and slowly emptied it in one visit as a kind of threat. He pulled himself up, stumbled through the gloom to Tom's chair and leaned over him, breathing whisky fumes right into his face. 'Yeah, she's all right as a shag, but I hate it when you get those bits of mud behind your teeth, don't you?'

30

As Julian quickly undressed, struggled into the extra-large T-shirt he was using as a night-shirt, and slipped between the sheets, he had a baleful premonition that this might be his last night in the marital bed and his heart seemed to sink into the mattress beneath him.

As he'd opened the door of the dining room after delivering his savage rejoinder, Tom had slammed it shut again to prevent him from leaving, and asked Julian exactly what he'd meant. Had he met Carly before? Had he been to her flat? But Julian had refused to be drawn on the subject and leaned back casually against the wall smiling impishly and raising his eyebrows in leering, cocky defiance.

Seemingly attracted by the opening and shutting of the door and the belligerent tones of Tom's penetrating stage whispers, Carly had pushed her way into the dining room and found Tom about to wrap his hands around Julian's neck in frustration.

'Tell him you've never even met before,' Tom had whispered angrily, and Carly's face had lit up with obvious pride to see the two men fighting over her.

'Just like a couple of bubblycocks,' she'd said, to their complete incomprehension, as Wendy, ever the perfect middle-class hostess, had bustled through unwrapping the Trivial Pursuit she'd bought in Fort William that morning and which she'd just fetched from the car. She'd suggested that they should all settle down to what she'd naïvely imagined would be an innocuous, dispute-free and slightly boring parlour game – which she'd also imagined she would win.

Julian had managed to grab a seat opposite Carly and had

sat well back so that she couldn't get at him, and he and Tom had slugged it out on the Trivial Pursuit board – Tom fighting hard to be the first to fill his little wheel with the different coloured 'cheeses', and Julian drinking hard and giving ridiculously flippant and inaccurate answers in an effort to show how little he cared about winning or losing, but desperate to win by accident all the same. The whole game was eventually scotched by Julian's blatant cheating – filling his own wheel with cheeses from other people's wheels with such annoying regularity that an argument finally ensued about who'd had how many of which, and the whole thing was given up as a bad job.

Just as they'd packed it in and decided with much common relief to call it a night, Carly had said, 'It'd be a much more interesting game if you were allowed to write a few questions of your own, wouldn't it?'

No one had taken her up on her enquiry. Julian's heart had skipped a beat.

'Like – have you ever been unfaithful to your wife?' Carly had said, pointedly looking at Julian before turning to Wendy and adding, 'or husband?' then looking across at Tom.

The room had gone very quiet, so quiet that Julian was able to hear the small brook outside, over two hundred yards away from the house. Tom had looked perplexed, Carly had grinned mischievously and Julian's heart had pounded against his ribs as he'd waited for what he imagined was the death blow. But as Carly opened her mouth to speak again Wendy had butted in.

'Have you quite finished?' she'd said, fixing Carly with a furiously indignant stare. She'd wanted to say, 'Because I'd just like to say that I have never met anyone as deliberately provocative as you. You seem to delight in using what little misinformation you have to play upon people's fears in a way that would have made Himmler proud – cracking the whip like the ringmaster in some kind of mind circus in the mistaken belief that your actions are justified by some form of outrageous philosophical mysticism. But you're wrong, you're nothing but

236

a pathetic hippy living in the twilight of ill-informed alternative doctrine – a quack medic, a quack psychologist and a quack philosopher – and the sooner you leave this house, the safer we'll all be.' But she hadn't been able to summon up the nerve and after a pregnant pause she'd just said 'Good-night' instead, scraped her chair back, and strode from the room. Julian had followed quickly after her, desperate not to be left alone with Tom and Carly, but mindful to grab the bottle of Jim Beam as he'd made his escape.

Now, as Julian lay in bed, waiting for Wendy to finish her ablutions at the washstand in the corner of the bedroom and to come and join him, and listening to the muffled sounds of Tom and Carly getting ready for bed in the room next door, he slowly came to the conclusion that a confession was all that could save him. He knew that the time bomb in the next room could go off at any minute – Carly was counting out his life like the midnight chimes of the worm-eaten grandfather clock in the hallway below were counting out the end of the day – and he felt he had to beat the clock.

He was thirty-eight, he thought to himself, over half-way through his life, maybe even more so taking into account his alcohol intake. Over the last week he had had his first glimpse of real happiness for nearly a decade. Not the two-dimensional, drunken, orgiastic partying of his lost nights in Soho, but a new kind of happiness that seemed to nourish his body and his soul, and that might have a future, might be ongoing and alive – and this discovery had come to him almost as a spiritual revelation.

Wendy slid into bed beside him and snuggled up close, wrapping her arms around him and clinging to him tightly, partly to get warm, but mostly out of relief.

'Christ, that was a day and a half, wasn't it?' she said, sighing heavily. Her relief at finding sanctuary made her suddenly realise that she had drunk much more than usual, and she felt moved to prolong the pleasantly light-headed sensation. 'Is there any of that Jim Beam left?'

'It's right here,' said Julian, quickly twisting round and snaking an arm out of the bed to reach for the bottle, overjoyed to find Wendy playing the kindred spirit, and lifted by a sudden hope that a greater degree of inebriation on Wendy's part might help the passage of his confession. He passed the Jim Beam to her under the bedclothes and she drank from the bottle, giggled, and handed it back to him. He was reminded of their courting days and the freezing cold room in the Glenthistle Highland Motor Lodge, half-way between Aberdeen and Glasgow, where they'd similarly shared a bottle of champagne under the covers, enjoying a delicious sense of misbehaviour and the smell of each other's bodies. As he took a swig of the bourbon and handed it back to Wendy he reminisced on the zigzag route from Bristol to Gretna Green and calculated that their courting period had amounted to exactly thirty-six days.

Wendy offered him the bottle again but he shook his head, deluding himself that sobriety was on his side. She took another small sip, then screwed the top back onto the bottle and leaned bravely out of bed, into the cold, to place it on her bedside chair and blow out the candle. The room was pitched into instant, inky blackness, and lying there with only the top of his head poking out of the bedclothes, unable to discern any shapes at all in the ebony void, Julian could almost feel the darkness closing in on him as if it had some material form, and felt as if his world was being made inexorably smaller, as if he were about to be smothered – and suddenly panicked to think that this might be the beginning of the end.

'Do you mind if we have the candle back on for a moment,' he said.

Wendy jumped up in bed in alarm at the tremble in his voice. 'What is it? What's the matter?' she said, striking furiously at the matches and breaking two before being able to light the candle, then turning back to confront Julian's confused and troubled face.

'Actually, I've got a confession to make,' he said. He felt

worse than he did on a first night but he had to get it out –
this was his baptism into the new church, the great purging
of his soul, and he shook in the belief that the confession was
his *only* chance at wiping the slate clean and starting again.
'It's about Carly,' he paused. 'She's Charlie Chaplin.'

In the flickering shadow of the solitary candle he watched
Wendy's face as she took a sharp intake of breath, and he
waited to see her grasp the full meaning of what he'd just said
before he continued.

'But she hasn't been around for years!' said Wendy, genuinely shocked.

'She has, I'm afraid. There's hardly been a day in the last
couple of months when she hasn't got me – it feels like she's
been stalking my every move.'

'But you never said.'

'I didn't want to worry you,' he fibbed, feeling as if he'd
dipped his pen in the ink but had just managed to hold off
from blotting his new clean sheet.

'Why didn't you tell me when she arrived?'

'I thought she was a friend of yours, and I didn't want to
hurt you,' Julian said, seeing an image of the pen knocking
against the sides of the ink bottle which rocked precariously
on the desktop above his clean sheet.

There was a pause as Wendy took in the information, during
which Julian thought he could hear Tom and Carly getting
into bed.

'The diary!' Wendy exclaimed suddenly. 'That's how she'd
have known where you were all the time. Whenever she came
round she was always flicking through the diary – the one next
to the phone in the kitchen. She only lives next door, you
know?'

'I know,' said Julian, solemnly.

'Christ, what's she doing here? She must be genuinely
touched! Do you think Tom knows? Quick, we ought to tell
him,' said Wendy in panic, shifting in the bed as if about to

239

get out and run into the room next door and warn him. But Julian pulled her back.

'I don't think it's a problem for Tom at the moment,' said Julian. 'Listen.' They both lay breathlessly still for a moment, cocking their ears, and heard the tell-tale rhythmical squeak of the iron bedstead through the wall.

'Oh Julian, you should have said straightaway,' said Wendy, turning back to wrap herself around him and feeling him starting to crumble emotionally. 'Oh you poor baby, you should have told me, we have to share these things. I can't help you if I don't know, can I? Oh, you must have felt just awful when you saw her standing there in our own kitchen! – I thought you were rather cool at the time.' Julian began to weep quietly at what a bastard he'd been to this kind, loving woman. 'Don't cry darling, don't cry, it'll be all right. Look, we'll just keep a close eye on her over breakfast, and then we'll just have to suggest that they go. As soon as they can.'

'The thing is,' said Julian, trying to hold back his self-pitying tears and steel himself for the moment of truth, perhaps the moment of absolution. 'The thing is . . .' and he paused, interminably weighing up the pros and cons in his confused and frightened mind until he thought his head would explode, then he took a deep breath and said, '. . . you couldn't pass me the Jim Beam, could you?' And as Wendy leaned across to her bedside chair for the bottle, in his mind's eye Julian saw the whole bottle of ink spill onto the virgin sheet of clean white paper, blanking out his good intentions and the new start for ever. And though he felt desperate to attempt a salvage operation, to somehow clean it all up again, the only solution he could think of was to wash it all away with bourbon.

'I don't think we should let her be alone with the boys,' said Wendy.

'No,' said Julian, finishing off the remaining quarter of a bottle in two concentrated visits, then dropping it out of his side of the bed to the floor. 'I think you can turn out the light now.'

Wendy blew out the candle for a second time and Julian fell into unconsciousness listening to the sound of Tom and Carly's increasingly energetic antics from the room next door.

31

The next morning Julian opened his bleary seeing eye and tried to focus on the small travel clock sitting on the chest of drawers. *Half past eleven?* He found it hard to believe, despite the leaden residue of whisky behind his forehead that seemed to be pinning his head back to the pillow. They'd been up with the lark since they'd arrived, except for one attempted lie-in which had proved impossible thanks to the constant racket the boys had made downstairs. *The boys!* His heart leaped into his mouth as he realised he couldn't hear them, and he couldn't help thinking something horrible had happened. *What had Carly done to them?* He shook Wendy urgently by the shoulder.

'Wendy! Wendy! It's half eleven! Where are the boys?'

'What?' said Wendy, snapping into consciousness.

Julian was up and hopping about the room trying to ram his legs into his jeans. 'The boys! I can't hear the boys!' His own shouting echoed round his head like a bowling ball in a dustbin.

Wendy was up and out of the room in a flash, wrapping a towel around her for modesty's sake and flying down the stairs, with Julian struggling after her, fighting to put on his jumper. Bursting into the kitchen together they were met by a scene of absolute calm: the whole place was tidier than it had ever been before, spotted here and there with little vases of freshly picked wild flowers from the valley; a beautifully plaited wreath of straw was hanging above the wood-burning stove; a steaming pot of freshly brewed coffee stood on the table beside an array of attendant cups and saucers; and across the table, leaning languidly back in his chair, was Tom, casually leafing through the *Guardian*.

'Morning all,' he said.

'The boys,' said Wendy, 'where are the boys?'

'They went for a walk with Carly. Up onto the Sgurr.'

Julian rushed to the window that overlooked the big, flat-topped Sgurr na Eanuill. Its walls were grassy and unimposing from this side but he knew there were cliffs on the other and his mind raced with images of the psycho flinging their tiny bodies way out into the nothingness and watching, with a smile on her face, as they broke onto the craggy rocks below and tumbled down the mountainside into the valley. He turned to find Wendy at his side, feverishly scouring the mountainside with the aid of Jamie's plastic Thunderbirds binoculars.

'I've got them!' she said, breathing a huge sigh of relief. 'I've got them – they're all right!'

'Let me look.'

'You see the big gorge with the shadowy bit?'

'Yes.'

'Well they're coming down the green "V" underneath that.'

Julian wildly cast the infuriatingly small binoculars about, cursing and huffing, until he picked up his sons in their bright yellow stormproofs, skipping merrily homewards down the hill, holding Carly's hands. The magnification wasn't strong enough to be able to see their facial expressions but their body language seemed happy enough.

'Heh, they'll be all right, they've got Carly with them,' said Tom. 'What's the panic?'

'Why didn't you go with them?' Wendy screamed at him.

'I didn't really feel up to it – my thigh muscles are a bit sore,' he said defensively, then added more lasciviously, 'Bit of a sex marathon last night, actually. Hope we didn't disturb you too much. Anyway, I borrowed the car and drove down into the village instead to get you some croissants, but they didn't have any. So, fancy a Scottish fancy?' he said, and pushed a plate of garish-looking pastries across the table towards them.

Julian and Wendy used the half-hour it took for the boys to reach the house to breakfast, wash and dress, then sat out in the late-autumn sun by the back door with Tom to keep a watch on them as they strode manfully back to the house.

'Hi you two,' said Wendy, opening her arms to receive them as they ran the last hundred yards towards her. 'You must have got up early.'

'We got up at six o'clock.'

'Carly woke us up.'

'Yeah.'

'She said we were going on an adventure.'

'And we did.'

'Yeah. We went right to the top.'

'With some sandwiches.'

'Yeah, and some orange juice.'

'And we made a cairn.'

'Which is a big pile of rocks.'

'And Carly told us all about Hercules.'

'Hercules?' said Tom, with an avuncular chuckle.

'Yeah, every hundred moons, which is olden talk for months, they used to kill a man called Hercules.'

'And get a new man called Hercules.'

'Yeah – they used to get him drunk.'

'With mead – which is like olden beer.'

'Yeah, like olden beer.'

'Then there was a circle of twelve stones, like cairns, and in the middle was a tree.'

'An oak tree.'

'They used to tie him up to a tree.'

'No, *onto* a tree.'

'*Onto* a tree.'

'Then they used to whip him until . . .'

They paused and looked at each other, then at Carly. She

244

gave them a little shake of the head and a patronising smile as if to say 'Come on, you can remember'.

'. . . until he lost his conscience?' Jamie asked Sean.

'Consciousness,' said Carly.

'Yeah,' said Sean, nodding his head wisely, 'until he lost his conscienceness.'

'Yeah.'

'Then they'd poke his eyes out.'

'With a stick.'

'Yeah.'

'And then they'd get a big knife and cut off his penis.'

'Penis?' said Wendy, darting a questioning look at Carly.

'Yeah,' said Sean, giggling, 'it means your willy.'

'They used to catch all the blood in a bowl and splash it all over themselves and water the garden with it to make everything grow bigger.'

'Then they'd get another big, sharp stick, and they'd stick it through his heart to make him dead.'

'Yeah, then they'd cut his arms off.'

'And his legs off.'

'And they'd cook them on a fire and eat them.'

'And they'd put his penis on a raft with his head and send it down the river.'

'And that's it.'

'Yeah, that's it.'

It had poured out of the boys like a flash flood pushing aside everything before it, and only when the stream of horror and brutality came to an end did Wendy and Julian have time to catch their breath. The silence seemed so sudden and so complete up in the highland wilderness. They looked at each other open-mouthed, then turned to Carly who grinned artlessly back, a teacher proud of how much her students had learned.

'And *then*!' shrieked Jamie, suddenly remembering.

'Yeah, and *then*!' echoed Sean, excited about this last part of the story they'd forgotten to tell.

'*Then* they choosed a new Hercules and all the holy ladies would get drunk and have sex with him.'

'Yeah, they'd all have sex with him!'

The silence came again. Even Tom found it hard not to express a note of disquiet in his face.

'What do you mean by sex?' asked Wendy finally, trying to sound composed.

Sean turned to Carly. 'It's when the man's penis goes into the woman's vagina, isn't it?'

'That's right,' said Carly.

'Yeah, you slide it up and down,' added Jamie.

'Carly says it's very nice.'

'You've done it, haven't you, Daddy?'

Julian paused. 'You'd better ask your mother.'

'Yes, your daddy's done it,' said Carly, laughing, and looking at Julian who clenched his buttocks together and waited for the knock-out punch. 'Otherwise you two wouldn't be alive now, would you?' Carly carried on, and Julian tried to relax again. 'Come on, let's go in and get some hot chocolate.'

'No, it's all right Carly, I'll do that,' said Wendy.

'I can manage.'

'No! I'd rather just have a word with them on their own if you don't mind,' said Wendy, forcing herself between Carly and the boys, and herding them into the kitchen. 'Tom, I wouldn't mind having a word with you as well if that's all right,' she said, and as Tom squeezed sheepishly past into the kitchen she closed the door firmly behind her.

'Come on, let's go and fuck in a shed,' said the psycho fan, shoving a hand up Julian's jumper and grabbing at his belt.

'Fuck off,' said Julian in an angry stage whisper, knocking her hands away and pushing her violently back against the hard granite wall. He roughly propelled her along the side of the building and around the corner to get out of earshot of the kitchen window and pinned her to the wall with his hands around her throat. 'This is crazy! I'm not having an affair with

246

you. It was a mistake, a one-off shag – and not a very good one at that. So stop fucking about. You've got to leave – now.'

'You know Wendy wants to have an affair with Tom, don't you?' said the psycho with a sweet smile, but shaking in the way she used to shake outside the stage doors, full of nervous excitement.

'Shutup!'

'And I know Tom would rather sleep with her than me. Even before I moved into the flat I used to see him waiting around the corner until you'd left, and then watch him go in. He's only going out with me to make her jealous.'

'Just shutup!'

'But it's fair really – the only reason I went out with him was to get to you.'

'Look,' said Julian, recognising an unfathomable scale to her madness and trying to keep a lid on the situation. 'You need help. You've got something wrong with you, and you need help.'

'I'm sleeping with him for you, Julian,' she said, lovingly stroking the hands that still gripped her neck. 'What are you afraid of? You want the life of a bachelor, don't you? I won't tie you down, I'll just be your mistress. One of your mistresses – you can have as many as you like – I don't care.'

It struck Julian that it was the offer he'd always wanted to hear, and if Catriona with the laughing Irish eyes from the National had made the offer to him not four weeks before, he'd probably have snapped it up in a trice. Then he closed his eyes and thought of Wendy, only to be disturbed from his day-dream by Carly who had begun to shake even more and was starting to moan and to gyrate her groin against his thigh.

'Just fuck off!' shouted Julian disgustedly, and set off towards the outhouses.

'You can't walk away from me, you know,' Carly shouted tremulously after him. 'You're mine. You're my Hercules. Nothing can stop that. You've been my Hercules for eight years!'

247

Julian spun on his heel and rushed back over to her, his face only inches from hers, shouting at the top of his voice, 'Well *you're* nothing special to *me*, all right? So just keep away. Keep away from me, my wife, and my family!' She looked deep into his eyes with a questioning, elfish look on her face. 'And don't bother thinking you've got a hold on me because I've already told Wendy all about us. OK?' He saw her flinch. 'I told her last night.'

Her face crumpled for a moment, then eased back into a tentative grin. 'No you didn't.'

'I did,' he said, and strode off purposefully towards the kitchen door.

She shouted after him. 'Sometimes, if they liked the present Hercules enough, they used to kill his tannist instead – his deputy – and keep him to themselves for another eight years!'

Julian pushed angrily at the kitchen door, went inside and slammed it behind him. Wendy was there with the boys who were sitting at the table looking subdued and confused.

'What's she shouting about?' asked Wendy.

'Oh, she's just completely fucking bonkers,' said Julian, wondering if his new ad hoc gambit of pretending to Carly that he'd told Wendy everything would work. 'I wouldn't bother talking to her if I were you. She's bleating on about Hercules now – I think she's cracked.'

'Is Aunty Carly not a nice lady?' asked Jamie timidly from the table.

'No, she's not. And she's not your aunty!' snapped Julian.

'Well, I've had a word with Tom,' said Wendy, resting a soothing pair of hands on his shoulders, 'and they're leaving tomorrow.'

'Tomorrow? Why not today?'

'His tickets aren't valid for today.'

'For Christ's sake – I'll buy him some new ones! What about flying? There must be an airport round here somewhere – I'll rent them a jet!'

She massaged his shoulders. 'Look, keep your voice down,

and let's just leave it as it is. He's my oldest friend. Or was,' she said quietly, looking distraught. 'Tomorrow will do fine.'

'Did you tell him who she was?'

'I couldn't.' She pulled Julian close and hugged him warmly. 'Please, just let it rest until tomorrow. I think this is the end of the line for Tom and me – just let us have one last supper and say our goodbyes. Then we'll be on our own again.'

Julian sighed and squeezed her back. 'Well, just don't expect me to talk to them.'

32

'Tom's just reading the boys a chapter of *The Railway Children*,' said Wendy, breezing into the kitchen later that evening. 'Now, what shall we have for supper?'

It had been a relatively successful day for Julian for he had both avoided Carly and denied her the opportunity of a one-to-one chat with Wendy. Admittedly he'd had to endure a three-hour round-trip to Mallaig and suffer the delights of its Marine World, but these were forfeits he'd been happy to pay.

Returning home they'd found that Tom and Carly had lopped off all the lower branches of one of the three trees by the house, a wind-battered Scots pine, and had built an enormous bonfire to 'entertain the boys'. But the wood had been too green to burn and Julian had been overjoyed when the wind had dropped, and the rain had come, and everyone had been forced inside, with Tom looking foolish and reeking of diesel.

The last twenty minutes had been the only time he'd been on his own with the psycho since their spat round the side of the house and she hadn't said a word. She'd just been sitting there looking introverted and subdued, making a persistent but minuscule rocking motion, and slowly rubbing her fingertips together, as if about to embark on a game of cat's cradle, while Julian pretended to read the *Guardian* in the frail candlelight, carefully eyeing her every few minutes to check for any signs of impending attack. He'd even begun to feel sorry for her – she seemed so obviously disturbed in quite a clinical way.

'I've got some salmon, but I don't know if I could face fish after this afternoon,' said Wendy. 'Mind you, it's going to go off if we don't eat it soon. What do you think, Carly?' There was a forced singsong quality to her voice as she tried to lighten the atmosphere of gloom and depression and make her last evening with Tom as convivial as she could. 'Hmmn?'

Carly lifted her head slowly and spoke with quiet and hard-won deliberation. 'Yesterday, when I said I was in love with Julian's work, I wasn't telling the whole truth . . .'

Julian felt the blood suddenly draining from his face.

'I know what you're going to say Carly, but the fact is I know already – Julian told me last night.'

'Know what?' asked Carly, as the last vestiges of colour in Julian's face disappeared and he became almost translucent in the half-light.

'That you're Lilith, Julian's big fan, the number one fan, the one who waits for hours and hours outside every place he ever goes – and I bet you're the one who rings, aren't you? It's all right, you can tell us, we're not going to hurt you. I'm only worried because I don't think you've told Tom, have you? And I think you ought to.'

If only he'd confessed it all, Julian berated himself. He'd meant to do it, to gouge out the canker of his past and start again from scratch, but the ridiculous hope of getting away with it had hung on by its fingernails.

A broad, beaming smile split the psycho's face. She turned to Julian and laughed. 'Is that all you told her?' She laughed again, triumphant, her eyes suddenly flickering bright once more, and turned back to Wendy. 'The fact is that we are having an affair, aren't we Julian?'

'That's a lie!' cried Julian.

'We had sex twelve days ago.'

'That's a lie!'

'Twice.'

'No.'

'In my flat.'

He turned to Wendy. 'It's a lie; you can't believe her.'

'I've got it all on video tape. I've got a copy upstairs in my bag – if you find a video machine you can watch it if you like.'

251

Wendy fixed him with an all-seeing stare. 'Is it true?' she said.

He edged back in his chair to pull his face away from the direct glare of the candles on the table and fought desperately for an idea of an excuse, but his moment's silence was enough to damn him. A hollow-eyed fury burned across Wendy's face and she ran from the room. Seconds later the roar of the Range Rover engine could be heard outside and the beams from its headlights flashed across the kitchen window as it spun round and sped off down the valley.

A heavy silence fell upon the kitchen. Julian sat gobsmacked, not by the suddenness of the betrayal but by the actual event of Wendy's departure. So many times in his life he had goaded and provoked her on the half-promise of her not being able to take it any more and of her storming out – and now it had happened without him trying at all. He looked at Carly. She was grinning from ear to ear. He expected her to fly across to him and start tearing at his jeans, but she stayed sitting where she was, no longer rocking, just casually leaning back with one foot on her chair, hugging her leg to her chest.

'The boys are asleep,' said Tom, sauntering into the room, 'where's Wendy off to?' Julian looked at him blankly. He was paralysed by the paradox of finally getting what he'd so often wanted just when he didn't want it. An immense sadness seemed to crush his spirit but he felt no tears, just an over-whelming and immediate sense of loss, and despair at the abysmal future stretching out ahead of him like the frozen wastes of Antarctica. He had no thought of Wendy coming back – as soon as she'd left that was it, he knew – the damage was too great to repair and she would never forgive him.

'She's gone to get us a Chinese take-away,' said Carly. Julian stared at her open-mouthed. She was so casual, he thought, so unnecessarily devious. But he let it go.

'What? In Strontian?' asked Tom.

'No, in Fort William.'

'But that's an hour away.'

252

'Yes, well, she didn't want to cook.'

Julian hung his head. He couldn't summon up the where-withal to challenge her. His mind was racing with ideas of how to get revenge – of spilling the beans about his shrine; about the way the panels must revolve, like in a James Bond movie; how many others were there? – but he felt too disorientated to talk. The inside of his head felt odd, his brain felt detached from his skull and he knew he was in no fit state to take on the madness of the psycho.

'She'll be at least two hours,' grumbled Tom.

'Never mind,' said Carly, rising and taking Tom's hand. 'Come on, I've got something special planned for you.'

'Oh, here we go again,' Tom said to Julian, raising his eyebrows in mock-complaint and grinning dirtily as she drag-ged him from the room.

Julian thanked whichever God was responsible for their departure. They could suck each other to death for all he cared, as long as they left him alone.

He stared at the stove for a while and tried to imagine what he ought to be feeling. He wondered how someone ordinary would react to the same turn of events, wondered what was expected of him. All he knew was that it seemed so unreal, and that he felt like an actor without a script. He thought of the boys upstairs and their mother tearing along the dirt track and onto the black highways beyond towards the sanctuary of some hotel, and he felt an urgent desire to get pissed. Going into the pantry he checked his supplies – two bottles of Blue Nun and a bottle of Baileys Wendy had obviously bought for herself. The boys would have to live with their mother of course, he thought to himself, he'd never win any kind of custody battle with his record as a parent. And he felt glad that the inevitability of this conclusion more or less absolved him of the need to worry about it. However, they were in his care for the night, with Tom and the psycho roaming free, and it occurred to Julian that perhaps he ought to stay sober. Standing in the larder looking at the tins of cling

253

peaches and packets of Coco Pops, Julian pondered on his future as a bachelor – he'd be free, free to get a pad of his own in the middle of town and shag as many girls as he wanted.

Girls like Carly! it suddenly struck him – and he grabbed at the bottle of Baileys.

Wendy parked up on the hard shoulder opposite the war memorial just beyond Strontian, turned off her headlights and looked out through the gloaming at the tranquil waters of Loch Sunnart.

She felt completely humiliated and ashamed, not so much by Carly's revelation of Julian's infidelity as by the ridiculous way she had been fooling herself for so many years, and how stupid that must have made her look to all of Julian's show-business friends. *And Tom!* They must have thought she was such a doormat; a meek, frightened little mouse of a housewife, innocently washing through Julian's smalls with almost comic insensibility.

Of course she knew that Julian slept around – it was obvious – no one stayed out all night so often when home was only three or four miles away unless they had something better to do. She'd just never admitted as much to herself in the forlorn hope that if she ignored it, it might go away. She'd even guessed the full truth of what Julian had been trying to confess the night before, but had refused to help the confession to the surface and buried it deep in the dusty corners of her subconscious.

Julian must have thought she was such an easy dupe, she reflected agonisingly to herself, and she imagined how that must have made her even less attractive in his eyes than she obviously already was. She looked down at her ankle-length jersey skirt, T-shirt and cardigan, and wrung her hands in despair at her drabness.

She wondered how many women Julian must have slept with. Had he slept with her old university friend, Clare? They'd certainly seemed sheepish coming back from the toilets the

New Year's Eve before last. Or Sally the babysitter? Or Francesca? He'd definitely slept with the actress who played Lady Anne in *Richard the Nerd*. What about the cleaner? Elaine? His wardrobe mistress? Her mind was filled with a bewildering array of women and she tried to rouse feelings of outrage and betrayal within herself, arguing rationally that she was definitely the aggrieved party in this situation, but she could only summon up greater feelings of self-loathing and disgust – *she'd brought it all upon herself by being so haughtily intellectual and dressing like a spinster* – could only think that it was her fault, that it was all a direct result of her self-delusion and weakness.

And now her frailty had been exposed by someone as low and obviously deranged as Julian's number one fan! She wondered briefly if they were all back at the house laughing at her, but then pulled herself up short – she knew that Julian loved her, the last week had seemed like an extended advertisement for how much he loved her, and how good life with him could be. It occurred to her that he'd been crying out for guidance almost from the first moment they'd met, and that she'd let him down.

Besides, where was she going to run to? Clare, in Manchester? Her parents? Tom? She was twenty-eight with two children. And she did love Julian, she thought to herself, she just hadn't given him enough care, hadn't got involved, hadn't protected him, hadn't fought for him – she'd just lain back and let him fend for himself against the world.

Her thoughts were suddenly interrupted by a loud rapping on her window and she turned to see a leering, drunken, unshaven face pressed up against the glass. Shocked, she grabbed for the ignition, rammed the car into reverse and spun backwards out onto the road. Turning the wheel and locking her door at the same time, she slammed the car into first and put her foot down, the wheels spinning and burning up rubber before she sped off back towards Strontian.

It was only as she reached the village that she realised the face at the window had been Dougal McIntyre's, but she couldn't think of going back – she was on a mission to fight for her husband, to rescue him from the forces of loneliness and abandonment. Life wasn't a question of simply side-stepping the difficult times, she told herself, but of taking them on. And as she turned onto the track that led up to Gleann a'Bhuic, and the tears at last began to fall, she started to daydream furiously of moving to the country, away from the lures and hollow temptations of the outside world.

Tom had never been so hard. He'd never dared to suggest bondage to any of his sexual partners, even Carly, and now here he was in Dougal's shed, spread-eagled and strapped tight to the wooden frame of the corrugated-iron wall, his head restrained in the vertex of two beams and his mouth sealed shut with three-inch-wide emergency plumbing tape. The only things he could move were his eyes and his penis, and he looked down proudly at his aching erection twitching in the yellow glare of the Tilley lamp.

Carly looked magnificent. She was naked save for the great sheaves of turkey feathers in her hair which she'd used to excite him into his fully engorged state, by turns stroking with the vanes and then softly flaying with the horny spines. As she danced a wild, primitive, pagan dance through the shadows cast by a pair of giant, rusting tractor wheels in the corner of the shed, Tom felt elated by the fantastical nature of it all. And yet he couldn't help wondering what it would be like with Wendy in this position. Carly was a sweet girl, he thought, and he knew he was being a 'bit of a bastard' in using her this way, but, after all, he reasoned, it was she who had seduced him first and she seemed to be enjoying it. And it wasn't every girl who got to sleep with the brightest young luminary of the British stage. He closed his eyes and thought of Wendy – he couldn't imagine her in the feathers and pictured her in a cardigan instead, but naked underneath, her small breasts shaking fleetingly into view through the gap in the soft folds of wool – but his fantasy was interrupted by a loud clattering noise, and he quickly opened his eyes again and searched for Carly. Her dance had taken her behind the gruesome-looking pitch-pole harrow where she had to try to narrow the scope of her exotic gyrations to avoid its razor-sharp tines, but she was in such a frenzy that her heels and elbows were banging into the corrugated-iron walls. She negotiated it safely and came back into the centre of the shed where the dance slowed gradually to a complete stop. She stood directly in line with him and marched in a stately, almost funereal way towards him, staring solemnly into his eyes like a priest at a wedding.

'Goodbye, have a safe journey,' she said, and solemnly knelt before him and took his penis in her mouth. Tom closed his eyes and silently chanted his mantra to himself, praying that enlightenment would be his. Perhaps this time he would really feel something spiritual, he thought to himself, and not have to keep on pretending. 'Om mane padme hum, om mane padme hum,' he kept repeating to himself as he concentrated hard on the seven chakras and the reversal of Genesis, whilst keeping a part of his consciousness on the look-out for any signs of blissful insight. But these beginnings of his transcendental journey were suddenly cut short by sensations of excruciating pain emanating from his penis, and he looked down to see that Carly had skewered his manhood with the sharpened quill-tip of a turkey feather. She let it go and it stood unsupported, blood issuing from its base at a steady trickle.

He wondered briefly whether this was some sado-masochistic ritual that would heighten his spiritual awareness, then looked on with increasing alarm as he saw Carly dancing over to Dougal's metal cabinet, opening it, and returning with the long, sharp knife that had been used to sever the turkey's neck. Tom tried to cry out for her to stop as she cavorted wildly in front of him, teasing him with the knife like some Maori warrior greeting Prince Charles, but the plumbing tape was so thick and sticky he couldn't raise more than a muffled whimper.

With one deft, high-arcing swipe she sliced through his penis

257

at the base and held it aloft. The pain, like a jackhammer drilling at his pubic bone, was numbed by the great shock of adrenalin that surged through his veins like a roller-coaster. Seeing Carly squat between his legs he looked down to see her washing her face in the stream of his blood and he passed out.

Coming round a short time later, his brain a raging cauldron of shattered nerve ends, he was confronted by Carly's blood-drenched face in front of him, slowly bringing Dougal's chisel up towards his mouth. Shrieking inwardly he struggled to get free but the leather belt around his neck cut into his windpipe, and his resistance was cut short as Carly rammed the chisel through the tape with the heel of her hand and hammered it through his lips and into his teeth which splintered and sang with a pain that gripped his face like a vice. Carly wrenched the chisel left and right to enlarge the opening, through which he screamed in fear and agony, but soon after he could feel the keen edges of the chisel cutting into the roof of his mouth. Blood poured down his throat and he began to choke, looking on stricken and helpless as Carly drew back her hand and punched it up into the haft of the blade.

Getting out of the Range Rover Wendy thought she heard a strange cry coming from the nearest shed, and was puzzled by the sound of furtive scurrying about, as if someone were trying to hide something. She edged towards the shed and her nostrils caught a powerful, warm, thick, livery smell, and carefully opening the door her breath was taken away by the sight of Tom on the wall. She struggled forward to see what she could do but it was grotesquely obvious that he was dead.

'Good evening, Wendy, I didn't expect you back so soon,' said Carly, rising up from behind Dougal's cabinet. Wendy stumbled backwards in fright and fell.

Emerging sheepishly from the house to investigate the sound of the car arriving, Julian heard the metal cabinet crash to the ground in the shed, heard Wendy scream, and dashed over, barging through the door just as a gruesome vision in blood and feathers sank her cleaver into Wendy's calf. The psycho turned to face him but was caught off balance by the cleaver refusing to come out of Wendy's leg, and Julian wildly charged her down, propelling her back onto the plentiful rusty prongs of the pitch-pole harrow, which sank deep into her and held her upright as her eyes closed and her head fell forward.

'Oh God!' cried Julian.

'The boys!' screamed Wendy, clawing her way across the floor back to the door, 'get the boys!' Julian rushed to help her. It seemed her shin bone had been split in two. The lower part of her leg was hanging at ninety degrees to the rest. 'Leave me!' she screamed at the top of her voice, using Dougal's work bench to help her get back onto her feet. 'Get the boys into the car!' Julian ran off back to the house as the psycho's eyes opened and she started to prise herself off the spikes.

Running out of the house again, sweating and out of breath, with a boy in each arm, Julian could see Wendy desperately hanging on to the outside handle of the shed door.

'What's going on?' he shouted, worried that he might not be able to take any more of this terror and that he could possibly collapse in a dead faint at any moment.

'Get them in the car first!' she shouted back, sounding weaker by the second.

'What's happening, Daddy?'

'Daddy, what's happening?' asked the twins, bursting into nervous tears.

Julian didn't have the breath to answer. He bundled them into the back of the car and dragged himself towards the shed just as the cleaver splintered through the wooden slats of the door. Wendy screamed and released the handle, letting the door fall open to reveal the badly wounded psycho kneeling behind it, struggling to pull the cleaver back out of the door.

Julian felt like vomiting with fear, but summoning all the

strength he had left he picked Wendy up in his arms and staggered back to the car, cramming her into the passenger seat and hauling himself round to the other side. He jumped into the driver's seat, turned on the ignition and pressed his foot down hard on the accelerator. *The car wouldn't move!* He turned to Wendy, panic-stricken. 'I can't fucking drive!' he shouted.

The psycho fan's cleaver smashed through the rear window and the twins began to scream.

'Left foot down!' shouted Wendy, slamming the gear lever into first, 'now up again!' and the car leaped forward, shaking off the psycho and kangarooing into space before crunching into the loose rubble of the road and revving off down the valley, the lights coming on only as it approached the first bend.

EPILOGUE

'Goodbye,' said Wendy, hugging Julian tightly, her tears dampening his ear lobes, 'I'll miss you.'

'Goodbye, Daddy!'

'Goodbye!' shouted the twins, hanging onto his legs and trying to squeeze in between their parents.

The guard who was slamming shut all the doors of the train was approaching Julian's carriage.

'I'd better get on the train,' said Julian, eliciting a fresh wave of sobbing and kissing. 'I'm only going for the day, I'll be back tonight,' he said, swallowing hard, and they reluctantly let him go, like adoring puppies shaken off by their doting mother. He boarded the train, closed the door and leaned out to hold Wendy's hands through the open window. Her face was stained with the tracks of salty tears but she was smiling through the heartache – they were tears of joy, confirming the new life between them. The guard's whistle blew and the train pulled slowly out of the station with the boys running alongside and Wendy limping behind them, waving her stick. Julian waved back until they were lost to view, then took his seat in first class – it was extravagant, he knew, but today he was going to earn at least ten thousand pounds!

The train cleared the outskirts of Newton Abbot and rolled into open countryside, and Julian could see the great mass of Dartmoor in the distance illuminated by celestial spring sunshine and his soul filled with a sense of belonging. Life on Stout's Farm was just fantastic! he thought to himself. It was as if he'd been orphaned as a child and suddenly found his real home – everything seemed so natural and so perfectly in place. Starting over with total honesty and a clean sheet had left him and Wendy giddy with enchantment. It had been like falling in love with each other all over again. He loved her laugh, her fund of knowledge, and her arse, even though it wasn't quite as perfect as it had been nine years before.

'Will, you be taking breakfast?'

The voice caught him unawares. He turned to face a steward. 'Er, yes, thanks.'

'Are you who I think you are?'

Julian sighed. 'I don't know. Who do you think I am?'

'Well, the other stewards think you're Julian Mann.'

'So?'

'Well, are you?'

'Yes, I am.'

'No, you're not,' said the steward, disbelievingly, as if Julian was just playing along.

'All right then, I'm not.'

'Aren't you?'

'No.'

'You see, I told you so,' shouted the steward down to his sniggering colleagues behind the door at the far end of the carriage, 'I knew it wasn't him – he's not fat enough!'

Julian turned his gaze back to the window and smiled. 'Advantage – Mann,' he said quietly to himself. He'd lost a lot of weight since the inquest into Tom's death and Kali (as she spelled it) or Lilith's, or as it finally emerged, Tracy's trial, when his picture had been splashed all over the papers. Five months of hard, manual labour learning the ropes as a stockman on his farm had toughened him up and given him a lean, outdoor look. And he thought it was just the most incredible work, so completely absorbing and set in the magical, ever-changing world of his own private bucolic idyll. It was spiritually uplifting without any seeming effort on his part. He wondered why he couldn't just stay there with his beautiful family and shut himself off from the rest of the world for ever. The answer was money, he knew. The insurance cheque for the house and the sale of the burned-out shell to some developer who was going to turn it into flats had paid for the farm, and although the farm could carefully support their needs in the future he still had two massive tax demands to pay off, legacies of his profligate past and the scrapping of *Blood Train*, which was why he was on his way to London to do a ridiculously overpaid TV voice-over for some crap new breakfast cereal.

He knew just how it would be. *Just give us your* Richard the Nerd *voice, Julian . . . Can we do it a bit wackier than that, do you think? . . . Oh no! Not that whacky! . . . We want it to sound like you but not you . . . Can you shave half a second off that? . . . I think we've got to concentrate on defining a character for the oat cluster . . . Can you do Orson Welles?* He looked down at the place that had been set for him by the steward, and at the small plastic phial of UHT milk with its annoying peel-back foil top – so different from the jug of warm, unpasteurised nectar he'd become used to at home – and he felt a familiar tightening in his chest.

The steward came back with two steaming pots. 'Tea or coffee, sir?'

'Listen,' said Julian, drawing the steward in conspiratorially, 'what time does the bar open?'

'Eleven o'clock.'

'Yes, thought so,' he said, reaching into his pocket and withdrawing his wallet. 'Look, here's a tenner, you couldn't get me just a small miniature of scotch, could you?'

The steward winked and nodded, and surreptitiously stuffed the money into his breast pocket. 'It'll take me a couple of minutes, mind.'

'Well, look then,' said Julian, getting another tenner out and sliding it across the table, 'get us a couple, would you?'

The steward nodded and took the second note, then making his way out through the door at the end of the carriage Julian heard him say to one of his cohorts, 'You're right, it is him.' And although he balked at this two-dimensional character

263

sketch in the face of the new man he thought himself to be, Julian couldn't help feeling a narcissistic pride at the remark.

As the cab from Paddington edged through Soho on its way to Covent Garden Julian remembered an adventure round every corner, monumental piss-ups in bars and clubs and upstairs office suites late at night, with friends and co-workers and one-night stands. He took another swig at the bottle he'd bought coming out of the station and chuckled at the memories. He hadn't been this drunk since the afternoon with Bill Tyndall in the Kensington Parkview Hotel, and he was frankly enjoying it. He rationalised out loud to himself in a patch of purple prose for his non-existent, self-congratulatory autobiography that the bottle was his crutch when Wendy wasn't there to support him.

Getting held up in heavy traffic towards the bottom of Frith Street he watched a young woman squeeze through the narrow gap between his cab and the one in front. She was beautiful – tall and blonde with an easy grace and an untroubled face. As she lifted her bags to negotiate the cab's protruding bonnet her jacket opened and he could see her breasts pushing lusciously against the thin weave of her polo-neck top, and looking up to her face he saw that she'd seen him looking. He smiled and mouthed, 'I love you.' She giggled bashfully and continued on her way, but glanced briefly back at him after six or seven paces. *Trapped! Caught in the act!*

Julian looked at the meter which read four pounds eighty, gave the cabbie a twenty-pound note and got out of the cab.